images of the future

images of the future:
the twenty-first century
and beyond

edited by Robert Bundy

ℙ𝔹 *Prometheus Books*
Buffalo, N.Y. 14215

Published 1976 by Prometheus Books
923 Kensington Avenue, Buffalo, New York 14215

Library of Congress Card Number 75-32697
ISBN 0-87975-048-0

Printed in the United States of America

Acknowledgments

When Paul Kurtz and I first met a few years ago during a television interview I had no notion that our biographies were soon to become linked. After the interview he asked me what important issue had not been adequately addressed in the growing literature on the future. My reply was immediate: "Why, images of the future, of course." I am not certain how he felt at the time about either the topic or my assessment of its importance, but he encouraged me to think about a special issue of *The Humanist* magazine devoted to images of the future. After this issue was published in late 1973, he urged me to go ahead with plans for this book.

I wish to acknowledge Paul's encouragement and the personal advice he rendered in the development of both these publications on images of the future. I wish also to thank all of *The Humanist* staff who were involved, particularly Rita Wilson and Doris Doyle, as well as Cynthia Dwyer of Prometheus Books for her editing skills. Finally, I thank my wife Rosemarie for the very practical advice and assistance she gave me on numerous occasions.

R.F.B.

Contents

Robert Bundy

Preface

This book is a collection of essays on images of the future. It is intended for people who are sensitive to humanity's awesome problems and who are deeply troubled by the ominous directions global trends are taking as we approach the twenty-first century.

Most of the contributors to this volume are internationally known. All are provocative thinkers from a wide range of fields and endeavors. The issue that brings them together here is the role of public images of the future in the history of a civilization. The central questions asked are: How do images of the future come to be? How do they influence the future that actually occurs? And, finally, which images will or should shape humankind's future over the next several decades.

To prepare the reader for what follows it may be helpful first to re-think a part of our conventional wisdom. We are accustomed to speak of the past as prologue to the present. In this book we are going to treat seriously the proposition that the future is prologue to all history. Such a proposition does more than put a customary view in a new light. It suggests a different causal relationship in human affairs.

By *future* is meant the public images, the focused expectations, of the yet to come. These images may be positive or negative. If positive—to borrow from Fred Polak's pioneering studies—they tell of a counterreality radically different from the present, of another and better world in another time. Whether these positive images speak of a heavenly kingdom or the good society here on earth, they provide meaning and hope. They pull a civilization forward in search of the destiny the images foretell.

Images of the future, of course, have their roots in the shared memories of a culture. The images are born and refined in the light of specific interpretations of the past. When the past is re-visioned by the charismatic leaders of the times, new images of the future emerge to replace or challenge the old. Nevertheless, in the consciousness of a civilization, images of the future speak to what will be or can be or should be. Thus, they have their own dynamics, their own power over the present, and their own dialectic with it. A civilization can be described in terms of its images of the future. But even more important, the actual future of a civilization—vigor and growth, or decline and breakdown—is prefigured in the shared images of the future possessed by its people in the present. It is in this sense that the future is a prologue to all history.

The importance and timeliness of this inquiry into images of the future derives from a crucial observation about Western civilization. In our time we seem to have finally exhausted the central images of the future that have pulled us on, however erratically, in the past. These images are not dead, for they still have their adherents. However, none seem to have the power to energize the public imagination in any collective sense. Instead, with the residual power they still command, they compete with one another to the point of extreme social divisiveness. In short, we have no comforting images of greatness and progress that speak to all of us; we have no common roots in some dominant vision, no shared dream uniquely fitting our historic period.

By what processes this exhaustion of images takes place is difficult to know. Sometimes, expectations are too long delayed and they lose their appeal, or, having been partly achieved, the images are discovered to be inadequate. At other times the images become too greatly at variance with the world that is. However it may be explained, what does seem clear in our historic period is that the spiritual center of Western civilization has been rent, many of our central dogmas have been seriously weakened, and no existing image of the future has sufficient attraction to possess the hearts and wills of the body politic.

Secularism in its many forms has certainly wounded the Christian world view and influence. Nationalism is not looked upon with the same fervor it once was, as the web of social and psychic interdependencies tightens about our tiny spaceship Earth. The promises of Marxism appear inadequate to capture the collective imagination in the West. The belief that human beings can take charge of their own evolution and destiny through the enlightened use of science and technology seems incapable of becoming a living faith for the majority in the immediate future. Nor does any return to primitive standards of cognition, as a rejection of a technicized civilization, seem likely to have any convincing mass appeal. George Steiner is thus persuasive when he speaks of our loss of faith in the following: (1) ascending progress, (2) the self-evident superiority of the West over other races and social histories, and (3) a belief in the necessary connection between literacy and politics, between the humanities and humaneness, in short, in the correlation between cultivation of intellect and feeling in the individual and rational and humane behavior in society. Indeed, concludes Steiner, the very notion of a high culture in the West as something worthy of being preserved is repugnant to many who feel alienated today. The totalitarian horrors of the twentieth century, they argue, were not prevented by the dominant cultural system, and the high culture was bought for the few at the price of suffering, poverty, and underdevelopment for the masses.

The foundations of Western civilization, therefore, appear to be shaken to their very core. However the accomplishments of the West are viewed, if we are without crucial dogmas, a common literacy, a centrality of values, and magnetic images of the future to guide us in a collective way, we indeed face a grim future: the prospects of devastation of the planet by nuclear war; social/economic collapse on a global scale; megadeaths from famine; the fatal pollution of our environment; and bizarre and inhuman applications of the new biological sciences. The present thus dominates our thinking because the present, with all its problems, is preferable by far to the grim future ahead. But our very pessimism, our failure of nerve to dream new images, our lack of a magnetic pull for the yet to come could well be prefiguring where we are headed. The death knell of Western civilization is perhaps being sounded unless we can find a new sense of mission, purpose, and reason for being—in short, new images of the future that speak to us in rich terms of human renewal and are appropriate to the problems and opportunities of our historical period.

These are the issues and questions this book addresses itself to. Included are nineteen essays by authors who in one way or another take our theme of images of the future very seriously. Ten of the essays originally appeared in the November/December 1973 issue of *The Humanist*. These essays probed in a beginning way the subject of images of the future. Because of the excellent response to this first effort, it was decided to solicit additional people in order to broaden and deepen this inquiry. The other nine essays are original contributions published here for the first time.

In Part I the epistemology and phenomenology of images of the future are explored. Here we are not so much concerned with particular images as we are with the nature and importance of images of the future in the historic process, and with how images are formed in the collective consciousness of a civilization. The writers in this section, sociologist Fred Polak, philosopher Thomas Green, poet Geoffrey Squires, social critic Jacques Ellul, and theologian Drew Christiansen, pursue their topics with great facility and insight.

In Part II the recent futures movement is reviewed by sociologist Wendell Bell and myself. Some significant conclusions are drawn as to whether the process of imaging in the social imagination has been enhanced or restrained by the movement.

The remaining five parts explore images of the future from the point of view of: (1) particular subgroups such as different economic classes, women, racial minorities, and so on; (2) specific fields of human activity including religion, education, economics, anthropology, science, and sociology; and (3) current problems of worldwide significance, most notably, the environment, hunger, war, energy, and global cooperation. In these five parts an unusual assortment of people have been brought together. They include economists Lester Brown and Herman Kahn; social scientists Manfred Stanley, Robert Jungk, Elise Boulding, and Ralph Wendell Burhoe; anthropologist Elaine Morgan; women's rights advocate Mary Lee Bundy; American Indian spokesman Vine Deloria, Jr.; theologian-scientist Robert Francoeur; and educators W. Timothy Weaver and Roy P. Fairfield.

An attempt has not been made to be comprehensive in all these areas. This is not a book detailing cultural movements, social experimentation, new life-styles, or utopian communities. Nor is it a book that summarizes major trends, forecasts, and predictions about the future. Elements of all of these will be found, but the main thrust has been to explore those deeper rhythms, those fields of meaning that characterize human relationships, imagination, and aspirations within contemporary society. Hopefully, we have been able to clarify issues, pose new starting points for discussion, and shift lines of debate over the future into more fruitful directions.

Like much of the futures literature then, the essays deal with obvious and pressing world concerns. Unlike most of the futures literature, the umbrella theme and guiding light throughout is images of the future and the way in which these images serve to create the future history of a civilization. This orientation offers an immensely powerful dimension to thinking about the future in fresh, bold terms. These essays are therefore, in this editor's judgment, an important contribution to the rapidly expanding literature assessing human prospects for the future as well as to that small but growing branch concerned with images of the future. In terms of the latter, this book fits into a modern tradition of thinking characterized by such works as Bertrand de Jouvenel's *The Art of Conjecture,* Fred Polak's two-volume work *The Image of the Future, The Image* by Kenneth Boulding, and *The Sociology of the Future* by Wendell Bell and James Mau; the writings of certain cultural critics and historians such as George Steiner, Richard Weaver, Ivan Illich, William Thompson, Theodore Geiger, Vincent Vycinas, and J. H. Plumb; anthropologists such as Clyde Kluckhohn, Ruth Benedict, and Anthony F. C. Wallace; and writers on the psychology of future-time perception, including W. Timothy Weaver, R. J. Kastenbaum, and Nathan Israeli.

Western civilization is the obvious focus of all that is said. But the drama we are engaged in is global; therefore an important underlying assumption in all the essays is that what happens to the West will significantly shape what the world will be like as the second millennium arrives.

The authors, of course, will speak for themselves. As editor, it has been my task to set the stage, organize the flow of thoughts, and draw out the pertinent questions and ideas. In the Epilogue I attempt to bring together the major conclusions from the essays and offer a perspective on finding a new meaning for the future.

Throughout, the reader is invited to participate in this fateful dialogue and answer for herself or himself this question: What images of the future shall guide us, instill hope in the possibilities of human renewal, and quicken the social imagination to cope with the apocalyptic days ahead?

PART $\boxed{}$

THE NATURE AND
IMPORTANCE OF
IMAGES OF THE FUTURE

These essays explore the social and historical dynamics of images of the future. Each brings different insights to the problem of understanding the nature of images of the future and how they become part of the collective consciousness. All the writers agree on the necessity for shared, inspiring images in human affairs and also that there is currently a poverty of such images to guide us through the difficult years ahead. Many provocative suggestions are given for the following: the kinds of images now needed; places to begin a search for new images; our limitations in being able to invent compelling visions of the future; and ways to avoid corrupting the process of searching for humanly fulfilling images.

Fred L. Polak

Responsibility for the Future

Fred Polak is an important pioneer in the study of images of the future. He reviews his earlier ideas on the nature of images of the future and his assessment of our imaging capacity. Today he remains moderately optimistic, despite a seemingly less hopeful situation.

Responsibility for the future is the central core and crystallized essence of all responsibility, always and everywhere. This responsibility for the future not only is *the* all-encompassing responsibility, but also is prior to and a primary condition of man's responsibility in and for the present. This function is considered to be fundamental for human behavior as *human* behavior, pertaining to both mankind as a whole and man as an individual.

Man is the one animal able to cross the frontier of present reality. Man is the only living being who consciously splits reality in two: into the existing,

This article first appeared in *The Humanist*, November-December 1973.

concretely observable situation and into another, an inventively conceived, not-existing state of being. Homo sapiens thus is "split man," and in this creative capacity he distinguishes himself from and rises above a purely animalistic or vitalistic state. He can behave purposefully as a "citizen of two worlds." The development of this typical dualism marks the most significant milestone in the almost unknown process of the birth and early growth of human civilization. It is the main explanation of the progressive bifurcation between nature and nurture. It starts the biological species of *homo* off on its amazing career as man, the maker of civilization.

Man cannot become truly and fully man, cannot attain the summit of human dignity if he cannot simultaneously elaborate and refine his mental picture of another world in a coming time. The image may be eschatological or utopian; but this image of the future, infusing man with the knowledge of a destiny of happiness and harmony, haunts him and challenges him to work for its realization. The search for the future has become basic to man's behavior, his attitudes alternating between eager hope and bitter despair, between the Faustian forward-driving faith and the frozen or frantic grip of fear.

As soon as man's eyes are opened to the flow of time toward the future, which probably will be different from both present and past, two insoluble enigmas are posed: the problem of change and the problem of meaning. Causal reconstruction seemingly goes on forever without any prospect of reaching the haven of universal validity for the historical past. More precarious still is the situation with respect to the interpretation and meaning of history. The former unshakable belief in a God who personally determines all historical events down to the smallest detail is no longer a living faith. Even His dramatic reappearance at the end of time for the final act of closing history has receded into the remoteness of heavenly shrouds. But the contrary belief—that man himself would direct history toward the ultimate goal for a good society—is equally shattered. Existential belief-systems about the utter meaninglessness of earthly history now tend to prevail widely in our world.

The previous failures of the social sciences to find sociocultural time-laws or general regularities of the same precision and constancy as the natural sciences have found, combined with the self-confessed failure of the philosophy of history to ascertain the inner *or* outer meaning of the historical process, have left most modern scholars discouraged or at the very least skeptical of all attempts to catch the elusive time-continuum in all-inclusive absolutistic systems. It is, indeed, now rather easy to ridicule many of the single links in a long chain of indomitable attempts to make history a science. It is easy to demonstrate the pitfalls, the completely subjective judgments, and the unscientific methods of our predecessors. Their dead-end trails, however, give indispensable clues to new paths of progress.

Unflinchingly, we must return again and again to the cardinal questions: Why and where did these systems of the great thinkers go awry? If we succeed in separating their true from their false statements, there is no reason, even less an excuse, not to try anew. The main objection that could be made against all existing theories in this field is that they all derive their predictions of the future from the past-present segments of the time-flow. I am convinced that a well-founded diagnosis and subsequent prognosis can be made and justified *only* if the segment of the time-flow labeled "future" is also included as an independent and codetermining entity. This means the unborn future, to be predicted, should enter into a preceding phase of the analysis, because it is already at work with us in advance of becoming an apparent part of reality. This has always been true, and the future is therefore absolutely indispensable in any time-formula that would illuminate the tortuous and mysterious path of history.

Just take a superficial look at history and see whether the course of future events would not have been better perceived in broad outline if more study had been devoted to the future itself. I mean to that *potential* future, which was foreshadowed by radiating "images of the future" working their way toward the real future through their magnetic mass-appeal and the massive expansion of influence-optimism in the forward strivings and active aspirations of man. These images of the future not only reflected the shape of things to come in the present but they *gave* shape to these things and promoted their very coming. The images of the future and their prophets were writing the history of the future—they *made* history by creating this future, by fulfilling their own prophecies. They were like powerful time-bombs, exploding in the future, releasing a mighty stream of energy flowing back toward the present, which is then pushed and pulled to that future.

IMAGES OF THE FUTURE

The term "images of the future" is used here for those condensed and crystallized expectations prevailing among peoples in certain periods and developed into systematic projections toward the future. They may be of a transcendental-religious character, pertaining mainly to the end of time or to last things (eschatological), or they may concern themselves mainly with social-humanitarian ideals for the good society on earth (utopian). The history of human civilization abounds with future-forming images of the future, supplementing and supplanting each other in a continuous golden chain, welded together by the world's greatest prophets, philosophers, poets, humanists, idealists, saints, scholars—by the visionary men of genius and thought-provoking pioneers. In short, the past is seen in another perspective when reviewed as the history of man's images of the future. These images tell the unfolding story of mankind. They foretell and unveil futures that in the meantime have become verifiable pasts. If the right questions are asked, they might today give the right answers to the unknown future, over which we now wonder and worry.

Let us here retrace the main steps through the history of civilization. First, and most important, is man's dualistic mental capacity to imagine another world and another time radically different from the present. Spiritual leaders and visionary messengers emerge. They evolve constructive images of the future, painting a picture of another, coming world as a better world. Through their intellectual insight, but even more through their emotional and aesthetic appeal, these images designed by the elite are communicated to the masses and arouse their enthusiasm and burning belief. The world is set aflame by these dominating, directing forces toward that other and better future. The promises and prospects contained in these previsions and predictions make for a purposeful choice between a great many possible futures and help direct the elected potential future into active operation. They also help to explain the specific uniqueness of each of these ancient cultures or separate culture-configurations.

The prophetic, inspired proclamation and stimulating propagation of positive, mass-moving images of the future form the main generating process of the birth and growth of culture-patterns. Cultures, in their realistic unfolding, tend gradually to climb a staircase of a spiritual progress carved out of the nonexistent with the tools of the mind and heart. Cultures are the human expression of the attempt to bridge the gap between the natural, factual environment and the idealistic and better world of the imagination. Human culture results from the enduring effort of man to create the world in the image of the preceding and prevailing image of the future. Culture is slowly advancing along a steep trail, split open by split man in his far-reaching visions of the future, wresting the world free from its compelling and cramping present.

The same causal process may also be seen in reverse, however. The disintegration of constructive images of the future, their weakening or even negativation, and the absence of equivalent, balanced, subline forecasts to replace antiquated, worn-out, or frustrated conceptions may spell a period of cultural decline and breakdown. Of the thirty known civilizations in world history, as distinguished and described by Toynbee, only one, we are told, is now in existence, and even that is threatened with the same extinction as the other twenty-nine. This last survivor in the gloomy graveyard of a cultural Stonehenge is our so-called Western civilization.

Images of the future always have to be reevaluated to be adapted to the passage of time and to be brought up to date. All ethics refers to the future—but to which future? What is the meaning of our cultural heritage of values and ideals now, and particularly what is at present their suggestive mass-appeal, their radiating and expansive force in shaping this very future? Social ethics, born out of the compulsion of free choice, now has to choose for itself between the extremes of mere existence and pure essence. It might be carried off by the stream of presently fashionable pessimism and negativism, denying the reality of a coming other and better world and stamping this as a dangerous delusion of our naive predecessors. To avoid this it must strive hard for a positive reorientation and revaluation, explicitly redefining the new goals for the future life so they can be understood and perhaps even acclaimed by this realistic and skeptical generation. The main responsibility of social ethics now, as always, is to assess and pass on to coming generations our responsibility for the future. This implies, above all, the ability and willingness to contribute to a responsible choice between potential futures and alternative systems of values. Not all images of the future, not even the positive and optimistic ones, should be automatically considered as good images of the future. There are ones on which a responsible position must be taken; if necessary, a clear yes or no must be openly given. Social ethics can no longer pretend to remain neutral and aloof.

MAN'S CURRENT POSITION

The red thread weaving through the entire course of this argument is that all responsibility—including our responsibility in and for the present—cannot but be incorporated in a wider framework of responsibility for the future. Either we ourselves must consciously try to make the future, or others are sure to make the future, both theirs and ours. It is not a choice between having or not having any images of the future but between the good images— worth living and dying for—and the bad images, which we cannot accept without betraying ourselves.

Let us try to determine our current position, find true north, and measure the velocity of the drift. We may use the image of the future as a fairly reliable criterion of primary driving forces: its strength or weakness indicates their direction and regulative power. My argument in 1955 was that there are three main fields for such observations.

1. Western Europe, which, thanks to a sweeping succession of exalted images of the future, has held the key to human civilization for a few thousand years, now seems rather exhausted. On the whole, the former potent images of the future (both eschatological and utopian) are mostly in their death throes or are already buried, without effective recharging of these indispensable generators of culture having taken place. There is now a marked tendency to deride and defame these spiritual fathers of our own time; there is a strong distaste for and revulsion against all idealistic and optimistic thought concerning another and better world. The inverse idea, that we are thrown into the worst of all possible worlds, a world that cannot be fundamentally changed, is making impressive headway on a broad front. This idea leaves no hopeful prospect for mankind on earth.

2. In the United States there was at first an astounding upswing and far-reaching renascence of images of the future among a genuinely excited people. The New World was erected right through rocky mountain ranges, barren wildernesses, and arid deserts, unwaveringly following the beaming and beckoning lodestar of the American Dream toward a wildly fantastic and yet factually foreseeable future. But this, too, has by now become past history. This is surely not the place to weigh the value and validity of the American Dream in the America of today and tomorrow. Still, the outcome of such inquiry will portend an all-pervading influence for the future outside of America also.

3. Finally, in almost all other parts of the world, whether we like it or not, there is unquestionably at work a churning upheaval of mass-appealing images of the future. These are already changing the faces of whole continents, perhaps of the whole world. The guiding principles and normative values of these images may not be ours; they may even be diametrically opposed to our cherished views, mutually exclusive. If so, there is but one response to this challenge: to have the better, clearer, stronger, and, above all, more aspiring and inspiring images of the future. In my opinion, the decisive struggle in this ideological combat will take place where the struggle began when man first started to split reality and time—in the minds of men and women. It will be won, in the end, by those peoples who have at their command the most highly charged potential of powerful and persistent images of the future. Bound to triumph are those images of the future that reach out

most convincingly toward the greatest vistas and highest prospects for human society.

If, in our time, we no longer feel responsible for undertaking the creative splitting from reality of a coming other and better time, then we have already regressed a long way. If we want only an increasing mastery of the forces of nature, nature and time will unite against man and his shortsighted civilization. If the pursuit of happiness is self-centeredly focused on today's problems, profits, and pleasures, then one day the reckless evocation of *après nous le déluge* may become a bitter reality for the descendents we have repudiated by fault. Then creative faith in the future may gradually but completely be superseded by an impotent fear of the future, leaving man an easy prey for a coming onslaught of apocalyptic catastrophe.

These speculations are not meant to be pessimistic or, even less, despairing. They are intended to draw attention to the sharp cleavage characteristic of the spirit of our time. The split is no longer between this and another, better society but between the so-called idealists and the so-called realists. The idealists say no to the present and yes to their chosen future. The realists say yes to the present and are not on speaking terms with the future. The protagonists of the here-and-now seem to be gaining ground. Their eventual success might lead to a Pyrrhic victory.

The Image of the Future contained a prophecy: Either the emptiness of utopian and eschatological images of the future will mean the emptiness and maybe the end of Western culture, or there will be a new and spiritual soul-searching for meaningful and magnetizing images of the future. I am inclined to think that there are now many signs of the latter under various names, although they may be partly ineffective or even destructive in the beginning. In that sense *The Image of the Future* might be regarded as a self-destroying and self-fulfilling prophecy at the same time. Now, as then, I am moderately optimistic, in a seemingly even less hopeful situation.

Geoffrey Squires

Poetry and the Future

Why is the current usage of poetic *and* poetry *so restrictive? Squires feels the problem lies in an acceptance of reduced images of human beings. It is not an image of the future we need, but an image of people and the world. The poetic shows the unreality of reductionism, for people are inextricably immersed in the world.*

The invitation I received asking me to contribute to this collection of essays invited me to consider ideas of the future from a "poetic" standpoint, the word *poetic* being placed carefully within quotation marks. Now this device—quotation marks—is used either for words that are newly minted and gaining currency or for words that have become a little doubtful. I hardly think it is the former. But in what sense is the word *poetic* doubtful?

This article first appeared in *The Humanist*, November-December 1973.

16

It is not simply that so few writers or poets engaged in analytic thinking about the future are professional "futurists," as John McHale has pointed out. I suspect it is because the word *poetic*, like the words *imaginative* and *sacred*, belongs to what are currently dissident or marginal realities, especially for those who deal mainly in shared public images: policy advisers, planners, technical advisers, newspaper columnists, and the like.

I have quite different doubts about the use of the word. On one hand, I feel that current usage (both of *poetry* and *poetic*) is so restrictive as to create a kind of ghetto, where poets talk mainly to one another. In this sense, poetry begins where other and more important things leave off; it exists at the limits of the rational, the empirical, the technical, the public. Sometimes I think it would be best if the word *poetry* disappeared, lapsed, fell out of usage for awhile. (Bertolt Brecht: "Certain poets whose poems I read are known to me personally. I am often surprised that many of them show themselves a lot less reasonable in their poetry than in their ordinary talk."[1])

On the other hand, I came round in my own mind some time ago to the conclusion that an analytic/discursive mode of writing was, for me anyway, inadequate for talking or thinking about the future. There are things, for example, that I want to say about an image of the future, which would themselves take the form of images. (So these notes represent, in a way, a compromise between an essay and a poem.) I see the necessity of poetic or expressive writing, not because of the adequacy of that mode but because of the inadequacy of any other.

I can put this another way by saying: poetry is not a kind of discourse that complements other kinds of discourse; it is the totality of discourse. It does not begin at the limits of something else (the scientific, the public, and so forth); it is there all the time, from the outset, but becomes most evident when we try to achieve a completeness or fullness of expression. (Maurice Merleau-Ponty: "This world is not what I think, but what I live through."[2])

The basic vice of our culture, then, is reductionism—an acceptance of reduced images of man—which leads to futile and obvious attempts to add on the poetic or the cultural or the creative or whatever else it is we feel is missing—much as the manufacturers of cereals add vitamins to try to replace the ones they have taken out in the processing.

There are many implications in all of this for writing and for poetry, which I will not go into here, except to mention two. First, such a view must restore to writing the dimensions of action, or praxis, which it loses when it is conceived of mainly as reflection, or reflection *on* action. In Paulo Freire's terms, the poet is, perhaps more than most people, engaged in naming the world, a world that he does not escape from but which is indeed part of his own definition. (Merleau-Ponty again: "When I return to myself from an excursion into the realm of dogmatic common sense or of science, I find, not a source of intrinsic truth, but a subject destined to be in the world."[3])

Second, we need to modify our notion of the authentic or the personal in writing. Robert Duncan has put this very clearly:

> The basic misunderstanding between Blaser and myself here, dramatically contrasted, seems to arise between his poetics in which the poem is to be authentic, i.e., an expression of what is really his own—the authority of his poetry must be first-hand, and the criterion of its reality is that it be actually his—and my poetics in which the poem is thought of as a process of participation in a reality larger than my own—the reality of man's experience in the terms of language and literature—a community of meanings and forms in which my work would be at once derivative and creative.[4]

All of this digression is necessary because of those quotation marks around the word *poetic*. I presume an economist, for example, would not experience quite so many difficulties of this sort. Now, to *The Image of the Future*. Four aspects of Fred Polak's argument: (1) the simple forward magnetic pull of positive images, (2) the less simple patterning effect of the nature of the images, (3) the interaction of image and event in the time-flow of history, and (4) the alleged absence of shared positive images of the future in contemporary culture. I cannot comment on Polak's historical arguments, except to wonder to what extent he confines himself to Europe. The rise of Islam, for example, might provide him with one of the most compact examples of what I think he is talking about. On the other hand, I wonder if Chinese or Indian culture or various parts of the Third World might not provide a very different perspective. If, as Marx argued, many subsistence cultures were timeless, may we not see the European preoccupation with the future as an aberration, an exception?

I wonder about these things because the first thing I asked myself about this argument was: Is it true of me? True of the people I know? By and large, I feel that there is a great deal of truth in it. At the very least, an image of the future, in this world or the next, can sustain one, and quite often, I imagine, it bends one's behavior in a particular direction. But the trouble is, both Polak and I are Europeans.

The *Tao Te Ching*, chapter 40: "'Returning' is the [characteristic] movement of the Tao."

Furthermore, I am not sure if Polak is complaining about the absence, in contemporary Western culture, of positive images, of admirable images, or of shared images. For example, the images of the future in the Third Reich were positive (in the sense that Hitler promised it would last a thousand years), but not admirable. Negative images of the future may, in any case, be a healthy warning system like physical pain. The absence of shared images is another matter altogether. Do we in fact need common images to the extent that Polak suggests? Can we not get along with a degree of pluralism in this respect?

However, Polak's argument worries me in a far more fundamental way. This is because I think we are in the middle of two distinct crises, not one. The first crisis, the one I believe he is talking about, is the crisis of belief, or hope or purpose, which must have to do partly with the decline in formal religious belief. Although this is real enough, it does not seem to me to be fatal; rather, it is a kind of malaise, a drifting. The second crisis has to do with the inter-action between technology and society, affecting population, resources, pro-duction, pollution, and their possible trigger effects on the nuclear balance of terror. Failure to resolve this crisis, or set of crises, would be fatal, not just for individuals but for society as we know it, and possibly the planet as well.

Let me try to describe the two crises in terms of the system. The first crisis is coming about because the system, for a variety of reasons, is unable to set appropriate goals for itself. The second crisis results from the fact that the system, in extending its own capabilities, has also extended, and compli-cated, its feedback information loops to the point where it cannot accurately —or quickly enough—perceive the results of its actions.

An added danger with the second crisis is that it is a new kind of crisis. The world has known crises in belief before—as well as ideological crises. And we all have personal crises. But this current crisis, which is an unfamiliar mixture of technology, ecology, and politics, doesn't fit properly into any of these categories, so that we even have difficulty in understanding that it exists. It is the kind of situation where one could imagine people saying afterward (if there is an afterward): "Well, it wasn't really anybody's fault." It is a rather abstract, complicated crisis.

Assuming that one recognizes the existence of the crisis—or cluster of mutually exacerbating problems, to be more exact—one can react in a number of ways. The first is to attempt to improve the feedback information, and I take futures studies to be a part of this. Given the habits and momentum of industrial societies, particularly those where the rationale of business and production dominates, I do not imagine futurists will have very much effect on the course of events. In general, futurists are taken rather less seriously than astrologers were in ancient courts. A second reaction is to rely on an "overshoot mode" to teach us a lesson—that is, if we are still teachable. I think this kind of fatalism is quite common. The drawback with this argument is that people in a crisis can react in two ways: either by a change in consciousness or by hysteria. We should watch the handling of the energy crisis and its relation to Middle East politics during the next five years, as an indicator.

The third way of reacting to the crisis is to say that the system must adopt a fundamentally new attitude toward the "extension of its own capabilities," that is, technology. It is here that we come back to the question of images of the future, since it is obvious that certain kinds of positive images would be absolutely disastrous in the present situation, as for example, images of endless growth and extension, of total mastery, and so on. So images that might help resolve the first crisis (of purpose) might very well exacerbate the second. In this respect, I find Polak's argument not only misleading but highly dangerous.

In my own mind, I see a deep connection between all forms of mastery, whether it is over the beasts of the field, nature, so-called inferior races and cultures, or one's own instincts and unconscious. I see a connection between mastery and the Judeo-Christian images of final victory, the triumph of good over evil, the proletariat as the mystical body of Christ, and the pervasive images in European literature of journeying and arrival, the Grail, the voyage of discovery. We are rapidly becoming aware of the mastery mentality in social organization, in the form of technicist-based social engineering, which is a more interesting and revealing phenomenon than sheer authoritarianism, since it makes the final and inevitable link with knowledge as a form of mastery. But mastery, or perhaps Empire in Blake's terms, has been around much longer than we think. As Joseph Needham has pointed out:

> It is generally known that during the European middle ages there was a considerable number of trials and criminal prosecutions of animals in courts of law, followed frequently by capital punishment in due form. . . . The legal actions fall into three types: (a) the trial and execution of domestic animals for attacking human beings (for example the execution of pigs for devouring infants); (b) the excommunication or rather anathematization of plagues or pests of birds and insects; (c) the condemnation of *lusus naturae*, for example, the laying of eggs by cocks.[5]

Needham also points out in Volume 2 of *Science and Civilization in China* that a culture that rears animals is more likely to talk about mastery than a culture that grows crops. It is as if we see beasts everywhere.

Surely it is not an image of the *future* that we need, but an image of man and the world. Within this, there will be images of victory and images of harmony, but all subject to a basic proviso: that man cannot stand outside the world. And here, Freire's notion of dialogue is a rich seed-image, a kind of open dialectic, the male/female interplay of the Taoists, Edmund Husserl's dialogue or infinite meditation. Contrast this with the dominant high-technology model of research, development, diffusion, adoption. (Perhaps writers are particularly aware of the dialogue with self; see Robert Duncan again: "I study what I write as I study out any mystery. . . ."[6])

Along with the image of dialogue, I find another image recurring in my thoughts, that of the "field" of which one is a part, in which one is located. And significantly enough, this is an image or notion that is quite common in certain kinds of science. I say "significantly," because it suggests that a rejection of naive and brutal forms of mastery does not entail a reversion to an antiscientific primitivism. Although the relation of Taoism was to protoscience rather than science proper, it is surely of interest that Feng Yu-Lan says: "Taoist philosophy is the only system of mysticism which the world has ever seen which is not fundamentally antiscientific." If we want a label, we are dealing with a kind of organic naturalism. But these are Western labels, and we should use them only as a point of departure in trying to understand the Chinese phenomenon. In particular, it is important to realize that the

Chinese distinguished carefully between (human) law and (natural) organization.

Is it that science (nineteenth-century science) gives one the illusion of standing outside the world? So that even in our visions of apocalypse, we are *watching* it? Or is it the illusion that we have arrived at a total description of the world? And can thus stand back from it?

Gary Snyder:

> One moves continually with the consciousness
> Of that other, totally alien, non-human:
> Humming inside like a taut drum,
> Carefully avoiding any direct thought of it,
> Attentive to the real-world flesh and stone ... [7]

I will not try to speculate here on the likelihood of such a major shift in our images of the relationship between men and the world, subject and object, controller and controlled. I see some signs of it (sometimes confused with a revival of romanticism or gnosticism), but they seem pitiful compared to the drive and power of the dominant images. Also, there are probably more subtle and basic links between the two crises I identified, but I shall not go into that. I would like finally to comment on the two notions that have been central to my argument: the technologic and the poetic.

I see the human technological experiment, which began largely in China but found its characteristic and most cumulative form in post-Renaissance Europe, as having reached its limits. Or, rather, we are beginning to perceive that it is an experiment. The limits may appear to be ecological, but these are simply consequences of a more important psychological stance, an inner condition. This is, of course, the experimental stance, where the experimenter, as far as possible, stands outside the experiment. The usefulness, but also the unreality, of the experiment consists precisely in this "standing outside," and it is just this notion that the poetic brings into question, since it shows man to be inextricably part of the world, immersed in it. The illusion of "standing outside" can be maintained so long as we believe that the reductionist descriptions we give of the world in our various modes of discourse and knowledge are complete. But the existence of the poetic is a negation, in language, of that completeness. (George Oppen: "You do not write what you already know.")

It is not that the technologic and the poetic are opposed but that they move on different levels. The technologic mode is a useful subsidiary mode, and the images of autonomy and control that go with it are useful subsidiary images. But if, through a reductionist description of the world, we come to believe that it is the primary mode, then we begin to imagine that man is outside the world, or above the world, or that, with a lever, he could move the world.

In a largely technologic culture, poetry will tend to be about the experience of being an experimenter. Perhaps another way of putting this is to say that it exists in the space between what we think and what we live through.

Is not our fundamental condition, however, that of being *in* the world, and are not our images those of immersion, incompleteness, location, and dialogue that this state of being evokes?

NOTES

1. Bertolt Brecht, *Notes on Literary Work.*
2. Maurice Merleau-Ponty, *Phenomenology of Perception,* trans. Colin Smith (London: Routledge and Kegan Paul, 1962), p. xvi.
3. Ibid., p. xi.
4. Robert Duncan in *Audit/Poetry* 4, no. 3 (1967): 49. Published in Buffalo, New York.
5. Joseph Needham, *Science and Civilization in China* (New York: Cambridge University Press, 1956), vol. 2, p. 574.
6. Robert Duncan in *The New American Poetry,* ed. Donald M. Allen (New York: Grove Press, 1960), p. 400.
7. Gary Snyder, *A Range of Poems* (London: Fulcrum Press, 1966), p. 76.

Jacques Ellul

Search for an Image

The Western world, argues Ellul, has no common values for constructing an efficacious view of the future. We can, however, begin a project that might eventually lead to a new view of the future. To forestall a Third World without a future, we need a total reconversion of the West's economic and technical system. This project is essential to our survival and for giving us a reason for being. But we must confront the "will to transgress" and build upon a reasserted individualism.

I am not going to present any image of the future, for I do not think that an intellectual can form out of his dreams or imagination any useful image of it. The views of the future held by Tommaso Campanella, Thomas More, or Charles Fourier do not seem to have played the slightest historical role in the past nor foretold any future reality. If, on the contrary, it is claimed that

This article first appeared in *The Humanist*, November-December 1973.

Jesus at least presented a real view of the future, I would reply that in fact he did no such thing, since his was an eschatological conception, the very opposite of an "image of the future." If anything, it is through his life, and his resurrection, that some concept of the future imposed itself on his disciples, but never through his searching, his problems, or his themes.

In other words, all that the reveries and imagination of a group of intellectuals can represent is a literary product for internal consumption, quite without potential for providing society with either energy or goal. As to the images of the future of Huxley, Orwell, or Kafka, they only produce negative reactions among intellectuals. It is certainly not without importance to learn at least about the kind of future we should avoid. But the problem remains that artists and intellectuals who denounce a negative future are those least likely to modify the structure and operation of the powers that produce it, and those who have such power ignore the work of an Orwell or a Kafka.

What it comes to is this: a view of the future cannot—if it is to be meaningful—result from the effort of a single mind. It cannot be produced by arbitrary or artificial means or arrive from nowhere. A certain number of conditions must be satisfied if one's view of the future is to be more than poetry or make-believe. By not taking into account the conditions for forming an effective view of the future, one is left to choose between two points of departure.

The first is that of utopia; but, unlike many writers, I fail to see a positive value in utopian views. They do humanity no good. Whenever men have taken utopian descriptions seriously, the result has been disastrous. From an ideological angle, the crimes of liberal capitalism are partly explained by the seriousness with which Robinson Crusoe is treated, and the fact that Étienne Cabet and Fourier have been taken seriously has certainly hampered the development of socialism. It took Marx to put socialism back on the track. He investigated the socioeconomic reality of his time and foresaw its probable evolution, but never did he describe a desirable view of the future. He never stated explicitly what he meant by a "socialist" society.

The construction of a utopia always seems an attempt to avoid reality. It is true that a society that lacks a living image of the future is condemned to disappear. On the other hand, the efforts of some intellectuals to provide such an image will scarcely be enough to save a society.

In fact, intellectuals, contemplating the failure of their society, realize their political impotence and characteristically prefer to create utopias. This is much easier than appraising reality and its probabilities, which in themselves never represent futuristic concepts. Prediction, an operation by which the probable evolution of a system is calculated, is unable to produce an image that gives meaning to society. It represents either a concrete presentation of rational choices (which P. Masse has claimed to do for planification) or an unconquerable determinism, in whose presence man revolts. Utopianism is the remedy chosen by intellectuals to cure their impotence, but it is without any use to society as a whole.

It is true, however, that a view of the future held by a single man can involve the whole of society and direct it forward. That is, by using propaganda for purposes of indoctrination, power can be gained and held. Perhaps it was because Plato did not use propaganda (the Socratic method did not prepare him to become a Pericles) that he failed to transform Syracuse into his image of an ideal city. We saw Hitler impose on an immense collectivity an image of the future manufactured solely by himself; he produced and directed a future experienced by the whole world—not exactly what ideologists had foreseen but the result nonetheless of propaganda.

Beliefs in a millennium are generally of this kind. We associate this kind of belief with an image of the future shared by an important group of people. However, it is brought about by propaganda, a fact as much ignored as it is decisive. The idea of a millennium is never a spontaneous group creation; the group is in fact dominated by propaganda. But propaganda for a chiliastic ideology is successful only as it reflects views already present in the conscious mind, and this was true for Hitler also. Hitler, in his visions of the future, gave concrete form to an ensemble of beliefs and opinions, sentiments, desires, and hates held by the Germans of his time. Before Hitler, these feelings and sentiments were essentially amorphous and had little effect. It was by taking existing values, synthesizing them into a compelling form, and equipping them with instruments of power that Hitler's vision of the future began to seem viable. He did the reverse of what intellectuals are tempted to do for their utopias.

THREE CONDITIONS

One must consider, then, actual conditions for forming an image of the future that is to be socially effective. There are a great many such conditions. A true image of the future must depend, first of all, on the real experience of a people, on their feelings, and on the manner in which they represent these feelings. For the way they represent them is often more important than reality itself.

Second, one must take into account the range of the possible as it is imagined. What counts is not the individual imagination but the collective one. What we have to consider is neither the desirable, as such, nor the simple, scientifically calculated possibility. We then have something situated between these two poles which, if it is not on the point of realization, is still more serious than a fairy tale. It is essential to take into account the kind of possibility imagined by the collectivity. Otherwise our image of the future will never see the light of day.

Finally, one must consider the existence of values held in common by the group. A view of the future rests always on the totality, or scale, of values held collectively and questioned by no one. If a group has no values of that kind, it can have no view of the future. What one might propose when values are not shared will never be anything but the affirmation of one group against the social body, a group that may perhaps impose its goals but can never truly represent the future image of society.

If all three factors are not present, or if the second and third are lacking, no invented concept of the future could possibly be implemented. None would possess the power to put the social body into motion, give it meaning and direction—a *raison de vivre*. For an image of the future to have some real value, it must appear capable of being lived, and not merely desired—not only by the individuals who believe in it but by the social body as a whole.

We must energetically reject the irresponsible attitude that says: "We don't know what is really efficacious. Let us dream up any image of the future that appeals to us; let us throw the bottle into the sea; it may reach land somewhere. An idea seemingly devoid of all consequence eventually will have, perhaps only after centuries, immense repercussions; therefore, let us not bother with real consequences but rather hold to our dreams and desires."

This sort of attitude seems completely undesirable, because we cannot expect to see a slow, secret evolution of the futuristic views of intellectuals suddenly explode after centuries to give new shape to reality. If we are responsible intellectuals, we should abstain from launching all sorts of images and ideas. Instead, we ought to rigorously seek out the *one* concept that can be implemented effectively, allowing our society to continue to create its future, giving it a reason for being and some force of will. It is not a dilettante's or an uncommitted artist's attitude that brings this about. It is simply that, in a society characterized by its power of action and which strives indefinitely toward rationality without ever reaching it, the projection of the purely imaginary appears to be totally inadequate.

Our primary difficulty then—and one on which I shall not elaborate because it is self-evident—is that in the Western world commonly shared values have disappeared. Ancient traditional values are out of date, and it is impossible to revive values that have been rejected by society. When a society has lived by certain values and then has progressively stopped believing in them, it is absolutely useless to defend them or try to re-create them. There is no point in saying that Justice and Truth are always Justice and Truth, and so forth. To the extent that it is possible to give definition to these words, it serves no purpose to believe in their perennial value.

In fact, when there is no longer consensus on the *meaning* of a value, its content or its richness, it cannot be re-created artificially. The group must then work to create new values, to reach a consensus on a new meaning, to create new symbols. And, if society is not successful, it surely will disintegrate. In other words, it is now a time for invention, and we must stop acting as though traditional values still existed. But beyond the classical problems often enunciated in this context, it seems necessary to bring up three present-day difficulties—perhaps impossibilities.

DIFFICULTIES IN INVENTING NEW VALUES

The first difficulty is that in our society—perhaps because of its bigness or variety, its internationalization, or perhaps because of the mass media—there is a disassociation between real problems objectively posed by situations and often formulated by specialists, on the one hand, and what public opinion generally considers to be a problem, on the other. The latter often takes the form of politics.

An image of the future should be constructed in the light of real problems, but, ignored by the masses, these are seldom taken into consideration. For example, a real problem that affects the world is the structure of technology as an autonomous system; a fictitious problem, one that excited public opinion, was the Vietnam War. I do not say that there was no drama in the war, but it is not in terms of dramas of this sort that one can conceive the future. One can only present as an image of the future one that has roots in popular concepts. But popular opinion—polarized as it is over current events, with passionate feelings tending to obliterate the truth—is incapable of comprehending a view of the future that attempts to deal dispassionately with fundamental problems.

Never before in history has this kind of situation existed—whether it is because the community used to be smaller, because it dealt with down-to-earth problems, or because the mass of the population accepted established authority and there was no division between the views of the governing and those of the governed.

A second difficulty lies in the acceleration of history. In traditional societies an image of the future was formed slowly through an accumulation of experiences, a deep consciousness of reality, habitual presentation of competing ideas (with confirmed attempts at synthesizing them), and a progressive working out of details for the future society. All of this sometimes went on for generations. Men used to move slowly, advancing toward the future step by step, taking their time to approach their ideal, changing it little by little as they went along, adapting it to changing circumstances without ever annihilating it.

But in our technological society, everything changes quickly. What we are being asked for is a dynamic view of the future that can be presented immediately and widely for exposure to criticism and experiment. And it must be capable of quick implementation. As soon as one points out that it is impossible to solve in a day the problems engendered by technology, that what is involved is, rather, an enterprise of long duration, requiring the progressive modification of social structures, behavior patterns, and the prevailing mentality, then one immediately discerns a lack of interest in the whole proposition. All problems must be solved tomorrow, and social patterns fitting the preconceived project must be constructed artificially. This attitude derives not only from the accelerated pace of modern life but also from the proliferation of means to accomplish things. One knows that everything needed can immediately be brought into being (or should be!); thus the realization of an idea should be within grasp of fulfillment.

And so, one finds serious projects for a future world raised to the heights, only to disappear quickly. For, faced with the test of immediate applicability, an image of the future soon loses its mobilizing power.

It is sufficient to compare the slow evolution of the Christian view of the future, which took four centuries to elaborate, with the revolutionary socialist view, developed in less than half a century, which, according to its partisans, can be made operative in a few years. Nevertheless, socialism too is a concept obeying a slow evolutionary rhythm. Since World War II, we have seen in France at least three concepts of the future emerge. They generated enthusiasm, united the young, filled the newspapers, took on a mystical importance, entered the stage of practical application, and then quickly lost their appeal and disappeared. All of this in a few years! Those who went through one of these "waves of the future" are now profoundly skeptical and disabused, and no new view of the future could move them, give them new

hope, or provoke them into action. One experience of this sort is generally suf-
ficent for one lifetime. Those who lived under the image of the future
spawned by Hitler were capable of nothing more than a closed, self-centered
existence, rejecting any kind of novelty.

Finally, the third difficulty in producing a coherent image of the
future is the division between two major possibilities, which are antithetical
and irreconcilable.

On one hand, we find an image of the future attainable with the
means at our disposal. This one belongs to the domain of prediction, the important elements here being the means and their possibilities. Such would be,
for instance, the idea of the Great Society, a society producing well-being, leisure, consumption, and so forth, or, at a higher level, the concept of the scientific society, a society representing a rational equilibrium in growth.

This is the idea of a reasonable and "normal" future, but it is interesting to observe that this is not the view generally found in anticipatory
novels and in science fiction, because it arouses little general interest. Nobody
reads a novel to find out that we will soon have a six-hour workweek and that
leisure will have to be organized. This view is a bit like that of the horse
pulling the plow that makes the furrow; it contains nothing very exciting and
is effortless. When progress has such an inevitability, interest in the future is
destroyed and passivity results. Why should one search for the meaning of
life in what is only a path that unrolls automatically?

Nevertheless, full of goodwill, adults do attempt to make real this progress and potential. We did engage in a great adventure, man mastering
matter and society becoming a world of abundance, and now, although this
goal is almost reached, nobody is interested any longer.

Opposing this approach and in total disagreement with it is the other
quest for the future, conducted without considering the means available and
the social reality, but with man and his potential for growth in mind. This approach, favoring contemplation, an affirmation of the "I" and its amplifica-
tion, has been called the "counterculture."

It is evident that we are confronted by two tendencies so radically
opposed to each other that it is impossible to formulate clearly a view of the
future acceptable to both.

The tragedy in all this is that those who control the means and make
the machine run no longer have an acceptable view of the future to propose—
not because of a lack of intelligence or imagination but from the very fact
that they belong to a technological system which, to function properly, renders all finalities, such as judgments and proposals about the future, evanes-

cent and obsolete. In opposition are those who, while capable of formulating a view of the future clearly desired by a great many, are at the same time ignorant of social organization; but above all they are an adjunct to the technological society and a supplement to the consumer society, without which they could not survive. The legend of the economic autonomy of hippies as artisans is just that—a legend.

Torn between these two orientations, modern man simply refuses to think about the future or to escape it, and jumps into some unverifiable beyond—into utopia and the irrational.

WESTERN SOCIETY AND THE THIRD WORLD

It is undoubtedly easier to explain why a concept of the future is practically impossible to develop than it is to propose one. I think it necessary that we resolutely discard everything that refers to yesterday's values or beliefs. We can no longer speak of happiness in regard to the future. Happiness does not have meaning any more, for its content is too vague and its association with consumption too close. The concept of happiness has lost its credibility and its activating powers, and as a consequence we can do away with those things associated with it—leisure, consumption, and so forth.

Those hopes and formulas belonging to the past can no longer activate humanity, develop a society, generate great ardor. The same holds true for the ideologies of equality and socialism. We are speaking of myths, which, acceptable at one time, are today outdated. One should not make the mistake of believing that the great movements in the Third World have anything to do with post-Marxist scientific socialism. They come closer to an emotional, spontaneous form of socialism that consists less of planning a fundamental reorganization of the world than of beginning an equitable distribution of the world's riches and resources. This is the equivalent in the Third World of the *partageux* of the 1830s. That all this represents perfectly valid and sufficient reasons to mobilize and fight is evident. It is, however, not a view of the future and is useless for the Western world.

What should concern us are the impulses toward generosity, solidarity, and fraternity that the West feels toward the Third World. If we want to avoid having a Third World without a future, engaging in mere revolt, it is necessary to consider a total reconversion of the West's economic and technical system. We are facing, not a view of the future, but a reason for continuing to exist, change, and live. If we feel really responsible for the Third World's achievement of some kind of affluence and also the possibility of future development in the social, political, and human sense (and I want to stress that here I am much closer to Ivan Illich than to anyone else), then we have good reason for continuing to develop our own industrial power in order to put it at the further service of the underdeveloped world.

Let us not take the problem lightly; this is not a matter of handing out surplus goods. What we have to do is to totally reconvert our financial, economic, and even technological system—but without setting up a socialist regime. Our aims can be achieved perfectly well under a semicapitalist type of organization. The difficulty is not in the technical and organizational aspects of reconversion; we have done many more difficult things since 1938. The difficulty, rather, lies in the lack of support for a project of this type.

Think, too, of the unbearable difficulties that come up in fighting racism. It is incontestable that, as long as we continue to have violent reactions on the basis of color, no healthy relations can exist between the West and the Third World. In fact, the only project that seems capable of giving meaning to technological growth *and* of inducing the young to interest themselves in such growth comes up against a fundamental obstacle—an obstacle at once psychological and ideological. For here we encounter a tendency that is becoming decisive with modern man: the will to transgress.

From different starting points, we are all now on the same road. Our real desire is to transgress—laws, limits, taboos. We will not put up with limitations. And I include all of us, not just the young. This is a powerful movement supported by every social stratum and by all generations. In the main, its discoveries have been bitter. The transgression of sexual taboos leads to discovery of the essential sterility of eroticism, even as the use of drugs leads to an even greater enslavement. For the real limit that Western man seeks to transgress, and around which he fumbles desperately, is himself. His error consists in believing that he goes beyond his limits when he denies his condition as a creature and hopes to become an angel. His real limit is self-imposed. It is his enclosure, not in the social context, but in an impatience to give himself to another being, to someone who is different, who does not resemble him.

Such is today the real problem for Western man. We are actually facing a "new frontier." We have to rediscover the life-style of frontier days, push it back ceaselessly, or transcend it. But there are only two possibilities for transcendence: one can either increase his power and possessions or give meaning to his life. Modern man suffers from having power and wealth, but he is quite without power to give meaning to his life. The only chance our society has of surviving is to adopt the project I have outlined. Perhaps it is old-fashioned to talk about a "conversion of the heart," but it is precisely this we need—nothing less than repentence.

If this reorientation of our economic and technical power in terms of cooperation rather than in terms of aid or charity does indeed imply a transformation of our structures and institutions, it can be the Great Crusade modern man requires. One of the typical errors made by all governments in their confrontation with youth occurs when the latter are told how laws, organizations, and so forth are going to be changed.

A NEW VIEW OF THE FUTURE

An image of the future for modern man must be something more than the description of a society of well-oiled machines whose legal foundation is satisfactory and in which problems are resolved by law. Our image of the future has to be a dynamic one. We cannot be satisfied with the ideal society of Plato in which everything is fixed and unchanging. What matters is a movement forward, the question being: toward what? That toward which we move cannot be a mountain placed before us nor a heavenly Jerusalem all decked out to delight us. That toward which we move must come into existence as we live and advance toward it. This is why the young try to experience what adults often reproach them about: a revolt that does not appear to have any goal and is without any kind of program. What matters is to live and not to attain an objective; the objective creates itself through lived experience. This in turn implies the complete subordination of all organizational means to our project.

When we talk about an image of the future we must think of a unanimous, rather than a uniform, society, in which the Third World will be able to *develop* (and not by merely committing itself to economic progress) in all of its own dimensions, independently of and in cooperation with the West. I do not have in mind the creation of an international fund for food or development or even new institutions to aid Third World countries. An institutional project can only be supported if the people have accepted it, been convenienced by it, been converted to this image of the future—if the people see in this image their raison d'être. Here is a way to resolve one of the most difficult problems of the West—that posed by the autonomy of its technique. If, however, a Great Crusade with material consequences stirs the souls of Western people, then the autonomy of technique will be questioned.

But the Great Crusade cannot be directed toward increased power and well-being; in such an orientation, the autonomy of the technological system can only grow. The technological system cannot develop in any way other than by making itself autonomous; it is a power directed toward power and cannot forbid itself means or sums. The Great Crusade must be resolutely oriented toward a decrease in power among the present holders of power and toward the nonenrichment of the owners of capital. This certainly implies a change of heart, but by this I do not mean some pious vow or spiritual appeal. What we are faced with is a matter of life or death. If the people of the West do not find a project worthy of maintaining their society, then the West, not having found some reason for living, will die—and this without a new war or a revolt of the Third World.

This crusade will not come about simply as a result of propaganda. No propaganda can lead to comprehension of the Other. It is necessary to start at the most profound human level; the collective project can only be stirred by a new thrust of the individual. If we do not want a mere propagandist's image of the future, we must have one that results from the individual's will to reassert himself in the etymological sense of the world (*individuus*: the central kernel that cannot be divided). We must think of a human being in this sense in thinking of the future, for without such an individual there will be nothing but the blind growth of the system behind a smokescreen of good intentions and idealistic chatter—proof of the impotence of man hidden by the multiplication of his powerful mechanism.

This is why I appeal to the individual. He is in danger of being destroyed as much by the system as by psychopedagogical means of influencing and manipulating him. Our first step should be to stop the flood of psychological and psychoanalytical activities, the wave of pseudo-Freudianism and Marxo-Freudianism, and the tendency to rely on the psychoanalyst and group dynamics. Otherwise, the West will miss its only chance, which requires the return of the individual to the struggle, a struggle conducted by him, for him. We must start with the individual, for he is the one most threatened. Our appeal corresponds to the appeal from today's youth and to their project; above all else they want to be individuals, even when they form communities. They want to be different, authenticate themselves! But the young are becoming individuals with an unhappy consciousness, imbued with feelings of fatality; theirs is a flight from rationality. We must now turn back to the individual in a critical, constructive, and creative way and rediscover the road—the oldest in the world and one least followed—of cooperation with and understanding of others.

Thomas F. Green

Stories and Images of the Future

Green insists that our visions of the future are always grounded in our uses of the past. Shared visions are transmitted from generation to generation through the telling of stories that provide a common mythological structure for belief and confidence in the future. The central problem confronting Western civilization may be that we have lost our capacity for shared stories.

Men and women do not possess visions of the future. They are possessed by them. On the whole, we are not free to decide what our visions of the future will be. We do not choose them. There is a sense in which they choose us. Indeed, it seems to me unintelligible to suggest that visions of the future shared by any large number of people were ever made up—invented or created for that purpose and then spread about as in some kind of evangelical or missionary movement. I do not doubt that such shared visions of the future can be transmitted from generation to generation. But it seems odd, nonetheless, even to suggest that they are learned. It would accord more with experience to suggest that they are planted. They take root. They grow and take possession of our consciousness.

But how? Essentially through the telling of stories. We are free to invent the concrete details of the stories, but we are no more free to invent what the stories are about than we are free to invent the past. If the capacity for shared images of the future is lost in the modern world, it is partly—perhaps even largely—because the capacity for shared stories is lost, stories that provide a common mythological structure for belief. Visions of the future have always been essentially mythological; they probably always will be. And it is the nature of mythology that it is conveyed in story and in art. Art in general, and stories in particular, are of course made up. They are acts of the imagination. To a literal-minded people, it may therefore seem that stories, especially those bearing mythological content, are only made up: they are not true; they did not really happen; they are not historical and therefore do not command belief.

Nothing could be farther from the truth. A mere product of the imagination that has no roots in experience, that does not reflect the truths that men and women know about themselves and their world, will not take root. It would be, as it were, *only* a piece of fiction and not the grounds for visions of either past or future. A story that takes root in consciousness will never add to what people know except as it sums up what they already know, and it will not take root unless it sums up what they already find in their experience. A successful mythological story vivifies the memories of people. Such stories do not provide the premises from which we are to reason about the nature of human beings, youth, power, nature, and so forth. Rather they provide the conclusions that give meaning to the truths we already know about these things. Indeed, it is the function of myth to render memorable those truths that are so timeless and basic that otherwise they could not be easily taught or recalled. Such stories, nonetheless, always rest on fact even though in detail they never happened, are not historical, and are only "made up."

In this way, our visions of the future are always grounded in our uses of the past. They derive without exception from memory. That may seem an odd, even contradictory, claim to make in a day when a common form of story telling is science fiction. Nonetheless, it is worth observing that there can never, in principle, be any stories of the future. There can be, and are, stories that are *set* in some future time. But they are always composed as from a past that is future. That we can develop stories as from a past that is yet to come is no more consequential than that we can develop stories from the perspective of a future that is past. There is no way to develop images of the future except by learning how to be instructed by the past.

THE NATURE OF HOPE

These claims may seem odd to us, even indefensible. Yet their truth is evident when we try to consider in detail the most conspicuous part of any vision of the future, namely, the nature of hope itself. We could not possibly understand the nature of visions of the future without understanding the nature of hope itself.

Hope is an astonishing human capacity. It is future-directed, never directed to the past; it is always factual, never counterfactual. It is, therefore, never wishful. It is an emotion, yet its existence requires a certain kind of world. It is neither prediction, forecast, nor expectation, yet it leads to all three.

Among the human emotions there are some, like love, that are indifferent to time. I can love what is past, present, or future or, for that matter, what is here or what is absent. With respect to time and place, love is an emotion whose object is ubiquitous. There are other human emotions or capacities that are peculiarly oriented to the past, like pride. I can only be proud of what already is, not of what is yet to be. And when the object of pride seems to lie in the future, it is always because in the past there is some event that assures its future occurrence. I can say "I am proud that I *shall* receive the Pulitzer Prize" only if there has been a decision to award the prize to me, that is to say, only if the prize *has been* awarded to me. In these respects hope is unlike love or pride or any other of the human capacities that are indifferent to time or directed solely to the past. I cannot hope for what is past, and I have no need to hope for what is present. Love is an emotion that *can* be directed toward something that is not yet. Love, therefore, *can* lead us into the future, but hope cannot do otherwise.

Though hope is exclusively directed toward the future, it is not wishful thinking. We may wish for what we know or believe to be impossible or contrary to fact or in the past. We can hope, however, only for what still lies in the future and for what we know or believe to be possible. We may say "I wish he had not been elected," but we say "I hope he will be elected." The verb *to wish* takes the subjunctive mood—which is to say that it extends to what never was and never can be. We say "I wish he were . . . "or "I wish I were . . . "or "I wish things were . . . ." The verb *to hope* has no such character. We do not say "I hope I were stronger"; we say "I hope to be stronger." Wishing can take in things that are impossible and contrary to fact. Hoping cannot. Therefore wishing can continue long after hope is lost. To be without hope is to be of the opinion that what might have been the object of my hope is incapable of realization. I can wish, however, even when I am without hope that what I wish for can be realized. In these respects, hope is to be contrasted with wishing. It is always based on the belief that the object of hope is possible. That belief may turn out to be false. But if it does, then hope vanishes. In that respect, hope is a kind of expression of confidence. It is a confidence, grounded always in fact, that one's world is able to sustain possibilities for the future. Hope, therefore, is not just any old attitude about the future. It is, on the contrary, a quite specific and positive belief about what the future will be like.

Hope is an emotion. It is an emotion that contains a belief. Like any other emotion it possesses a logical structure that we can describe, but unlike most other emotions, it also has a social structure. It requires a certain kind of world, a world that provides abundant factual evidence that good things can be. And without memory, that evidence cannot be bundled up to be the bearer of any person's hope. Hope cannot exist without a world that is believed to be pregnant with *good* possibilities, and *that* belief cannot exist without memory. We would all recognize that a person whose life is filled with wishes rather than hopes is either someone who has lost all touch with reality or someone whose world has provided no memories sufficient to sustain hope.

In this respect, we can also see that hope is a value-laden emotion. It is a feeling of confidence, containing a belief about what is good. We can predict, forecast, or even expect what is evil, but we cannot hope for it. We hope only for things that are good. Socrates claimed that knowledge is virtue. Philosophers have argued endlessly about the consistency of that claim and about its adequacy as grounds on which to rest the search for moral knowledge. But at the level of human emotions, there is no doubt that it is true. The Socratic point was that no one does evil because it is evil; he does so only because he believes that in it there is some good. That is the essential premise. From it one might derive the conclusion that people do what is not good because they have mistaken beliefs about what is good. Correct their beliefs about what is good, and their behavior will be remedied. I suppose that Socratic premise might be doubted. Perhaps it is false that people never do what is evil except as they see in it some good. But surely, it is true that no one hopes for what is evil. That cannot be doubted. This is a primary feature that sets hope apart from expectations, predictions and forecasts. We can and do predict, forecast, and even expect what we do not hope for.

Still, having hope, we have expectations. We sow seeds that we expect to harvest. We invest and expect return. We expect the harvest and the return of good things. Hope requires that kind of world. Yet, it requires something else as well. In a world where luck is the only god, there is no hope. Good fortune, of course, may nurture one's confidence in the future. But it can also strengthen one's fear of misfortune, and therefore confirm a person in a kind of sickly caution. If I believe that the good things in life come only as a consequence of luck, then I must also believe that the future is filled with insecurity and therefore so is the present. Luck, after all, has a way of "running out." In good times I would seek to guard against bad times. I would hedge my bets. Instead of venturing freely into the future with that sense of confidence associated with hope, I would seek to guard against it.

That kind of world would be a poor seedbed for hope, although it would seem to provide fertile ground for the growth of prudence. In fact, however, where luck is the only god, there cannot even be prudence. For the exercise of prudence presupposes the kind of world in which something done now can affect the future. But in a world where there is only luck, there cannot be such human potency. Where luck is the only presiding force in life, people are impotent. And where people are impotent, there can be no point to prudence and no grounds for the confidence that is at the heart of hope.

Good luck, in short, is not enough for hope. What more is needed? Competence and potency. If I live in a world that is pregnant with good possibilities, then I live in a world that contains, among other possibilities, the possibility that I am—or can become—good. But from the vantage point of the interior life of men and women, to be good means always to be good *at* something or good *for* something. In short, the experience of being good, of having worth, is the experience of competence, but an experience in ways that demand the witnessing and endorsement of other people. The experience of competence that I am trying to describe is the experience that any person has when he is able to point to or describe something he has done and say in effect, "See that? I did that. Isn't that good?" The implication sought is "Therefore, am *I* not good?" A world that allows that kind of self-validation also allows action, potency, competence, and the possibility of good things in the future. It is a world that allows hope, a world that permits the memories of good things to be shaped on the basis of something more than luck. And because hope demands this kind of competence, it demands also the presence of other people. Hope, in short, brings us to the edge of community.

THE POWER OF HOPE AND MAJOR MOVEMENTS IN WESTERN HISTORY

As against this analysis of hope, it might be argued vigorously that men and women, even whole cultures, have sometimes been guided by visions of the future even when the world permitted neither potency, competence, community, or even partial escape from luck. Perhaps it is one thing to describe the conditions under which individuals may have hope. But it may be still another to describe how people come to be possessed by visions of the future, and how in times of deep disarray, like our own, they can come to be repossessed by some shared vision that will suffice to lead them on. Having a vision or image of the future is not the same as having hope. Or is it?

The question deserves serious thought. It seems to me however that there are five, or possibly six, periods or movements in Western history that come to mind when we try to think about the power of presiding images of the future and that in every one of them the conditions I have described are satisfied. Whatever we may mean by an image of the future, it cannot be a power in life or in history unless it can be rendered as a reasonable hope. That is at least the minimum condition that any image of the future must satisfy if it is to be a power in the lives of people and history, instead of a mere wish.

Consider what we know of such examples. There is the experience of ancient Israel with its evocative pictures of the "Day of the Lord." There is the rich and conflicting mixture of visions that belong to the Christian era. There is the Enlightenment, and within it the secularized versions of Christian eschatology. There is also within that movement the Marxist versions of the eschaton, and over and against it is the romantic vision that the way forward is the way back. To these one might add, of course, nationalism, a movement that has swept the world and has been the source of powerful and different visions of the future. Each of these movements has given content to human hope because of the way that each has used the past. In each case the presiding image of the future is, in fact, an image of the past and, moreover, a mythological image of the past. That would be too strong a statement to defend in all particulars. But is it not too strong a statement to make the point, especially in a time when people often do not know, and think they do not need, the uses of the past.

For example, the images of the future found in the experience of Israel are altogether unintelligible except in relation to stories about events past. Implanted in the memories of people, those visions of the future reveal the hidden meaning of these stories, and the visions are learned and their meaning grasped only by telling the stories. The events recounted in those stories, in turn, provide grounds for the confidence in the future that transforms those images from being mere wishes to being real hopes.

The Christian vision is perhaps unique in making the future rest squarely in the past. The central Christian doctrine, perhaps the only one that Christianity cannot do without, is the doctrine of incarnation. It is the story of an event that is claimed to have actually happened. Within that tradition, if we wish to know what the future will be, then we can always turn to the story of the incarnation. All the essentials are present in it. Confidence in the future is possible in the framework of that tradition precisely because the problem of the future has already been settled. It has only to be brought to completion.

Such a vision of the future, grounded as it is in a story of the past, could not be cut off from its roots in memory by a people already deeply familiar with the story. Even Marx could not escape conceiving of the future within a Christian framework. But he did so in the secularized version of the Enlightenment. In the introdution to his *Lectures on Political Economy,* he observed that bourgeois society is the last stage of prehistory. In this one observation Marx places the eschaton—which is usually understood to be at the end of history—in the future and at the beginning of history. He conceives of it as the beginning of history, however, because he conceives it as the beginning of human freedom, action, and agency. It is to be that time when men are indeed liberated from history as a process to which they are subject and begin to embark on true history as the story of deeds done. They are freed from mere luck. Marx's entire effort was bent to rest that image of the future upon solid scientific grounds, to transform it, as it were, from the status of a mere utopian wish to the status of a real and reliable guiding hope. This was to be done by providing a secular and scientific structure to the story of history so that men, having an understanding of the past, would have the patience, perservance, and incentive to hasten the inevitable dawn. The problem of the future was thus resolved by providing a rational structure to the past. The remaining task was merely to hasten the future, to cooperate with the coming of what was to come in any case.

Similar observations can be made about the romantic movement of the nineteenth century and the renewal of the romantic impulse in our own day. The image of the future is to be found in the evocation of the past. And there can surely be no doubt that within the nationalist mood, in all its forms, the visions of the future are framed only by recounting—some would say by inventing—stories of events and deeds long past.

These are generalizations of course. They are generalizations about enormous movements in Western history. They probably suffer the defects of most generalizations, namely, the omission of exceptions and counterarguments. However, it is not my concern here to defend their factual accuracy. My point is rather to make vivid, if not clear, what I mean by the claim that our visions of the future are grounded always in our uses of the past. Whether that claim is true is a decision I can leave to others; but what it *means* is a matter I cannot defer.

With the addition of two observations these generalizations will serve clarity well enough. The first need is to see in what special and ambiguous way it is that memory enters into our visions of the future. The second is to see in what rather special and unambiguous way I mean to refer to the past.

HOPE, MEMORIES, AND STORIES OF THE PAST

Memory lies on the other side of hope. Memory relates exclusively to the past, hope exclusively to the future. Yet they are so related that Gabriel Marcel, in a stunning turn of phrase, can speak of having a "memory of the future." In his hands that is a successful metaphor, and like every successful metaphor it has its roots in the facts of experience. What are those roots?

We have observed already that hope cannot exist at all without memory of rather concrete and specific events. Hoping differs from wishing in its peculiar dependence on fact. It involves a sense of confidence that the future can be good. And such confidence can have no other foundation than the memory of good things. It rests on the sense, derived from nowhere but memory, that the world contains promise. It is worth observing, by the way, that many other human capacities are similarly dependent on memory. Without memory, there can be no friends. Someone incapable of memory, in fact, cannot even have acquaintances. Every encounter would be wholly fresh, new, and unique. There is value in the idea that every human meeting should contain something fresh and new, but there is no virtue in the reality if the cost is the sacrifice of friendship. There is hardly a human virtue that does not similarly rest on the possibility of memory. Promising, for example, is a peculiar act. It is one of a small class of moral practices whose purpose it is to fix the future, to render it stable. Yet the very possibility of such a moral practice rests on the capacity of human beings to remember what was promised and when. Hope and memory, future and past, are tied together by the human capacity for such specific memories. I shall describe this kind of memory as *factual*, though in doing so I have in mind, not the kind of acts that enter into our knowledge of the academic disciplines, but the kind that enter into autobiography.

But there is another kind of memory, a kind that is more expansive and less factual but which is just as vital to visions of the future as factual memory is to hope. I shall call it *social memory* because it is the kind of memory that provides self-understanding by explaining to people their place in some social history. Social memory is therefore always a shared memory or, at any rate, a memory of a shared past. Still *history* is not the word to describe the kind of past involved in social memory. J. H. Plumb in *The Death of the Past* (Boston: Houghton Mifflin, 1970) has drawn "a sharp distinction" between the past and history. History, according to Plumb, is the truth of what happened; the past, by contrast, is a story. It is, as it were, the family album, the symbols, pictures, and metaphors of a collective. A vision of the future is always grounded in a story of the past, not in history. The past is always, therefore, to a large extent mythological. It may contain much that is historical, but it is not the same as a history. Stories of the past contain truth and histories contain meaning, but what is important to history is its truth, not its meaning, and what is important to a story of the past is its meaning and not its truth.

Plumb celebrates the death of the past and the rise of history. "Above all," he writes, "one hopes that the past will not rise phoenix-like from its own ashes to justify again, as it so often has, the subjection and exploitation of men and women, to torture them with fears, or to stifle them with a sense of their own hopelessness. The past has only served the few; perhaps history may serve the multitude" (p. 17). What Plumb celebrates others might justifiably regret. We can all share with him the knowledge that specific stories of the past have been the source of oppression and endless mischief and join him in the hope that that will not occur again. But one cannot help wondering on what historical grounds Plumb permits himself such a hope. Or is it better voiced as a wish?

It seems to me implausible in the extreme to suppose that history, as opposed to some compelling story of the past, will ever provide the grounds for a reasonable hope, much less the fertile basis for any vision of the future. Men rely on mythology. They have done so in every vision of the future that

I know of, and I assume they will continue to do so. They require stories.

CONDITIONS FOR NEW VISIONS OF THE FUTURE

What visions of the future might reasonably prevail in the years ahead of us? I do not know. Nor do I believe that anybody else knows. But I believe I know what the problem is. It has three parts. The first is that we shall have to provide the kind of world that can sustain and nurture hope. That means one that permits the accumulation of good memories, the exercise of competence, and escape from the tyranny of luck. It means, secondly, that it is a world in which men and women do not confuse the limited stories of particular pasts with the vision of human limits and possibilities. The tyranny of the past that Plumb so much regrets stems not from the pervasive power of stories, but from the human capacity to confuse national stories with the stories of the human race. Stories and myths there must be if there is to be anything like a compelling shared image of the future. But those stories and their understanding of human limits should not be understood in limited ways.

The third requirement is the renewed capacity to see that the story of any particular person can be in fact the story of every person. If there is any certainty in our knowledge of visions of the future, it is that those visions always involve the consciousness of some collective. The I-We tension is as essential as I-It and I-Thou in the formation of any serviceable vision of the future. The dismaying fact of so many contemporary visions of the future is their thorough individualism. We shall have to learn once again that the story of any particular person's life is essentially the same as everyone's.

Drew Christiansen, S.J.

Blind Prophets and
Quick-Witted Kings

Christiansen begins his essay with a basic question: Why are we looking for a science of the future? He concludes that the primary reason is not to develop methods, policies, or images of the future but to find new attitudes toward collective symbols and new habits of mind for living with them creatively. Within this orientation he has assembled a challenging assortment of books by a number of contemporary thinkers.

Why are we in search of a science of the future? We are looking for new vigor in our public life. Our hope is that a new discipline for the study of the future will provide us with new aims to elicit our commitment and thereby stir up new social energies for the enhancement of life.

    The primary work of this prognostic science will be neither the development of methods for thinking about the future nor the formation of poli-

This article first appeared in *The Humanist*, November-December 1973.

cies that minimize undesirable trends and maximize desirable ones. It will not even be the development of images of the future. What we need from futurists is more than new aims and goals. We need new attitudes toward collective symbols and new habits of mind for living with them creatively.

We are in search of a second naiveté, in which purposeful, yet conscientious, action is our pleasure once more. In this mature innocence, social energy will be released in the pursuit of a common life that nurtures the freedom and the intelligence of every man. We are a long way, however, from attaining such social innocence.

Our consciousness is anything but innocence. We are everywhere aware of our fallibility. Once upon a time, we thought a separation of fact and value might provide for the rational guidance of life, in which commitment would not produce blind zealotry and public symbols would not be an excuse for intransigence. But after Vietnam and more than a decade of social turmoil, such solutions seem simpleminded. Now we ask: How can we supersede the opposition of fact and value, of the rational and the conative in public life?

Answers do not come easily. Unrestrained adherence to inflexible symbols was the source of social distress for so long that we hesitate to surrender readily the tools of rational criticism and construction by which we broke the tyranny of the past. Yet systems analysis and other tools of late industrial society are symbolic systems as well, and they have been found wanting. They too have been overdetermined, and our commitment to them has been irrational. Not so long ago one data-processing giant was telling us that its products gave us not information but reality. No better token might be found for the hubristic use of symbols than their slogan.

Our own use of symbols has been as insensitive and manipulative as that of any dogmatism of the past. As a result, we are caught between a desire for public purpose, which we fear is atavistic, and an unrestrained technicism, which we fear will be our death. There is a growing consensus among those who think about our societal destiny that this cultural ambivalence has brought us to a dead end.

In *Between Two Ages: America's Role in the Technetronic Era* (New York: Viking, 1970), Zbigniew Brzezinski sees the source of our cultural impasse in the triumph of liberal skepticism. Once the traditional integrating institutions of society faltered as a result of critical opposition, liberalism itself was also destined to collapse. "Skepticism," writes Brzezinski, "was simply not enough when it emerged as the triumphant antithesis of traditional religion. . . . What they [liberals] were forced to ask themselves was to be the substance of a victorious skepticism."

If writers on the future might be categorized as analysts, critics, pundits, or visionaries, Brzezinski might best be called an analyst. He is an astute observer of the conflicting and often contradictory forces counterpoised in the modern world. He is at his best in dissecting the ambivalences of political and social systems. One of the major themes of *Between Two Ages* is that the explosion of technical possibilities has set off a social implosion and caused a collapse of human imagination. Brzezinski is disturbed by this condition, but as an analyst he offers no vision by which we might escape it.

Like Brzezinski, Daniel Callahan is agitated by the pervasive Pyrrhonism of our age. People in every quarter, he complains, are asked to pose "unbearable questions, bringing no solace, yielding no ready answers. . . . Everything should not be demanded of everyone." Callahan's *The Tyranny of Survival* (New York: Macmillan, 1973) makes a bold move in an unpopular direction. What is needed, he argues, is a culture that will instill "good habits, sensitive emotional responses, ennobling desires and healthy repugnances." He presents no visions of what this new culture might be like. He pleads, in fact, not for more visionaries but for antivisionaries who know their own limits.

The Tyranny of Survival examines two allied moral pathologies: the justification of coercive restraint in the name of survival, and, in the name of individualism, the legitimization of the fulfillment of every desire promoted by the technological materialism that has dominated our recent history.

Callahan is a critic. He is wary of sentimentality yet conscious of the limits of reason in human affairs. The result of this singular combination of attitudes is a flirtation with a Freudian theory of culture—as a prelude to more specific questions—to provide a theoretical foundation for ethics in a technological society. Although I do not believe Freud's thought can undergo an interpretation that calls for renewed subjection to a cultural superego, Callahan's use of Freud provides helpful insights into the human sources of technological disease. If we understand Freud, he suggests, we know that satisfying unlimited desires will always put the individual and society in opposition. The pathologies of technicism are due in part to the insatiable demands of libido but, in part as well, to the development of false satisfactions of real needs, in a society that exploits every want for its own profit.

In *The Farther Reaches of Human Nature* (New York: Viking, 1971) Abraham Maslow argues for the integration of individual and societal satisfactions and of the skeptical with the integrating mentality. The normative social psychologist must ask, he writes, "How [do we] integrate enthusiasm with skeptical realism? Mysticism with practical shrewdness and good reality testing? Idealistic and therefore unattainable goals (needed as compass directions) with good-natured acceptance of unavoidable imperfections of means?"

Pleas for a new policy science, such as are found in Fred Polak's *Prognostics* (New York: Elsevier, 1971), do not answer Maslow's question. The heart of the futurist problem is not in the value-free objective realism of sociology but in the dynamics of society as a whole. How does any group balance commitment with responsiveness, and the relatively static symbols required for social cohesion and determined action with the shifting needs of a plurality of factions?

Prognostics is the work of a pundit. It applies a great deal of conventional wisdom to a current problem. The result is less than stimulating. Polak has two immediate tasks in mind. The first is to present the case for normative social science that will overcome the value-free sterility of sociology. The other is to win over European policymakers from their genteel reluctance to engage in research and development.

Polak's central insight is that Western imagination has been hampered by an uncontrolled desire for certainty. While the physical sciences have grown philosophically sophisticated about the role of human intervention in knowing, social scientists, he contends, have adhered to a classical objectivity in their epistemology. As a consequence, the social scientist has failed to fertilize modern institutions with new social inventions.

Abraham Maslow was a social scientist who broke with the orthodoxies of his own field and consequently furnished us with a whole new humanistic vocabulary, new disciplines, social inventions, and new orientations in old fields of study. He was a visionary, and the effects of his work are a witness to the fruitfulness of visionary thinking for society at large.

Maslow never stopped growing. His early works, *Motivation and Personality* (2nd ed.; New York: Harper and Row, 1970) and *Toward a Psychology of Being* (2nd ed.; New York: Van Nostrand, Reinhold, 1968), went through several editions, and each showed a refinement of insight and a broadening of perspective that betray the humility of a genuine learner. *The Farther Reaches of Human Nature* is a posthumous collection of essays Maslow wrote over the last thirteen years of his life and which he himself had begun to revise for publication. There is little that is utterly novel for those who have read Maslow's earlier work, but refinements, new formulations of insight, hints of new problems, and questions will delight and enlighten those already familiar with his work. Especially significant is his growing concern that what he had learned from the study of self-actualizing people be applied not only to the norms of individual psychology but also to the reconstruction of our social institutions. His use of American Indian and Eskimo tribes to illustrate what these social institutions might be like suggests that we must forego the illusion that we are an advanced society with nothing to learn from economically less-complex groups.

Maslow was concerned with how we might advance beyond our present cultural impasse. In thinking about how we might do just this, we converge on four themes: (1) the decline of materialism, (2) pluralism, (3) self-control, and (4) conviviality.

The first point, on which there is wide agreement, is that we have reached the limits of economic materialism. The development of a human society depends, in this view, on a shift from economic activity to the expanding sector of symbolic interrelations as the heart of public life. In *The Limits to Growth* (New York: Universe Books, 1972) the Club of Rome, for instance, argues that equality and justice will be possible only when the myth of economic growth is abandoned.

By now *The Limits to Growth* is a significant force in public discussions of the future. The Club of Rome's studies of the multiple relations between economic and demographic growth on the one hand and the depletion of natural resources on the other is a milestone in social-science research. It has alerted the world to the perils of continuing on the present course in pursuit of affluence. But perhaps the work came too late. For the most awesome trend revealed by these studies is the lag between the application of curbs on present trends and the appearance of results from the curbs. Whether we choose limits for ourselves or not, we shall have to face life in an economy of constraint.

In *The Active Society* (New York: Free Press, 1968) Amitai Etzioni projects "a decline in the obsession with material assets and rewards." In a society where participation in public life is esteemed, he proposes, "the strains of scarcity will be reduced more readily, since symbols—unlike objects—can be given away and still retained." Similarly, Maslow sets up as ideal those high-synergy societies in which people are esteemed not for what they have but for what they give away.

Such a paradoxical system of rewards means an inversion of our puritan instrumentalism, in which more for one means less for another. The correlates in utopian designs of this sort are our tools on the one hand and our creative powers on the other. The goal is to obtain an equilibrium in which tools extend human powers without becoming instruments for the dominance of some people over the rest of mankind.

Proponents of economic limitation differ with establishment futurists, who extrapolate from present trends to an era that will see a growing gulf between the advanced nations and the developing ones. Brzezinski calls this process the "global ghetto." The ghettos of the global city will exhibit the characteristics of a revolution of rising expectations, as their consciousness of their needs, increased by education and mass communication, outstrips their ability to meet these needs.

Lester Brown, in *World without Borders* (New York: Random House, 1972), surveys global problems that must be met in the next two decades: environment, poverty, unemployment, hunger, urbanization, education, population, and transportation. He argues that such massive difficulties cannot be controlled without international organization and control of population. His solutions would tend, however, to strengthen uniformity in culture and the control of individual life for the sake of the common good. One of the social inventions, for instance, that he thinks will affect the future for the better is the multinational corporation. It is difficult to imagine, however, how the multinationals, without strong international controls, would serve the people rather than their own self-interests.

One of the trends Brown misses, but which is recognized by both the opponents of growth and those who accept it, is pluralism. Both economic austerity and further growth in the global city, as seen by Brzezinski, are understood as the conditions of creative pluralism in social life. Pluralism means more than tolerance for a variety of ethical and religious traditions. Ivan Illich contends, in *Tools for Conviviality* (New York: Harper & Row, 1973), that pluralism means the diminishment of those radical monopolies—the automobile-petroleum lobby, funeral directors, home builders, and professional educators, for example—whose control of some sector of life prevents the use of alternative means.

Pluralism will also witness the emergence of new sociopolitical organizations. These will not merely represent collective viewpoints on all problems of the day; more significantly, they will help activate new groups around a variety of interests. It is possible, says Brzezinski, that political parties will decline in importance and that organized local, regional, urban, professional, and other interests will provide the focus for political action, and, further, that shifting national coalitions will form on an *ad hoc* basis around specific issues of national import.

Brzezinski sees a blurring of distinctions between private and public bodies already, as a result of more widespread participation in decision making and the interpretation of a broader range of interests as general concerns. He views the continuance of this trend as being more likely than the rise of repressive regimes. "The dynamic congestion of the global city is inimical to a disciplined, centralized organization whose purpose is . . . to create a globally uniform social order."

Nonetheless, pressures for uniformity may be difficult to resist. Not everyone values self-imposed austerity. The possibility is considerable that a fascistic technologism would impose a highly centralized social system in order to maintain life at near-present levels of material consumption.

Uncontrolled scientism tends also toward homogenization of man. In *The Tyranny of Survival* Callahan warns against proposals, made in the name of science, that aim at the creation of a perfect man through genetic engineering. "An image of man based on a pluralistic conception of reality has been hard won. It would be a supreme irony if in the name of ever greater progress, there was to be re-introduced the old monistic, nontypical kind of thinking, this time, as before, in the name of value, good order, and a mythical notion of perfection."

The third condition for renewed social agency is self-restraint in our symbolic social processes. An excellent treatment of this topic is found in Etzioni's *The Active Society*. For those whose minds are filled with questions on how a high-participation society can be created and how images of the future relate to power and the realization of values, this theoretical study is recommended.

A more intuitive and practical book that also proposes restraint as a condition of a livable future is Illich's *Tools for Conviviality*. One of Illich's intuitions is worth a tome from the Hudson Institute. He has probably the most versatile imagination of any social critic writing today. The concrete criticisms of medical care, education, home building, **and** marketing techniques form a perfect balance for Etzioni's theoretical speculations.

The self-control envisaged by Etzioni, Illich, and others is not inhibition brought about by outside manipulation. It is a self-regulation that enriches the quality of life. "The active man is a self-restraining one," according to Etzioni. "To know is to delay action until information is collected and processed. To be committed is to defer rewards in favor of higher realization of goals. To apply power for activation . . . is to use it within limits determined by and in the service of shared values and not individually held ones. . . . " Shortly before his death Maslow also argued that "Apollonizing controls" enhance gratification of needs "by doing something well rather than just doing it."

Self-control is in large measure a matter of exercising wisdom in commitments to common goals and allegiances. Up to the present, our commitments have outlasted their purposefulness, and techniques have dulled our sensitivities. Self-control means striking a balance between these elements. It means forestalling premature closure and sustaining responsiveness, even as one focuses on a select hierarchy of goals. It means restraint of self-interest in order to engage one's energy in a common cause for a sustained period, despite pressures to attend to alternate needs—but it also means giving place to new needs as they arise. It means inhibiting that endless questioning that makes concerted action impossible and disciplining the instinct for action until thought is taken.

Limits to growth, pluralism in political organization, self-restraint in the use of symbols and commitments are all conditions for *conviviality*. This is Illich's term. Etzioni speaks of "activation," Maslow of "synergy" and "eupsychia." All three men see the coordinating ideal of future society to be "institutions . . . set up to transcend the polarity between selfishness and unselfishness, between self-interest and altruism," as Maslow has said. It means surpassing the tension between society and the individual so that the more one gives away, the more one will have.

"I choose the term 'conviviality,' " writes Illich, "to designate the contrary of industrial productivity. I intend it to mean autonomous and creative intercourse among persons and the intercourse of persons with their environment; and this in contrast with conditioned response of persons to the demands made upon them by others, and by a man-mind environment."

Etzioni takes up the same theme. "In all post-modern societies, the reduction of man is a multiple affliction, appearing in all sectors from education to politics." The difference between the active society and the one we have known would be that the former "is in charge of itself rather than unrestructured or restructured to suit the logic of instruments . . . "

With his relentlessly concrete imagination, Illich attempts to identify those points at which the utility of specialization, professionalization, and technical virtuosity is surpassed by their social inutility. In the area of health care, for example, he considers band-aids, antiseptics, pure water, and nutrition as convival technologies that contribute to the physical well-being of the majority of people. Unrestrained growth in medical technology, however, has led us to the point of diminishing return. Organ transplants, renal dialysis, and radiological therapies give only marginal assistance, at excessive costs, to narrow segments of the population.

This does not mean that technology itself is evil. Illich believes that "tools are intrinsic to social relations." The problem, as Callahan puts it, is, that we are asked to accept false satisfactions for real needs. The solutions to problems created by technology create in turn a bizarre inversion of normalcy: iatrogenic disease, technological controls for technological afflictions, moral perplexities that threaten every moral achievement of the last four hundred years. Population growth, for example, is a threat to survival in many regions of the world, but what do we say about a people who weigh the survival of their children against maintaining a level of unheard-of opulence? Balances must be found, balances that make tools the instruments of genuinely convivial purposes and of political self-direction by many groups in one society.

Illich, Etzioni, and Maslow are visionaries who suggest what a human future might be like. They understand the disproportion of means to ends under which we now suffer, and they offer wholesale solutions by which to reconstruct society. Callahan, Brzezinski, Polak, and Brown are the analysts and critics, who see the problems facing us to be a result of the untrammeled growth of technology. Until recently, the visionaries have been ineffectual. Power lay with the rational managers. The visionary was like the aged and blind prophet Tiresias, who vainly prophesied to the vigorous and quick-witted Oedipus about the unexpected consequences of his action. His words were given no hearing. But as critics and analysts teach us to realize the limitations of a culture dominated by economics, perhaps the rational managers may come to suspect that they have something to learn from dreamers.

The time has come for an integration of rational and managerial intelligence. History has proved that each without the other is a threat to civilized life. If prognostics is to give us not only images of the future but also a future in which we can have hope, it must seek new ways to deal with symbols and commitments. It must integrate both kinds of intelligence in an active society.

PART 2

THE FUTURES MOVEMENT
AND
IMAGES OF THE POSSIBLE

If we are to find new public images of the future, the current futures movement, with its emphasis on systematic forecasting and planning, presents our most reasonable hope for generating such images. Or does it? The following essays explore this question from two different points of view.

Wendell Bell

Futuristics and Social Behavior

Social futuristics should include the study of values, goals, and purposes of individuals and groups. Basic ideas such as equality, and its twenty-first-century forms, should be the direction futuristics takes if it is to fundamentally influence the character of society and culture. Despite the debatable track record of futuristics, Bell feels there is no acceptable alternative to that of moving toward some deliberate social design and conscious guidance mechanisms.

One can reasonably argue that the only useful knowledge is knowledge about the future. That is, as people make their way in the world their behavior is organized by a complex set of expectations. Knowing what to expect and when to expect it are essential in order to make adequate and effective responses to the environment, both the natural and the humanmade.

From the social point of view, of course, the society that generates expectations that have a reasonably good chance of being fulfilled might be

57

said to be functioning smoothly, to be orderly and articulated in a coordinated fashion. Obviously, this is not to say that such a society is necessarily a happy or congenial one, because the expectations might not be desirable. Certainly, to know that one will get only a small bowl of rice every morning or will be whipped every night at midnight is highly unpleasant but is, on the other hand, indicative of some order at least. The society in which predictions cannot be made accurately about patterns of social behavior can hardly be called a society. It is chaos.

Humans are time travelers, who chart their courses through time with maps of the future. These maps of the future contain the congealed knowledge about the future that individuals have. They are only more or less accurate; thus, behavior based on them is only more or less appropriate or effective. Society, then, can be usefully viewed as a set of more or less shared expectations about the future and the behavior based on them.

But there is a contradiction here. In a strict sense, there is no knowledge of the future. As philosopher Robert S. Brumbaugh has said, there are past facts, present options, and future possibilities, but there are no past possibilities and *there are no future facts*. Although the only useful knowledge with respect to making one's way through the time stream of the world may be knowledge about the future, there is no such knowledge, there are no future facts.

THE MAJOR PROBLEM AND OPPORTUNITY OF FUTURISTICS

Though this is certainly elementary, it contains in a nutshell both the major problem and the chief opportunity of futuristics. It is a problem, because we must act as if we know the future, even though we cannot really know it until it becomes the present, and our effectiveness depends, in part, on how good our predictions about it are. It is an opportunity, because the future has some degree of openness; there are often alternative possibilities, things that we can change more to our liking and things that we can prevent if we do not like them.

If we cannot literally study the future, we can do a variety of things to approximate knowledge of it, to make some guesses on which to act. Thus, we study the past and the present, and assume that some patterns of behavior will remain the same or continue a trend of change at the same rate or a changing rate of change. This is probably the most common practice both in our daily lives and in formal planning. For most times and places and for most aspects of social behavior, such assumptions are reasonably safe in the short run. We can make forecasts, projections, and predictions based upon data analyses of present conditions, past change, and known relationships among variables. Past facts are thus transformed into future forecasts.

More is being done of course. Scenarios are being written giving alternative futures; experts in various fields are being asked for their predictions and these are then synthesized; simulations and games are being played as microcosms of the real world; cost-benefit analyses are being projected into the future; and designs for the future are being constructed. Furthermore, a number of things related to "knowing" the future are real and can be studied. Images of the future *are* real and they may, as Fred Polak claims, summon forth a future reality. The actions of humans create the future, and one can study their design implications. The intentions that people have about the kind of future they are trying to achieve are real, as are the choices that they make among alternatives. And alternative possibilities for the future are, in some sense, real and deserve some ontological status.

This is a liberating way of thinking. If the conscious effort to get more accurate predictions about the future is successful, this clearly increases our ability to cope with it. This may be a matter of being prepared for the future when it arrives. If a hurricane is coming, windows can be boarded up. Beyond that, more freedom and power can come from a conscious effort to create the future, to decide what it should be, and to engage in the acts that will bring it about when it is possible to do so. The weather may prove intractable for some time, but social organizations can be designed or redesigned.

Humans of course, unlike B. F. Skinner's pigeons, are constantly creating the *causes* of their own behavior, whether or not they are conscious of so doing. Thus, increased responsibility, as well as freedom from compulsive repetition under the rules and norms of society and culture, can come with an understanding of the routines of current behavior, their operational codes, and their consequences for the future. Certainly, one cannot be casually optimistic about changing human behavior quickly on a mass scale—whether it is patterns of reproductive behavior or beliefs about what is food or what is God—yet understanding and insight into the empirical relationships involving interdependencies of behavior and networks of reciprocal commitments do permit persons to alter their behavior in such a way that the empirical relationships will be changed. It is not merely that knowledge permits some people to redesign the social environment for other people, thereby changing the latter's behavior and therefore their future; perhaps more importantly, it is that individuals themselves become enlightened and aware of the causes of their behavior. The translation of such enlightenment and awareness into imagined trajectories of their future permits individuals to evaluate and choose alternative actions to try to bring about more desirable futures, thus transforming themselves and their environments as they emerge into another time.

Furthermore, a good prediction may as often—or more often—be one that reorients behavior to prevent the prediction from being fulfilled, as it is one that seems to come true in the future. The balance of payments or rate of inflation may be predicted to be moving to such amounts as to be judged intolerable. But monetary policies can be changed and the predictions over-turned. A political scientist may show how past and present developments are leading to a military oligarchy—as Harold D. Lasswell predicted in the mid-forties about the United States, using the concept of the garrison state—but he can still urge that freedom-loving people take actions to prevent it from happening. Of course, such predictions are contingent, although not always explicitly so, and there are other predictions lurking in the background. "If one doesn't stop smoking, one's chances of lung cancer will be relatively high" is matched by "If one does stop smoking, one's chances of lung cancer will be relatively low." What should be stressed, however, is that knowing past facts and present options is not what makes action effective; it is their translation into forecasts. It is accurately knowing future consequences.

THE AGENDA OF SOCIAL FUTURISTICS

For sociology—which, since Émile Durkheim and especially in its American tradition, has tended to ask, "How does society shape people?"—the implications of such a view are clear. Only one side of the coin has been closely studied and the other side must also be examined. We should also ask, "How do people shape society?" Deterministic assumptions are still relevant and causal analysis still appropriate, but the implications of the latter question lead to a different body of knowledge as well as to an expanded agenda of sociological investigation. Generally, sociologists in exclusive pursuit of answers to the first question depict the social world as impersonal, condemned (happily or not) to the limitations of the present, organized around the needs and functions of society, largely beyond the conscious control of individuals, and limited to single slices of time. Conversely, sociologists asking the second question tend to see the social world as personal, problematic, rightfully subservient to the goals and purposes of individuals, to some extent within the conscious control of individuals, and as part of a continuous time flow. Futurists find their natural home with sociologists of the second group.

The agenda of social futuristics should include prominently the study of values, goals, and purposes of individuals and groups. Once society is made problematic and responsibility for the future becomes a conscious struggle to be free from blind routines and sacred compulsions, humans are further burdened, as Polak says, with the task of choosing the direction of social and cultural development. Much can be learned simply through the current study of the distribution and strength of various values, especially as they are manifested in hopes and fears for the future. But the role of the social scientist may have to be enlarged or somehow merged with the role of the humanist, since that challenge includes finding some basis for evaluating competing values and, possibly, of inventing new ones.

This brings us to the fact that decision making is perhaps inherently linked to future-thinking. As Lasswell has said in many of his writings, decision making involves the simultaneous consideration of facts, values, and most of all, expectations about the future. This is true in the everyday lives of ordinary people, as well as in the centers of power in corporate boardrooms and government organizations. Past and present conditions are viewed as implications for future developments, which are then evaluated with respect to some goals, purposes, or values used to guide a decision to take an action (sometimes even creatively) aimed at altering, preventing, or accelerating trends that will make the future conform more closely to what is desired. Of course, the extent to which such conscious decision making occurs varies widely from culture to culture, group to group, and individual to individual. But the spread of awareness can greatly increase the numbers of those who are both liberated and burdened by the necessity of consciously choosing their own future. For the rest, they may believe—or have been told—that they have no choices, yet alternative possibilities for their future are real too, although the possibilities may be hidden from them and dormant. Thus, if society can be viewed as complex sets of expectations, it can also be viewed as complex sets of decisions, more or less consciously made from among more or less "known" alternatives for the future. Thus, decisions too should become a basic unit of sociological analysis.

Clearly, we need to spend more resources for studies related to understanding the future, especially those that will make decision making more effective, both in setting goals that will maximize human happiness and potential—and resolve whatever conflicts or incompatibilities there may be between them—and in creating the means to achieve the goals. One solution to the former is a basic social policy that maximizes informed choice, such that a diversity of life-styles is encouraged to the extent to which individuals who have been given information about the consequences of each life-style decide to live them. No plan will work too well, however, unless it is dynamic and reactive, changing its form while remaining committed to the goals of choice, diversity, and acceptance.

FAILURES OF FUTURISTICS

The track record of futuristics up to this time can be debated. Crackpots still abound, astrological forecasts by computer are available for a few francs on the Champs Élysées, doomsday forecasts can be found in reports from the Rand Corporation or the Hudson Institute, and both nightmares and daydreams are for sale.

Among the most horrendous and miserable failures of futuristics are some of the most influential, widely accepted, and seemingly rational and scientific of methods. Systems analysis is a good example, especially its two most widely known forms, cost-benefit analysis and planning-programming-budgeting studies. These are methodologies for managing the present and designing the future. The aim is to achieve some goal, such as the biggest bang for a buck. Possibly my criticism is misdirected at systems analysis, when it should be directed at those systems analysts who do sloppy, even evil and corrupt, work. Still, Ida R. Hoos' *Systems Analysis in Public Policy: A Critique* (Berkeley: University of California Press, 1972) is necessary reading for anyone beginning to float into futurism on the lofty pronouncements of its adherents.

As is well known, Robert S. McNamara brought systems analysis to the Department of Defense in 1961 in an attempt to solve the enormous waste and inept managerial practices then existing. The result of the sophisticated techniques applied since 1961 has been inefficiency and mismanagement that, if judged by the billions of dollars involved, are worse than before, although, as Hoos says, the abuses were frequently rationalized and camouflaged by "scientific management." For example, cost overruns, production underruns, and delivery delays have plagued the Department of Defense. In the past decade, 7 billion dollars have been wasted on weapons systems that were simply abandoned. A recent audit of forty-five weapons systems being developed showed cost overruns of 31.5 billion dollars.

A dreadful example of "slipshod procurement practices, of elusive and imprecise accounting procedures . . . and a horrible example of management practices" (Hoos, p. 60), the Department of Defense quickly became a model for other organizations, and systems analysis spread from weapons systems and space programs to, among other things, health, education, welfare, traffic control, urban redevelopment, world population and food studies, and pollution control. Most of Hoos' criticisms of systems analysis also reveal why it is attractive to its clients: (1) its definition is not entirely clear; (2) results and performance are seldom evaluated; (3) its interdisciplinary tendencies often become undisciplined; (4) the goal of constructing a management system frequently deteriorates into the creation of a mere information system; (5) the stress upon quantification limits any analysis to variables that can be measured, no matter how many important variables are thereby left out of consideration; (6) it appears scientific and systematic although it is frequently based upon untested and unrealistic assumptions; (7) it gives the false impression that objectives are being scientifically set; (8) it can be used to rationalize and justify any policy; (9) subjective biases frequently determine whose cost becomes whose benefit; (10) even the empirical data on which projections are made are often shaky and inadequate; (11) the quantitative forecasts are more often than not completely erroneous; (12) the *Weltanschauung* of the analyst can be a dominant factor in the results; (13) the systems analysis of a problem itself may substitute for the action necessary to solve the problem; and (14) the farther away in time the future is being discussed, the more airy-fairy the results will be.

Hoos' account is frightening and threatening as an augury of a time when even a larger part of more human lives (and deaths) will be affected by social design. Yet one can see no acceptable alternative to that of moving toward some deliberate design and conscious guidance mechanisms. Can the future of society be left to private greed? To corporations? To luck? To the haphazard sum of individual acts? One has cautious hope in the vision, and works toward practical methodologies that may better achieve the promise. Most importantly, both creative and critical functions should be given full play.

THE CONCEPT OF EQUALITY: NEW FORMS FOR OLD IDEAS

Furthermore, by working at quite different levels of abstraction and technique and by using a wider span of time, one can find examples that give such hope foundation. Take, for example, an idea such as equality/inequality. In the sociological tradition it stands alongside other general concepts such as community, authority, alienation, rationality, and the sacred and the secular. It is conceivable that it could someday function for sociological theory as do the concepts of energy and mass for physics. It is useful in understanding a wide range of situations, although the specific referents in each concrete case may be different. It can be applied, obviously, to differences or similarities in race, ethnicity, social class, age, and sex—to mention just a few major sociological variables.

Equality is also something about which value judgments are made—often in highly emotional terms—about which political and social movements have been organized and in the name of which revolutions have been fought. There is no society whose value system does not somehow define how much equality or inequality, applied to which of its members in what institutional sectors, is right or wrong, legitimate or illegitimate. And of course at any given time there may be considerable conflict over the question of the legitimacy of the existing system of inequality and the amount of equality that is considered morally right. The long-term, historical trend for Western civilization is clear: more equality for more people in more aspects of civil, political, economic, social, and cultural life has been considered proper. The actual distribution of various rights has tended to follow the same pattern, although important contradictions exist.

No society is without inequality. Yet viewed as an image of the future and as a social design, the ideology of equality may have existed for as long as there has been an ideology of inequality. Some important part of the history of humankind and centuries of intellectual life can be seen as experiments with various forms of equality and inequality and as philosophical probes into their meaning and justification. Equality has meant leveling, establishing minimums, providing equal opportunities, guaranteeing equal inputs or, more recently, equal outputs (even though unequal inputs are necessary to achieve them). At different times and places equality has meant freedom from torture and slavery, freedom of religion, a fair and public hearing by competent and impartial tribunals, freedom to take part in the conduct of public affairs, voting, equal access to public service, the right to fair wages, equal pay for equal work, reasonable limitation of working hours and periodic holidays, the right to form and join a trade union, the right to a free choice of a marriage partner and to establish a family, the right to free primary education and equal access to secondary and higher education, the right to an adequate standard of living including adequate food, clothing, and housing, and the right to take part in one's own chosen cultural life, among many other things.

It is to basic designs such as equality that futuristics should turn if it is to have the impact some envision for it—to have a fundamental influence on the basic character of society and culture. In the case of equality, we need to clarify, perhaps invent, its new, twenty-first-century forms. In the meantime, methodology must be made more adequate, pomposity and self-delusion eliminated. The social engineering of immediate concerns and of limited time spans have their place when carried out properly. Hortatory efforts can spread the understanding of the importance of future-thinking. Some individuals will continue to plan their daily lives through the social maze and initiate action to achieve their personal utopias. But there remains a largely unexplored opportunity to come to terms with possible future manifestations of basic values (such as equality) toward which humankind seems to be groping, because they are our "inspiring, magnetic images of the future." The past facts, present options, and, most importantly, future possibilities of such basic values need to be known and understood if we are to carry out the tasks necessary to creating a world of tomorrow in which humankind can live and grow happily.

Robert Bundy

Up the Downward Path: The Futures Movement and the Social Imagination

Born out of legitimate human concerns, the current futures movement has become stunted and misshapen—a social menace. It is plagued, Bundy argues, by technicism, racism, sexism, elitism, and poverty of information. Only a radical redirection can save the movement from becoming the subservient arm of government, the military, and Madison Avenue.

During the past fifteen years, systematic planning and forecasting have become powerful techniques for change throughout the world. While it may be stretching things to speak of a full-scale *futures movement*, something of the sort has definitely developed.

By *futures movement* I mean all those organized attempts, mainly by institutions, to plan, forecast, study, and predict the future. Included within the movement would be planning and think-tank activities in government, business, the military, academia, and the professions; formal courses of study on the future; published literature exploring the future, including specialized bibliographic and information services; and regional, state, national, and international conferences dealing with some aspect of human concerns for tomorrow.

The practical *time* spectrum of activities within the futures movement extends from short-range operational planning (for example, designing a new educational curriculum) to longer-range studies (such as demographic projections for the year 2000 or scenarios of alternative worlds in the twenty-first century). The *institutional* spectrum runs from the smallest organization in which systematic planning techniques are used to corporate planning in the giant multinational companies. The *content* spectrum includes virtually everything human beings find of interest or importance.

As in the past, today's futures movement expresses a human concern for tomorrow. But unlike the situation in the past, today's movement is characterized by the following: (1) the belief that the future cannot be predicted but that it can be invented; (2) the study of alternative futures rather than a single line of the future; (3) a major focus on historical causality, rigorous methodology, and strategies for social intervention; and (4) interdisciplinary studies in recognition of the complexity of modern social forces. Planning and thinking about the future are not new in human affairs, but today's futures movement can be viewed as a new genre: a serious and broadbased attempt to make more explicit and orderly a natural activity of the human mind, and a concerted effort to invent the future by bringing it under human control rather than relying on blind faith or good luck.

The reasons behind the growth of the futures movement are many and complex. For some, exploring the future is intriguing because of the technological capabilities likely to be developed, or there is a peculiar fascination with the approaching millennial number. For others, there is a profound fear of impending catastrophes unless interventions occur in time. And for still others, systematic planning is felt to be necessary to accomplish social progress, or it may act as a substitute for philosophies of historical determinism, or it may offer a way to maintain vested power.

Despite the often mixed motivations for interest in the future, most serious futurists agree that the world is in a profound transitionary period. There is further agreement that the outcomes of this transition could range from a desirable future for mankind to planet-wide destruction. To prevent the latter we must learn how to clarify the major alternative lines of the future open to us, make our present options more explicit, increase our ability to anticipate opportunities and cope with problems before they become crises, and, finally, discover how to invent a future consistent with our highest ideals of justice and freedom.

With these comments as a prologue, I wish to address two central questions. First, how should the futures movement be appraised in terms of its contributions to solving the enormous problems confronting the human race? And second, has the movement brought us any closer to finding new images of the future desperately needed for our historic period and if not, why not? The importance and timeliness of these questions are obvious, in view of our current global situation, the widespread interest in and acceptance of planning and forecasting, and the promise made about these techniques by those within the movement.

To begin with, I believe that some important material gains have been made with the aid of systematic forecasting and planning techniques, that many people have been drawn into a healthy debate over the future, and that some important issues have been given high visibility. However, after more than a decade of personal involvement in this area, I am deeply disillusioned about the movement. To me the evidence is unmistakably clear that the movement has become stunted and misshapen and is fast becoming a social menace. Born out of legitimate human concerns, the movement has not become what it must if radical thinking about humankind's dilemmas is to occur in time. Nor, if present tendencies continue, will the movement become more than a powerful arm of government, the military, and Madison Avenue. I draw these conclusions reluctantly, because I had hoped the movement would help expand the imagination and humanity of a country and world seemingly bent on escalating its own collapse.

In offering my reflections on the futures movement, I shall emphasize developments in the West, since I am most familiar with these. My intentions are to describe the major problems within the movement and what must be done to redirect its evolution. Despite my pessimism I hope the movement may yet become an important catalyst for stimulating the consciousness necessary to build a more humanistic future.

Five basic problems plague the movement at this time, problems that are also characteristic of the larger society. They are technicism, racism, sexism, elitism, and a poverty of information.

TECHNICISM

Technicism is a world view and moral outlook that has been studied by a number of contemporary thinkers. The main characteristics of a technicist culture and orientation are as follows.[1] There is a bending of human reason to instrumental rationality so that efficiency and utility dominate the search for social goals. This confusion between means and ends results in obedience to the mystification of our social and technical tools, and human purposes end up being organized by the logic of techniques. Expertise becomes so elevated in importance that individuals are made increasingly dependent on specialists to define reality for them. Issues of human values, feelings, and purposes are labeled "nonobjective" and "private" and are therefore forced out of the public domain and deprived of their status as facts. The pathways to certainty are no longer traditional authority or transcendent truth but are instead morally neutral principles of rigorous scientific methodology and functional relevance. There is a progressive loss of mastery over our own language, as metaphors from the nonhuman world, especially machine and communications theory, are used increasingly to describe and explain human action. These metaphors conceal the voluntary, personal, and spontaneous dimensions of human experience, with the attendant danger that even the *awareness* that these metaphors are linguistic borrowings recedes from the public consciousness. Finally, there is a reduction of the individual, because personal agency and responsibility are given up to the technicians. Alienation increases as the masses discover their basic illiteracy about how their own society works.

If we accept the fact that strong technicist tendencies exist in our society, it should not be surprising to find these same tendencies in the futures movement. Currently, the movement shows its technicist orientation in several ways: (1) overdependence on statistical data, technical language, and rigorous scientific methodology to define and solve human problems, and an overallocation of resources to technical and scientific forecasting; (2) a pernicious "materialization of values," which makes human aspirations merely technical problems in disguise and therefore the proper domain for experts and technicians; (3) a lack of critical questioning of industrial symbols, assumptions, and tools (for example, an inability to seriously explore the implications for international justice when the planet's resources are not shared, and the suicidal distortion of modern tools in human relationships); (4) an insistence on credentialized expertise as a prerequisite to planning the future, together with the belief that increasing control must be exercised by global engineers because participatory politics is unable to achieve public consensus on social goals; (5) the development of planning systems—and sophisticated social/technological tools created by these systems—so complex that the majority of people cannot understand them (whether people could understand these systems and tools is often unimportant because they are led to believe such understanding is beyond them); (6) a mystification surrounding the techniques for planning and forecasting. These techniques are couched in technical vocabulary and are given such an aura of importance that they appear to take on magical properties and thus become immune to critical questioning by "nonexperts."

Consequently, people must constantly turn to specialists for guidance on how and when to use planning techniques. This chronic dependency is rooted in acceptance of the specialist's claim to define human problems in terms professionals can solve, the specialist's lack of faith in what people can do for themselves, and a scarcity of information (deliberately created by specialists themselves), which people would need to break this chronic dependency.

There are notable exceptions to this orientation in the futures movement, but there is clearly no major search for the ideas of the mystic, the artist, and the visionary wherever he or she may be found. Neither, broadly speaking, is there evident a deep concern for reexamination of basic human needs and values beyond pious platitudes, nor a celebration of other modes of knowing beyond the scientific. In short, there is no large-scale effort to redefine humanism for our times and no authentic moral fervor to bring the most obvious global injustices into line with traditional humanistic ideals. Not all futurists and forecasts can be labeled *technicist*, but the moving spirit behind the movement reflects many of the worst technicist tendencies of the larger culture.

RACISM

The futures movement is racist, because it is dominated by white, Western intellectuals and professional managers. The requirements for futures centers, business and government planning, publishing, and the teaching of courses on the future are one or more of the following: credentials, reputation, experience in planning, and a research and publishing record. As in the larger racist society, these requirements are most likely to be met by white Westerners. Those nonwhites who qualify are often faced with two further obstacles: discriminatory hiring and tokenism. This means, on the whole, that nonwhites have no more than marginal opportunities to contribute at important levels of forecasting and planning in business, education, and government. In addition, there are no influential centers in the United States for the study of alternative, nonwhite futures nor any well-known existing centers where the future of nonwhites is given serious attention. The issues here, however, are not just unequal social privileges, hiring discrimination against nonwhites, or tokenism, but the *absence of a nonwhite consciousness* in the growing dialogue on the future. (In the 1960s there was real hope this situation was changing, but it largely disappeared in the 1970s.) Instead of a cooperative dialogue between whites and nonwhites, we find the blatant production of scenarios that do not even include nonwhites; or that speak of dissolving the "lower Negro class," siphoning off the nonwhite population from central cities by dispersal into suburbia, and physically repressing minorities under certain conditions; or scenarios full of vicious platitudes about "raising" racial minorities to become contributing members of society. These kinds of scenarios are widespread and are produced by white liberals and conservatives alike, who find the problem of nonwhites, as well as poor people, an inconvenience or even a threat. Underlying these scenarios, of course, is the reluctance to permit the vast majority of people in the world (nonwhites) to obtain middle-class privileges, because then the privileges of the existing middle and upper classes would be eroded.

Racism is the major cause underlying the absence of a nonwhite consciousness in the futures movement. This racism may be overt or institutional, conscious or unconscious on the part of those who hold power in the futures movement. The destructive effect is not simply that the dominant images of the future flow from a white, Western mentality; rather, the real evil is that *only* these images make their way into the public consciousness. In short, the social imagination is severely limited because images of the future from a nonwhite perspective cannot enter the public awareness or do so only in a random and haphazard way. The result is a dangerous crippling of the social imagination and an immoral exclusion of whole segments of the population who should be part of the search for solutions to humankind's common problems.

SEXISM

As in the broader society, few women are involved in the futures movement and their ideas and perspectives are not taken seriously. The movement is dominated by a male psychology and, with some exceptions, the few women involved are only token or are poor spokeswomen for the feminine point of view. Again, the real danger is that only male-dominated images of the future are generated and broadcast to the larger society. The right of women to hold influential positions in the movement, as well as their own points of view, values, feelings, and questions, is lost at the very time when the movement should be redirected and when the most creative images of the future are desperately needed. This is not merely unfortunate; it is morally unjust. Fortunately, the situation is beginning to improve. In a very slow and piece-meal fashion the ideas of women are beginning to move into the mainstream of the futures movement.

ELITISM

For many of the reasons just cited the futures movement is elitist. Control of resources allocated to forecasting and planning, as well as access to the public media, is held by a small group. And this group clearly does not represent all of the people nor does it include those who would qualify as the creative minority of our age. Most damning of all is the fact that many well-known futurists show no evidence that they understand their elitism. In their arro-gance they believe they have a duty to think for others and therefore the right to shape visions for the broader society. The results are often the most crass attitudes toward whole peoples and their dire circumstances.

In recent years, for example, eminent futurists have produced reports, books, and statements that clinically dissect hunger and poverty in the world and forecast the number of deaths to be expected from famine. If the intent were to shock the rich nations into some moral responsibility, these forecasts would have redeeming value. Unfortunately, their intent is often to show that the problems of poverty and hunger are created by the poor and hungry themselves. The rich nations are thus asked to be more charitable or to be-come more wealthy so the poor nations can become a little richer.

At another level elitism occurs precisely at that juncture where plan-ning is transformed into decision making. The vast majority of people in this country, particularly the poor, are prevented from participation in the very decision-making processes that control their everyday lives. The result is often hopelessness and apathy on the part of the poor. They cannot take ser-iously the planning efforts to deal with today's and tomorrow's problems when they know, first, that the events that will most affect their lives are being designed by specialists whom they never see or talk to and, second, that the "system" can outplan and thus manipulate whatever planning the poor and oppressed do engage in.

At present, therefore, people are excluded from deliberations about the future and the search for solutions to their problems at most levels of political life unless they are experts, professionals, white, and male. Anyone who merely has some interest and wishes to participate cannot get into the systems of planning except with great difficulty. Many futurists themselves do not believe that all those likely to be affected by the debate should be involved in the debate on the future. Rhetoric espousing citizen involvement is often used, but the behavior of futurists belies this rhetoric. Therefore, the only remaining channels open to the masses of people are (1) physical confrontation, (2) uncertain, vague, and often ineffective forms of political representation, (3) legal redress for those fortunate few who can command the necessary resources, and (4) community power groups. Community power groups represent the most effective and hopeful channel. Unfortunately, these groups are often reduced to mere survival operations because they can be easily controlled by people or groups who have the resources to do longer-range planning.

Thus, the futures movement is oppressive because it is a highly controlled enterprise operating on the belief that experts should make the important decisions about the future. The masses are considered dangerous because of their irrationality and inability to think creatively. Published forecasts are often thinly veiled slogans and propagandizing based on the flimsiest assumptions and calculated to convince average people that all these deliberations are beyond their comprehension. If the futures movement links up further with Madison Avenue, then the control of images of the future will reach the status of self-fulfilling prophecies, and the movement will become the propaganda arm of the industrial-military organizations.

POVERTY OF INFORMATION

The fifth problem is a direct result of the preceding four. Ironically, in a society that has been called "information rich," dangerous levels of information deprivation exist. Since most of the images of the future presented to the public come from white, male, middle-class intellectuals and managers, the perceptions of social reality that underlie these images must by their very nature be limited. Only certain information is attended to, gathered, and analyzed in the creation of these scenarios. Likewise, ideas about trends, problems, opportunities, priorities, issues, questions, and problem solutions that form the basis for public discussions about the future must of necessity be narrow in perspective. Inevitably, the needed range of thinking does not take place. For example, the nightly news analyses on television describe the injustices and economic hardships created by the Arab oil cartel but never discuss the fact that the United States has been using food as a political weapon for years. Nor is any attention given to the enormous profits the United States makes on the sale of military equipment and how this is tied to instability and hunger in the Third World.

Poverty of information goes unrecognized in the public consciousness because there is a prevailing illusion that we have too much information and that only specialists can really understand what is going on. The future is dangerously constricted because poverty of information leads inevitably to poverty of imagination in forecasting and planning.

But poverty of information and imagination have even more insidious effects. The white middle class believes, foolishly, that they are part of the "we" who make the crucial decisions for the future or, at least, that the decision-makers have their best interests at heart. This kind of poverty-of-imagination cycle allows the middle class to be easily exploited by the needs of the giant multinational corporations. Nonwhite peoples, on the other hand, who have not been allowed to benefit from the dominant system, are not fooled by these myths. They know they have few spokesmen in their search for the self-determination that will enable them to alter the often inhuman conditions they are confronted with every day. However, those nonwhites and whites who are trapped in a physical poverty cycle can also be trapped in another kind of imagination poverty cycle. Their current condition is desperate, their future condition likely to be relatively the same or worse. Having no power or access to the kinds of information that could ultimately reshape their lives, they must rely on the dehumanizing benevolence of the larger society. Part of the information they need relates to everyday survival (jobs, food, education, and so forth). But another part of the information needed relates to alternative possibilities for the future and the means to invent a different future through self-determination by individuals and communities.

What is needed for whites and nonwhites alike to break out of their respective cycles of poverty of information is articulation of a broadened range of future possibilities for living, sharing, and working together. With the current futures movement, this cannot happen in any serious way because nonwhites as a group have very little access to the important planning councils and media, and the councils and media are unwilling to alter the images they have carefully constructed over the years. Options are thus closed, but the underlying ferment, fear, hatred, and hopelessness of many nonwhites *and* whites continues. At a time when the mind and imagination must be unlocked to conceive of the new and radically different, almost the exact opposite seems to be happening. Poverty of information leads to poverty of imagination, which ultimately leads to poverty of options and a poverty of humaneness in planning for the future.

REDIRECTION OF THE FUTURES MOVEMENT

The futures movement, while flowing out of a deep human need, has thus been stunted and deformed. The majority of activities making up the movement are directed, consciously or unconsciously, at protecting vested power and privilege, rather than opening up the future to new possibilities for human life. This situation could be changed however if there were a systematic attack on each of the five problems identified here.

To combat technicism, we must place the emphasis in planning and forecasting on the personal, voluntary, responsible, and self-determining dimensions of human experience. Human beings have to become the basic units of social analysis, not systems within which humans are inserted and processed. Issues of values, justice, equality, human purposes, participatory politics, human relationships to society's tools, and dignity of the person have to become central to discussions of trends, social change, and emerging national and global problems. Such a humanistic thrust would press forecasting and planning techniques into the service of people, put these techniques in their proper perspective as means, and make clear that they are not substitutes for clarifying human ends and goals.

To combat racism and sexism, opportunities for women and nonwhites must be opened in every phase of the futures movement. In addition, we must develop futures centers devoted to disseminating ideas about alternative futures for nonwhites, futures in which new male and female roles and responsibilities are explored, and futures that demonstrate possibilities for all peoples to cooperatively shape their social order.

To combat elitism and poverty of information, we must have public forums in which planners can be criticized and challenged and new ideas can enter the social imagination. One approach to accomplish this is the establishment of people's centers, which focus both on specific community problems and on broader national problems and are designed to serve different cultural groups and mixtures of cultural groups. The only entrance requirement would be an interest in participating in a dialogue on the future. All the activities of these centers would serve to instill confidence in the ordinary person's ability to think about the future and his or her basic human right to do so. Ultimately these centers would become new political institutions. I do not imply, of course, any antagonism toward specialized knowledge. What I seek is to prevent the specialists from monopolizing society's public channels and to open up new action channnels for people to build their visions of social order.

If the futures movement were to be redirected along the lines proposed, I believe we would do the following:

1. uncover an unbelievable range of original, exciting ideas about future possibilities in key social-problem areas;

2. give wide visibility to ideas on the future from a feminine and non-white point of view;

3. develop numerous forums for people to come together who wish to discuss and plan the future at all levels of social life;

4. encourage the expanded imaginations of people from all walks of life and cultural experiences about alternative futures and ways to deal cooperatively with emerging problems and opportunities;

5. make available a rich and diverse collection of social pictures of the future for the United States and of America's relationships to the rest of the world (such pictures would inevitably include scenarios radically different from current pictures of linear industrial growth and from perpetuation of existing social institutions that pervade our thinking);

6. establish a link between media people and artists (and fine-arts associations) that could creatively communicate these new ideas about the future.

These things, of course, are easy to state. Accomplishing them is an entirely different matter. The five problems discussed run so deeply in our society that the scenario for change I have presented seems almost impossible to implement. Also, it must be understood that studying the future is no substitute for compelling visions of the future to motivate a collectivity. The purpose of the futures movement is not to develop these visions or even a smorgasbord of potential visions; rather, it should serve to create a climate for cooperative effort, to open up channels of thinking and feeling that have been closed off up until now, to expand our awareness of the humanly possible, to demystify the tools and techniques of planning so they no longer are the monopoly of a few, and to bring a focus to those ideas and projects that are most viable for healing the enormous divisions in our society and that can ensure a humanistic thrust to our planning for the future.

If the futures movement can help accomplish these things, we in the West might find the courage to go on and develop a leadership that could be accepted and emulated by the rest of the world. I have some optimism about this but am aware that everywhere the powers of totalitarian governments, gross social inequities, and monstrous instruments of warfare are on the increase. The old saying "time will tell" must be amended in our situation to "a little time will tell." The inertia of the past is plunging us headlong into the darkness of an uninspired future. What the future will be is still pliable and subject to human choice and action, but we must not continue searching for the future by going up the narrow pathway that can only lead downward.

NOTES

1. See Manfred Stanley, "Literacy: The Crisis of a Conventional Wisdom," *School Review* (May 1972), pp. 373-408.

PART **3**

IMAGES OF WORLD
TRENDS AND PROBLEMS

Any serious study of images of the future must include an empirical analysis of world economic and demographic trends, together with projections of the future social consequences of these trends. The search for new images of the future cannot fail to include these economic and demographic factors if collective action is to be aroused to inhibit destructive trends and enhance desirable ones. Two well-known futurists offer their analyses of trends and their projections. They also make suggestions on how to alter the negative effects of the trends they discuss. It will be evident how crucial one's basic assumptions are in this kind of discussion.

Lester R. Brown

Issues of Human Welfare

Brown gives us a far-ranging view of current and projected world problems as we approach the end of the century. He argues that this period will at best be traumatic and at worst, catastrophic. A new social ethic is necessary if we are to have a more humane set of global priorities, new global institutions, and new levels of global cooperation.

Today, more than at any point in history, we live in a world of great contrast in the human condition. An affluent global minority is overfed and over-weight, but close to half the world's people are hungry and malnourished. Some of us can afford heart transplants, but half of us receive no health care at all. A handful of Americans have journeyed to the moon, but much of mankind cannot afford a visit to the nearest city. Several thousand dollars

This article, which first appeared in *The Humanist*, November-December 1973, was adapted from the author's book *World without Borders* (1972).

are spent on a college education for millions of young Americans, while many of us lack the limited resources required to become literate. Some of us live in families with three cars, but others of us cannot afford even a bicycle.

The contrast in the human condition has many dimensions, but when distilled it means simply that we live in a world where some of us have the opportunity to realize our full potential as human beings, while many of us do not. The circumstances in which we find ourselves in the late twentieth century suggest that it may be in everyone's interest, rich as well as poor, to create a world order where everyone can reach his full humanity.

If one judges the existing world order by whether it is solving the important problems facing mankind, then one must conclude that it is not working very well. A listing of mankind's most important problems shows that, with few exceptions, these problems will get much worse before they get better. Among these are the continued persistence of widespread hunger and malnutrition, widespread illiteracy, the massive migration from rural areas to cities, the spreading unemployment in the developing countries, the growing pressure of population on resources throughout the world, and the progressive deterioration of our natural environment. And, while the more perplexing problems man faces today are global in scope, the institutions to cope with them are largely national.

Continuing demographic and economic growth are putting great pressure on the earth's scarce finite resources. As we begin to press against some of the earth's finite limits, we find ourselves confronting the issue of social justice within an entirely different framework. The issue is becoming less the traditional one of how charitable the rich countries should be toward the poor and more one of how to distribute the earth's finite resources and capacities more equitably among its people.

In the late twentieth century, pleas for equal rights are becoming demands. Equal rights is the cry of Black Americans, Soviet Jews, Western women, and Third World poor. It is the inevitable result of historical forces already in motion, the culmination of centuries of evolution in human rights.

The nation-state, with its sacred borders, embodies a concept of territorial discrimination that is increasingly in conflict with both the emerging social values of modern man and the circumstances in which he finds himself. The dimensions of the problems confronting late-twentieth-century man are unique in their scale.

Given the scale and complexity of the many problems we confront, the remainder of the twentieth century will be at best a traumatic period for mankind, even if a frontal attack on the principal threats to human well-being occurs. At worst, it will be catastrophic. The basic questions are: Can we grasp the nature and dimensions of the emerging threats to our well-being? Can we create an integrated global economy and a workable world order based on a global rather than a national perspective? Can we reorder global priorities so that the quality of life will improve rather than continue to deteriorate?

THREATS TO HUMAN WELL-BEING

The world today is rapidly polarizing along economic lines into two camps—rich and poor. A line separating English-speaking North America, Europe, the Soviet Union, and Japan from Latin America, Africa, and Asia delineates these two camps. A majority of the human family lives south of this line and, except for scattered pockets of affluence, is desperately poor.

Unfortunately, poverty is not an economic abstraction; it is a human condition. It is despair, grief, and pain. It is the despair of a father with a family of seven in a poor country when he joins the swelling ranks of the unemployed with no prospect of unemployment compensation. Poverty is the longing of a young boy playing outside a village school but unable to enter because his parents lack the few dollars needed to buy textbooks. Poverty is the grief of parents watching a three-year-old child die of a routine childhood disease because, like half of mankind, they could not afford any medical care —even if any were available.

The current north-south polarization of human society along economic lines and the associated failure of the rich northern hemisphere to demonstrate any meaningful concern for the poor constitute a new form of discrimination, one based on place of residence. At issue is whether an accident of birth should deprive an individual of enough food to fully develop his physical and mental capacity, of the opportunity to become literate, or of any other basic amenities of life in a world where resources are more than adequate to meet these needs.

Each of the rich countries accepts internally the *principle* of income redistribution, through progressive-taxation systems and a wide variety of welfare programs, including such things as free medical care and unemployment compensation. But internationally, the rich nations only nominally accept this concept and provide only token amounts of financial assistance to the poor countries. In terms of aggregate resources at the disposal of rich countries and in terms of pressing human needs, transfers of resources from rich countries to poor across national boundaries are only crumbs from the table. Total United States assistance to poor countries with two billion people is only moderately larger than the New York City welfare program, and most of the assistance is in the form of loans requiring repayment.

Recognition of this territorial discrimination is strong among the young. The older generation tends to take poverty and serious inequities in the distribution of income and wealth for granted because in the past it was not possible to seriously consider eliminating all poverty in the world. For those born into the postwar era of affluence and rapidly advancing technology, there is a much stronger realization that the resources to eradicate global poverty do exist.

Uncontrolled human fertility may pose a greater threat to our future well-being than any other single factor. Slowing population growth is a prerequisite to solving many of mankind's most pressing problems, including widespread hunger, rising levels of unemployment in the poor countries, the widening north-south gap, widespread illiteracy, and a deteriorating physical environment for all mankind. We delude ourselves dangerously if we think there can be a humane solution to these problems within this century, without a pronounced reduction in birthrates.

At an earlier point in history a 5 percent economic growth rate would have brought widespread and unquestioned improvements in the quality of life, but such was not the case during the 1960s. While the per capita supply of goods and services produced by man was increasing at a record rate, the supply of those amenities provided by nature was also declining at a record rate. The global population increase of nearly 700 million during the sixties was roughly the same as that occurring between 1800 and 1900. This increase of more than 20 percent in one decade brought a corresponding decline in per capita natural amenities, which are in fixed supply. For each of us there was nearly one-fifth less fresh water, mineral reserves, arable land, energy fuels, living space, waste-absorptive capacity, marine protein, and natural recreation areas in 1970 than in 1960.

Closely related to the worsening distribution of income in most poor countries is the continually growing number of people without jobs, a phenomenon that has become one of the world's gravest social ills during the seventies. In many poor countries, entrants into the job market outnumber new jobs being created by two to one, creating levels of unemployment far in excess of any the rich countries have experienced.

Employment and employment-related issues are likely to dominate international development in the seventies, much as the food issue did in the sixties. Stated otherwise, the food-population crisis of the past decade may become the employment-population crisis of the current decade.

With the number of young people entering the job market swelling year by year, the day of reckoning with the impact of the population explosion on employment has arrived. In some poor countries the labor force is now growing at a rate three times that of the industrialized countries. As a result the number of potentially productive but unemployed people is rising. In Latin America the number of unemployed climbed from 2.9 million in 1950 to 8.8 million in 1965, tripling in fifteen years. The unemployment rate went from under 6 percent to over 11 percent during this period. Since 1965 the ranks of the unemployed have grown still further.

The level of unemployment in India is estimated to have increased from 11 percent of the labor force in 1951 to 15 percent in 1961, a trend that continued through the sixties. India's labor force is projected to increase during the 1970s from 210 million to 273 million. Already plagued with widespread unemployment and underemployment, India is now confronted with one hundred thousand new entrants into the labor force *each week*. Fifteen percent or more of the labor force is now unemployed in Pakistan, Ceylon, Malaysia, the Philippines, and probably Indonesia.

The continuing, swelling flow of people from countryside to city in the poor countries is creating a social crisis of many dimensions, one so serious that it could directly or indirectly affect the quality of life for all mankind. The returns from the 1970 world census showed that the populations of the poor countries are converging on the cities at a record pace.

Urban populations in the poor countries, now totaling 600 million, are expected to increase to three billion over the next three decades, a 500 percent increase in scarcely a generation. Since urban services and facilities are already overburdened, one can conclude that, in the absence of massive external assistance, the level of services will deteriorate dramatically in principal urban centers. By future standards, the Calcutta of today may appear to be a model city.

As things are now going, it appears that the twentieth century will be the one in which human society will be transformed from a primarily rural society to one which is primarily urban. The human habitat is being transformed from one close to the land and close to nature to one where most of mankind lives in intimate and continuous association with a vast number of other human beings.

In the late twentieth century, an era of unprecedented affluence for many, hunger is still the common lot of a majority of the human race. For this hungry majority, the quality of life is influenced more by the lack of food than by any other single factor. For them, daily existence is largely circumscribed by the quest for food, reducing life to very fundamental biological terms. This is not new, but what distinguishes the current era from earlier ones is that hunger is unnecessary today. As it becomes less necessary, it also becomes less tolerable.

Few problems facing mankind are as challenging as that of devising an educational system capable of responding to society's needs in the late twentieth century. If the quality of life for much of mankind is not to deteriorate, far-reaching changes in human behavior must occur in the years immediately ahead. Education becomes crucially important as a means of informing people of the need for change and for stimulating acceptance of new attitudes.

Education is now recognized as the principal vehicle of social change. Education is no longer simply a matter of mastering the three Rs, nor is it merely a matter of skill acquisition, of preparing for a vocation or profession. For much of mankind, education is the door into the twentieth century; it is the means to improving the quality of life, achieving social mobility, and participating in the world's affairs.

Five centuries have passed since the invention of the printing press, yet by 1970 two-fifths of the world's adults lacked the capacity to take advantage of this invention. UNESCO estimates that the illiterate share of the world's adult population declined from 43 percent in 1960 to 39 percent in 1965. Although the proportion of the population affected is diminishing slowly, the number of illiterates is greater today than it was twenty years ago because of growth in population. Our modern world is very much a world of words, and, despite the new opportunities for learning made possible through radio and television, the illiterate person is severely handicapped.

MEETING BASIC SOCIAL NEEDS

The advance of technology, the growth in human productivity, and the accumulation of wealth in global terms have now evolved to the point where it becomes difficult to argue against providing a minimum level of living for all mankind. Such a level is best expressed in social rather than economic terms, including particularly the availability of food, education, and health services.

A minimum nutritional objective for 1980 should include not only enough food to fulfill caloric needs of all people but also the right kinds of food to prevent malnutrition and to ensure full physical and mental development. Neither the intellectual development of children nor the productivity of adults should be constrained by inadequate food supplies.

Virtually every national government has adopted a goal of compulsory elementary education, but many in Asia, Africa, and Latin America lack the financial means to achieve this goal. Though the cost of this is substantial when compared with present investments in education, global society has evolved to the point where we can and must begin thinking in terms of universal literacy. To allow large numbers of today's youth to remain illiterate would be too costly—both in terms of forfeited productivity and their capacity to comprehend and cope with the rapidly changing circumstances in which they find themselves.

A third component of a minimum standard of living is the provision of at least rudimentary health services for everyone. At a minimum this would include protection against infectious diseases through vaccinations, provision of safe water supplies, and family-planning services free upon request.

By defining development objectives in these social terms, we go a long way toward coping with the question of how wealth and the benefits of external assistance are distributed within the recipient countries. Traditional methods of establishing objectives in terms of economic growth rates do not take into account income distribution, often permitting the further concentration of wealth among elite groups. If the focus is on providing the basic necessities as outlined above, then by definition the focus of development efforts is on the less fortunate members of a society. Providing a minimal level of social amenities for the world's poor is not only a moral imperative but also will serve the practical interests of all mankind. The historical record indicates that birthrates generally do not decline substantially in the absence of such elementary advances in living standards. The rapid population growth that currently threatens both global political stability and global supplies of finite resources will not be adequately arrested without these improvements in the lives of the world's deprived majority.

SOCIAL JUSTICE AT THE INTERNATIONAL LEVEL

Although we are approaching the limits of the ecosystem in some areas, we do not yet know what the population-sustaining capacity of the earth is for a given per capita income or life-style. We do know that the earth cannot support nearly as many rich people as poor ones.

The rapid expansion of global economic activity until it strains some of the earth's finite capacities will force mankind to address the issue of social justice on a global scale—and against a backdrop far different from any that has existed in the past. Always before, the rich could urge the poor to wait, arguing that the benefits of growth would eventually trickle down. But when opportunities for further growth are limited or nonexistent, the dominant issue becomes not how to expand the pie, but how to divide it. In our finite system it may be possible to narrow the gap satisfactorily only by slowing the rise in living levels among the rich; thus the stage is set for some revolutionary questions of distributive justice at the international level.

TECHNOLOGY FOR HUMAN NEEDS

Recent years have witnessed a growing tendency to question man's capacity to manage technology effectively. Symptomatic of this is the antitechnology mood among youth, the technology-assessment movement in Congress, and the loss of public confidence in the relationship between technological advance and improvements in the quality of life. It would be a mistake, however, to view the questioning and uncertain attitude toward technology as limited to technology itself. Rather, it is part of a more profound questioning of the goals of society. It is within this context that we must examine the need for new technologies to meet social needs.

The contrast between the actual uses of global research and development expenditures (totaling 70 billion dollars in 1970) and the needs of mankind does not inspire confidence in man's ability to manage technology. If one constructs a list of the ranking R & D expenditures today and a second list of mankind's most pressing technological needs, one finds distressingly little relationship between the two. A breakdown of the global R & D budget shows weapons research claiming the lion's share, followed by nuclear and space research. Indeed, the more pressing social needs—a better contraceptive, a high-protein rice variety, efficient cure for schistosomiasis, improved literacy-training techniques, and a pollution-free internal-combustion engine —still claim only an infinitesimal share of the total expenditures.

A closer examination of global research and development activity shows two sets of institutions—nation-states and multinational corporations —controlling expenditures for all but a small fraction of the total, most of which is accounted for by nonprofit groups, principally private foundations. R & D expenditures by the nation-state are heavily weighted by "national security" considerations; hence, the massive expenditures on new weapons systems. Those of the multinational corporation are directed largely at R & D activities that can potentially yield a profit. National security and the profit motive are the principal forces shaping the worldwide R & D program.

Human or social needs are treated indirectly or only insofar as they coincide with the security or profit objective, which is all too infrequently.

The real challenge now before mankind is to develop more efficient technologies for the world's poor to use, technologies that will permit people to attain a higher level of living at a much lower cost.

What has been lacking to date is a mobilization of scientific resources to focus on pressing social needs. Where efforts have been made, they have been extraordinarily successful. The notion of starting with a human need and utilizing existing technology to attempt to alleviate it can pay enormous dividends, as the work of Nobel Peace Prizewinner Norman Borlaug illustrates. His award for breeding new high-yield wheats, which resulted in the Green Revolution, was not so much for the discovery of new knowledge as for the application of the backlog of existing knowledge to the problem of hunger in poor countries.

Close on the heels of the agronomic breakthrough by Borlaug was a breakthrough in the use of television for educational purposes. The imaginative innovation of "Sesame Street" may, if properly exploited on a global scale, make attainment of near universal literacy through the use of village television a much more likely prospect.

Such strategic investments to exploit basic technologies may dramatically improve the human condition on a global scale. Significantly, each of these two revolutionary advances was achieved with an expenditure measured in millions of dollars, in each case less than .001 percent of the global R & D investment—or, stated otherwise, for *less than 1 percent* of the American R & D investment in the now defunct supersonic transport plane.

Rising unemployment and massive urbanization represent socioeconomic problems that few countries are well-equipped to handle. We need to know much more, for example, about how to distribute employment within a society that has a given level of economic activity, about the relationships between both the agricultural and industrial technologies used and their impact on employment levels, and about how to deal with the complex of socioeconomic problems associated with rapid urbanization. Each deserves an international institute that could focus on the interdisciplinary resources of the global community.

Using a more efficient combination of transport technologies selected from the panoply now available could permit a society at a low stage of economic development to satisfy its transportation needs far better than is possible by adopting the American model. An automobile-centered transport system absorbs the limited budgetary and foreign-exchange resources of a poor country for the benefit of the small urban elite that can afford automobiles. A system that uses the same resources but relies heavily on public transport, combined with the mass manufacture of simply designed, low-cost bicycles and motorscooters, would provide a far higher degree of mobility for the population as a whole and would also distribute the benefits for a given cost much more equitably throughout the population.

Attaining a higher level of living with a low investment of resources may be much easier with the adoption of one development model than with another. It might be appropriate to emulate one country in one sector and a different country in another sector. A country might do well to adopt the Japanese system of agriculture, the Chinese approach to providing health services with paramedical personnel, and the American system of public education. Taiwan, for example, has modeled its farm sector closely after that of the Japanese, but it has formulated a distinctly Taiwanese approach to foreign investment. It has closely paralleled the American approach to family planning rather than the Japanese, by emphasizing contraception rather than abortion. By carefully selecting the technologies imported from abroad, by devising indigenous Taiwanese approaches where necessary, and by stressing the redistribution of income, the Taiwanese have achieved a remarkably high standard of living at a low level of income, one comparing favorably with Mexico, for example, where average incomes are twice as high.

Scientists, residing preponderantly in wealthy countries, have been unresponsive to human needs elsewhere in the world. In order for science to improve the quality of life, global R & D expenditures must be guided much more by improved knowledge of prevailing social conditions throughout the world and by a social vision of what society should and could be like, rather than by narrow national-security or profit motives. The new technological frontier is not outer space or nuclear physics but, rather, socially oriented technology, technology designed to meet the needs of the people. National priorities must be reordered so as to reorient the scientific establishment, mobilizing at least part of it to the technologies that meet pressing human needs.

There are within the United States a few encouraging signs indicating an interest in managing technology and in focusing on human needs. One of these is the technology-assessment movement mentioned earlier. Perhaps the most encouraging action to date was the refusal by Congress to provide funds for further development of the SST in early 1971. This decision was significant not only because it avoided a major source of noise pollution but probably even more because it indicated that the American people were ready to abandon the pursuit of technology for technology's sake.

A NEW SOCIAL ETHIC

The sixties witnessed a quickening of the social conscience of people in many parts of the world, but particularly among the young, and more particularly among the young people in the United States. This increase in social sensitivity took many forms: concern over racial discrimination, Vietnam, sexual discrimination, and poverty and hunger. In every case the issue became a matter of social concern and political action. New values were being formed; indeed a new ethic may be emerging.

A social ethic is a set of principles, a code of behavior that enables society to function and, hopefully, to survive. The social ethic that guides much of mankind today—in matters of childbearing, the production and distribution of wealth, and the relationship of man to nature—has evolved over the centuries. By and large it has served us well. Not only have we survived as a species but we have greatly multiplied our numbers and in some instances prospered as well. But now the old ethic is no longer adequate. Some values must be modified or abandoned and others strengthened, creating a new ethic, one dictated by the circumstances in which we find ourselves in the late twentieth century. But the crucial factor may not be the changes themselves but the limited time available for man to adapt successfully.

The values the new ethic embraces in turn define the new society that is just beginning to emerge. It is a society that is much less ideological and, hopefully, more humanitarian than those of the recent past, one whose essential character is determined by the desire to survive and to improve the human condition. It is even conceivable that the common crisis confronting all of us could draw mankind together, giving rise to a new humanism.

One of the most basic tenets underlying modern societies is that man should have dominion over nature, subjugating the environment to his needs. It is this tenet that is partly responsible for the worsening environmental crisis. The new ethic encompasses a new naturalism, which places greater emphasis on man's harmony with nature and less on his dominance over it. The prevailing view of man as the center of the universe must be abandoned in favor of one that sees man as an integral part of the natural system, rather than apart from it. The new ethic recognizes the finiteness of our biosphere, the only place in the entire universe known to be capable of supporting human life.

In seeking a more harmonious relationship with nature, our emerging global society needs to formulate a new childbearing ethic. Throughout most of man's existence large numbers of children were necessary to ensure survival of the species, since death rates were high, particularly among infants. Indeed, even with high birthrates, population growth was often scarcely perceptible within any given generation. But continuation of today's birthrates for many more years could threaten the very life-support systems on which man depends. Man must abandon the old "be fruitful and multiply" ethic, replacing it with one designed to eventually stabilize population.

Another central component in the existing ethic is a nearly exclusive emphasis on production and on the acquisition of wealth as an end in itself. A by-product of thousands of years of material scarcity, this ethic must give way to a much greater emphasis on distribution and sharing. Poverty exists in the late twentieth century not because of a lack of technology to raise individual productivity above a minimal level but because the diffusion of technology and wealth on a global scale has received so little attention. Modern man has excelled at production but failed at distribution.

An affirmative answer to the Biblical question "Am I my brother's keeper?" needs to be strengthened and broadened to encompass all of mankind. The new ethic must seek to eliminate territorial discrimination along with the more commonly recognized religious, racial, and sexual discriminations.

The new ethic must broaden the social scope of decision making. Modern societies encourage individuality and applaud individual initiative and action. But man's survival in a deteriorating biosphere requires that he be much more cooperative, acting in terms consistent with the collective welfare. Traditional loyalties to the nation must be expanded to include all mankind. Circumstances require that nations give up outdated notions of independence and sovereignty, replacing conflict and competition with cooperation.

That we urgently need a new ethic there can be no doubt. It must not be a culturally biased ethic, but a universal one, a response to the circumstances in which late-twentieth-century man finds himself. Such an ethic has far-reaching implications for the behavior of both individuals and national governments. Its adoption would certainly result in new life-styles and a new society, one far different from the one we now know.

REORDERING GLOBAL PRIORITIES

Our efforts to improve the quality of life are handicapped because, although a global community is emerging technologically, we have not yet established a set of global priorities. The sum of national priorities does not add up to a rational set of global priorities consistent with the new social ethic required. Indeed, there is little relationship between global needs and global priorities, as measured by the current commitment of resources.

Circumstances in the mid-seventies call for a major shift in the use of public resources from military to social purposes. Global military expenditures in 1970 totaled an estimated $204 billion, *a sum exceeding the total income of the poorest half of mankind.* In the United States, a military budget of $78 billion currently consumes 37 percent of the federal budget, compared with only 1.5 percent for economic assistance to poor countries.

Currently there are limited but hopeful signs that the conditions influencing the global level of military expenditures are changing. Political leaders within both the United States and the Soviet Union are beginning to ask publicly whether war is becoming obsolete as an instrument of foreign policy.

As economic and social ties between East and West increase and as cooperation expands between the two major powers in space exploration, pollution control, and other matters, conditions are being created for a major reassessment of global priorities and expenditures. The renewal of contacts between the United States and China also enhance the prospect for reordering global priorities. Even a modest shift in resources from military expenditures to education, agriculture, and family planning could make a great difference in efforts to improve living conditions for the world's poor.

A second major shift in the use of resources, which the times demand, is from the pursuit of superaffluence to the elimination of poverty. Superaffluence is the consumption of goods and services to a point far beyond any conceivable, purely necessary relation to individual well-being.

In the United States, where incomes now exceed four thousand dollars per person yearly, further gains in income among the vast majority do not have much effect on well-being. As Americans, we must begin to ask ourselves what right we have to consume a third of the earth's resources in our pursuit of superaffluence when we are only 5 percent of its people. We must ask because others are beginning to do so, and we must be prepared to respond.

CONVERTING IDEAS INTO ACTION

The new ethic requires a new political man. Voting regularly will not be enough. Individuals must become actively involved in major political issues lest the special interests continue to prevail, to the detriment of society. For many, self-realization can take the form of involvement in a cooperative effort to solve society's problems. The magnitude and urgency of the problems facing human society today are such that opting out, though a great temptation, is a luxury that society cannot afford.

You and I must adopt and propagate this new ethic, translating it into political action. Our future well-being depends on how quickly the new ethic now emerging can be translated into a new, more humane set of global priorities, new global institutions, and new levels of global cooperation. The future requires a commitment to society in its totality, and the number so committed must expand rapidly in order to reduce the damaging impact of special-interest groups, whether they be the highway lobby in the United States, the military-industrial complexes in the United States and the Soviet Union, the beet-sugar interests in North America and Western Europe, or the rice interests in Japan. Unless the gap between the broader global social interest and these special interests can be narrowed—and soon—the prospects for a better world are dim indeed.

What specifically can you and I do to insure that the quality of life for all mankind improves rather than deteriorates? What can we do to help create a world in which greater numbers can have the opportunity to realize their human potential? In my opinion, we should focus in the immediate future on three specific and interrelated objectives: (1) the elimination of global poverty, (2) the stabilization of world population, and (3) the reduction of global military expenditures.

Each of us must examine our own priorities in terms of how we use our time and money. There are endless numbers of useful causes and organizations, but we must distinguish between those that are critical and those that are merely useful. The former will measurably affect the world in which we and our children live. The three interrelated objectives outlined above— eliminating global poverty, stabilizing world population, and reducing global military expenditures—are truly critical, deserving of a total commitment by all of us.

If our society is to survive and progress in the seventies and eighties, we need a new ethic, a reordering of global priorities, and fresh leadership. Continuing improvement in human well-being on a global scale is tied to the emergence of an increasingly unified global society. Forces at work are moving us inexorably toward a unified world or toward a deteriorating one. We can still exercise that choice, but not for much longer. The most urgent item on our agenda in the years immediately ahead is the creation of a world without borders, one that recognizes the common destiny of all the peoples on the earth.

Herman Kahn

On Economic Growth, Energy, and the Meaning of Life

Herman Kahn, an outspoken and controversial futurist, shared some of his ideas in an interview in 1973 with Paul Kurtz, editor of The Humanist. *In a far-ranging exploration of issues Kahn discussed the energy situation, economic growth, the possibilities of nuclear war, population control, the gap between the haves and have-nots, alienation, his image of the future, and differing attitudes toward affluence.*

THE RESTRICTION OF ECONOMIC GROWTH

KURTZ: What do you think about the image of the future advocated by the Club of Rome, that is, the necessity to restrict economic growth?

KAHN: I think that it is almost unbelievably childish. More specifically, I

This is a shortened version of an interview that first appeared in *The Humanist,* November-December 1973.

think it reflects narrow technicism and an even narrower class interest. We've spent a fair amount of time examining the report [*The Limits to Growth;* see the discussion on p. 49 herein.] but, while I happen to like the people who did the study as individuals, it's just not professionally done. It is not a well-done study in any way that I would care to name, except that it states one of the important problems. They say, in effect, that it's hard to look at the interests of our grandchildren and great-grandchildren, and they are trying to do this. That's legitimate enough, and that's its great virtue. It has also attracted much attention to our current pollution problems but in a way that is often counterproductive rather than productive.

KURTZ: It's futurist oriented, but in that sense—

KAHN: In any other sense it has no virtues. It does not understand the whole system; it's not a good computer study; its assumptions are awful; its technique is bad.

KURTZ: Now what about their notion concerning the use of energy, resources, and production; that is, if consumption continues at the same rate, by the year 2000 we'll be in a terrible energy and ecological crisis.

KAHN: Absolutely not, given only one caveat: you don't do things that are incredibly dumb. There are two kinds of problems you can get into. One kind of problem is similar to the thalidomide problem. You introduce a drug and a lot of people are crippled. Now that drug also did a lot of useful things, by the way. It may have done more useful things than harm. But the harm is very visible and we don't care to have it. Some aspects of industry are like that. They do both good and harm. There are mistakes like the methyl mercury problem in the United States. With this kind of problem it takes a long time for the effects to show up.

KURTZ: On the fish you mean?

KAHN: On human beings also. And if you don't watch and move fast you can poison a lot of rivers, and it can be very hard to unpoison them, though this can be done. Now, assuming that we will at least learn from the more obvious mistakes, it doesn't take very high-quality decision making to make sure that we don't run into pollution deaths of any great magnitude or that we don't have mass starvation on the order of hundreds of millions of people. Let's go to the next one hundred years. If the population grows 2.1 percent per year, and if it continues unchecked, we'll have fifty-four billion people by 2100. We don't expect to hit that. We expect to taper off way before that, probably at around ten or fifteen billion.

KURTZ: When?

KAHN: I'll say probably ten or twenty billion in the early or mid-twenty-first century and very slow growth or a decline after that.

KURTZ: Well, where do we get predictions that we may be overwhelmed by 2020? We hear a great deal about that.

KAHN: It could happen, but I don't think it will. I think there is a systematic overestimate of the likely future rate of population growth.

KURTZ: How do you explain this great concern? Is this country in the throes of great hysteria worrying about the future?

KAHN: The hysteria has to do with a number of issues put together, and it originates with an attitude held by a certain class of people. These people want to believe certain kinds of things for various reasons. The most obvious reason is self-interest. Say you are living on ten, fifteen, or twenty thousand dollars a year in a country like Portugal, Spain, Mexico, or Brazil. You live very well. First of all, you have two to five live-in servants. (Incidentally, one good servant is better than a household full of appliances.) Second, you have easy access to the more sensual pleasures of life, including girlfriends or mistresses. Third, you have immunity from the petty cares of life. You have cars without traffic jams, you have status, you have importance, you have a kind of safety, when other people have none of these things. Now, compare this life with that of someone making fifty thousand dollars in the United States. Who do you think lives better?

KURTZ: Who does?

KAHN: The guy who is making ten to twenty thousand dollars a year in Portugal and has the servant is living better than the American who makes fifty thousand dollars a year. If you are one of the 5 percent who have cars, you're living great. If you have a Cadillac, maybe you also have a Chevy.

KURTZ: But only a small class in Portugal lives like that.

KAHN: That's right. All I'm saying is that the standard of living in upper-class elites all around the world goes down both absolutely and relatively as the world gets richer. And they recognize it. Now why are our middle-class young in the United States playing poor? They play at being poor in order to differentiate themselves from the lower-class kids who are proud of no longer being poor and who like to dress and act in a way that shows off their affluence. Playing poor is a form of snobbishness directed against the lower-middle class. Nobody plays poor in a country where there are really poor people. Hippies come from very well-off countries in which the poor basically don't exist.

KURTZ: The affluent societies?

KAHN: Not only affluent but affluent with almost an absence of the absolutely poor. Now some people think of the United States, for example, as having poor people, because they define *poor* as having three to four thousand dollars a year. But I mean *poor* as the world uses the term.

KURTZ: Then don't you think that there is a class of poor people in this country?

KAHN: No, there's practically no poverty in the United States.

KURTZ: You think poverty is just relative?

KAHN: There is relative poverty in the United States, which will presumably continue throughout history, but very little absolute poverty.

KURTZ: Is poverty another notion that in your view needs to be discarded?

KAHN: No. You do have some very poor people in Appalachia and the South, but throughout the country the improverished tend to be people who can't, who don't know how to, or who don't want to cope with the system. That is, there are people who really know how to fill out the forms, but just don't want to fill out the forms, or people whose state is conspiring against them, as may be the case in some parts of Mississippi and Louisiana.

KURTZ: Then how do you explain the well-nigh mass hysteria that has invaded the advanced industrial nations? You've got people like John D. Rockefeller III, arguing that growth is the overwhelming problem and that the industrial nations have to restrict their growth.

KAHN: You've put it quite clearly. This is mass hysteria.

KURTZ: Where does it come from?

KAHN: The issue is very complicated. The first thing to recognize is that for the upper-middle-class guy, not for John D. Rockefeller III, growth is a disaster. Now take myself; we were poor, not middle class, when I was a kid, but I lived better than most kids ever lived. We went to California, and I've worked since I was about thirteen, earning a man's salary. When I was fourteen I bought my own car—a Model A, for seventy-five bucks. I used to drive down to Mexico for Mexican meals and up to San Francisco for Chinese meals. When we went to the beach, we went to Malibu, where the movie stars live now, and had the whole beach to ourselves. If anyone else came, we went north to another beach. We used to hike in the High Sierras. If we met someone there on the trail, the day was ruined. Now that's the way you could live if you wanted to thirty or forty years ago.

KURTZ: As you describe it, it sounds like a beautiful life.

KAHN: At any level of income, modern kids could not live this way. I make roughly twenty times as much now, and I can't live as well.

KURTZ: Isn't this due to overpopulation and the underdevelopment of the country?

KAHN: It isn't the population; it's wealth. Really poor people don't disturb anybody. They are quiet; they don't move around; they don't take up much space. It's people with money who cause problems. People with money to buy cars and boats and who have time for vacations and travel. These are the ones who fill the country.

KURTZ: This level of affluence is growing; it is worldwide, and it may continue to grow.

KAHN: Yes, and that means a loss to many with upper-middle-class values. But the middle class will enjoy it. The middle class doesn't mind applying ahead of time to get into a national park. I do. I will not go to a national park if I have to apply ahead of time. It's got to be there when the mood moves me.

KURTZ: Do you think the upper class is impatient?

KAHN: The upper classes want privileges; they want spontaneity, large amounts of privacy; they want to be able to do what they please when they feel like it, as they feel like it. They don't like traffic jams.

KURTZ: And that's why they are worried about growth, you mean.

KAHN: Partly, yes. They lose by growth. Some of them don't like suburban sprawl. Eighty-five per cent of Americans have a huge commitment to suburban sprawl. You know how in most European countries people used to live in villages and go out to the farm? In our country farmers always lived in widely separated houses—even during pioneer days—and this meant accepting the high risk of Indian attacks, and so on. And that commitment to suburban sprawl has continued right up to today. Now I doubt if you could find many city planners who think suburban sprawl is a good thing. Most city planners hate suburban sprawl. They want Corbusier-type ribbon cities; they want green belts. They do not want Levittown; unfortunately, the middle class does.

KURTZ: In your book *Things to Come,* you talk about the eventual overflowing of the technological bathtub.

KAHN: We talk there about the dangers of growth. They are very real. I talk about the 1985 technological crisis. In one part I list seventy problems that could cause really terrible troubles in the next ten to twenty years.

KURTZ: But are these not caused by growth?

KAHN: They *are* caused by growth. In this world nothing comes for free.

KURTZ: Is the problem then, not to limit growth, but to redirect it?

KAHN: Not so much redirect it as control it. As a matter of fact, I would be willing to limit growth if we could do so safely and equitably. But I'm relatively well off; I'm not poor. I'm not sure how I would vote if I were making five thousand dollars a year. I am perfectly prepared to say that a number of problems are made easier if you limit growth. And few problems get more difficult for me personally if you limit growth.

KURTZ: The growth of others you mean.

KAHN: The growth of everybody. I want to include others. Absolutely. The argument for limiting growth is, I think, fairly good. But there are also very good arguments against limiting growth. It's very hard to get a reasonable balance. All I'm saying is, first, that you can't totally limit growth and, second, that the pluses for increased growth are probably overwhelming. On the other hand, many problems are alleviated by slowing down growth. But that's mainly true in the rich world. In the poor world you have the population problem. I believe the only way to solve this problem is to make people rich. In other words, the American girl who normally has about two children has set this limit, not because of pollution or starvation but because of wealth. Middle-class people simply don't want too many children. Benjamin Franklin once made the comment that the easiest way for a young man to get rich was to marry a widow with seven children. That is a formula for bankruptcy today. If you want to stop the population growth, I believe you have to make the poor countries richer. And the easiest and fastest way to make them richer is to make the rich countries richer. One major argument for making the rich countries very rich is to increase the gap, which pulls up the poor countries.

KURTZ: Yes, but isn't the gap supposed to be increasing?

KAHN: It is increasing. The dumbest argument that was ever made by middle-class Americans and AID people is the following calculation that they make every year: Rich people make two thousand dollars per capita, poor people make two hundred dollars per capita, and the gap is eighteen hundred dollars. In one or two decades both incomes will be double. The rich will make four thousand dollars, the poor four hundred. The gap will then be thirty-six hundred, and the poor will be twice as badly off. You can't make a dumber remark than that. The poor people of the world are delighted to double their incomes from two hundred to four hundred dollars. You know something? They don't care what per capita earnings in rich countries are.

KURTZ: As long as they can increase their own?

KAHN: Yes. They couldn't care less whether you doubled, tripled, quadrupled, or halved your income. Their interest is solely in increasing *their* income. Now let me discuss gaps, because it is important to understand the concept. The greatest gap in the world is basically between the first and the second son of the king. One heartbeat away from everything, the second son feels the gap. The two vice-presidents, only one of whom makes president; the two authors, only one of whom gets the prize. Intellectuals really feel gaps, careerists do, and so on. And they think that everybody feels the same way. The next big gap is where somebody who has been up has gone down. England felt this when the Germans and French passed them. They are going to feel even worse. By 1985, very likely Italy, Portugal, and Spain will have a higher per capita income than England.

KURTZ: Spain and Portugal will have higher per capita incomes than England?

KAHN: It's a reasonable statement.

KURTZ: And the English will feel very bad about this.

KAHN: Older Englishmen, yes; young Englishmen much less so. They have no idea why the older Englishman turns white, blue, green, and orange when you say this. They're used to thinking of themselves as a second-class nation—or, better, not thinking in terms of hierarchy. Older Englishmen just can't stand the idea. The possibility of being patronized by visiting Italians or Portuguese horrifies them. But, let me say this, the gap thing is important. A lot of things revolve around the idea of social gaps.

Now take a chauffeur from a Rockefeller estate. He is not depressed because Rockefeller lives many times better than he does. You know, he expects it; he couldn't care less. He's not even depressed if the upstairs maid makes 50 percent more than he does. He knows that upstairs maids are scarce. You tell him though that another chauffeur makes ten cents an hour more, and he gets ulcers. That's the gap. It's the gaps within your own socio-economic status group that are really felt. Now if you're rich, you may not understand that. Rich men's children often have trouble talking to chauffeurs; they feel guilty about their money. But that's the kid's problem, not the chauffeur's.

KURTZ: But you don't think that the advanced countries ought to limit growth at this point?

KAHN: Just the opposite. They have a duty to make the rest of the world rich.

KURTZ: And you think if they grow they will export?

KAHN: It is the so-called trickle-down theory. And the trickle-down theory has worked in all cases. I don't know of any case where it doesn't work. The fact that people don't want to believe that it works is again a problem that the people have, but it is not an objective problem.

KURTZ: You mean if advanced countries limit growth, then this will tend to limit growth in the underdeveloped countries?

KAHN: Absolutely.

THE ENERGY CRISIS

KURTZ: But take the energy crisis of today. Suddenly great shortages have occurred in this country. You've been predicting it; other people have been predicting it.

KAHN: Actually, we've been very lucky. If we had had one very cold winter or one very hot summer, we would have had a shutdown altogether.

KURTZ: But doesn't this suggest that the problems of growth are getting out of hand?

KAHN: The problems of mismanagement. Here's an important example of mismanagement: We took something like natural gas, which is the most convenient fuel you can have, and we priced it at twenty cents a thousand cubic feet. It was grossly underpriced. The average price of gas today is twenty-five cents a thousand cubic feet. This is fuel that clearly should be sold at one dollar per thousand cubic feet. So naturally everybody uses gas instead of oil or coal, and you get a complete distortion of the market. This is not the same as a real shortage.

KURTZ: Do you think there are new sources of energy that can be used?

KAHN: There's plenty of energy in the world, but there will be a more or less permanent shortage of very cheap energy. In fact it's a reasonably good bet that energy at twenty cents a million BTUs will no longer be available, except in the Far East and Middle East. If people are willing to pay a dollar for the same amount, they will have all they want for at least a century or two. If they want to pay two or three dollars a million BTUs, there is all they want for the rest of history. If you are rich you can afford to pay the higher price. Now one of the big advantages that the United States has is that if we want to produce our own oil we can mine about two or three trillion tons of coal, which would produce about ten trillion barrels of oil. The most oil you have in the world from undiscovered oil is two or three trillion. From coal alone we could get three times as much in American oil.

KURTZ: Wouldn't this process be costly?

KAHN: It would cost five or six dollars a barrel. This is what we expect we are going to have to pay for oil anyway. So we don't have to buy it from abroad if we don't want to. Now in oil shale we have about two trillion barrels available. We do have serious problems of strip mining but I think they can

be worked out. They are serious problems, but they are hopeful problems—
that is, they can be solved, and their solutions do not lead to worldwide death
and destruction. The difficulty is that you may have to sacrifice major portions of at least four or five states, including Colorado and Wyoming.
Wyoming has unbelievably large coal deposits, and Colorado has both coal
shale and gas reserves.

KURTZ: Do you think the energy problem has been manufactured by the
media for the public?

KAHN: No, it is a serious problem. You have a serious shortage of refinery
capacity in the United States. We haven't built a single refinery here since the
late sixties, and there are no plans for building any.

KURTZ: Is this in part because of efforts to repeal the oil-depletion
allowance?

KAHN: It has nothing to do with taxes. It's because of environmental
objections. For example, you start to build a road. No matter where you build
it, anybody who lives right near that road is unhappy. Anybody a little dis-
tance away is very happy. The road is clearly good for almost everybody, but
it's definitely bad for the guy whose house is torn down. States don't want refineries, for they louse up large areas. Now I agree with the right of every state
to protest refineries. But I don't think their protests should always be successful. In other words, this is the eminent-domain issue. Often somebody
will be hurt.

KURTZ: Do you think the objections of environmentalists and the over-
emphasis of dangers by groups such as the Sierra Club will have negative
consequences?

KAHN: Well, both negative and positive. You do have to worry about the
environment, and it's very good to have movements that are worried about it.
But the way these groups act is counterproductive. Ninety-five percent of the
American people used to support environmental protection. Now it's eighty-
five percent. People have been driven out of the movement by the excesses of
environmentalists. The latter are really acting irrationally. But it may be good
to have some conflict in such situations. If you want a lot of pressure groups
on both sides, even extremist movements can be useful. On the other hand,
the leading environmentalists appear to some people as if they had gone
crazy.

KURTZ: So you need some balance on this?

KAHN: Yes.

IMAGES OF THE FUTURE

KURTZ: Well, I wonder if we can go on to images of the future. Do you think that in some sense the images that we have of the future determine the kind of future we will have?

KAHN: They affect the future. Obviously, there are both self-fulfilling and self-defeating prophecies, and it is possible for the two to cancel each other out. On balance, however, I believe that self-fulfilling prophecies are more important.

KURTZ: I'm interested in the images of the future that you think will emerge.

KAHN: Let me give you one commonly held image—the neo-Malthusian theory: resources are running out; pollution is going to kill a lot of people soon; disastrous gaps are opening between the rich and the poor. The humanist left would add that, not only are rich countries in trouble, but they were bastards who got rich by criminally exploiting men and the environment. This is an inflexible position. The progressive center sometimes says that there are different kinds of growth, but it tries to weasel about the situation. This more moderate position, I think, is closer to being correct.

KURTZ: And you hold the position that almost everyone is getting richer, some faster than others, and that if growth is properly managed, there will be plenty of resources. Is that your image of the future?

KAHN: That is the image I hold. It is completely accurate. It's carefully stated and not an extreme view. I can give you all the supporting data you want on it. Now there are some converts to my position. The future we foresee looks all right by middle-class standards and middle-class interests—but not by upper-middle-class standards or interests. You do have to worry about some far-fetched and unlikely but terribly important problems. It takes a moderate level of decision making to overcome the problems we can imagine, but no extraordinarily good behavior. And I do not promise that if you're rich you'll be well off. In fact, my basic point is that the miseries of the future are likely to be due to the ambiguities of wealth, rather than to the pressures of poverty.

KURTZ: By *ambiguity* you mean the psychological problems?

KAHN: There are all kinds of problems in the world. Wealth is not necessarily good for people.

KURTZ: Then your image is fairly optimistic.

KAHN: Optimistic at the material level with important subjective problems. For example, we talk about a technological crisis in 1985. This crisis brings with it a lot of subjective problems, such as the loss of privacy. That's ten to twenty years away, not fifty or one hundred. It's with us right now.

KURTZ: Is your view concerned with the need for population restriction?

KAHN: I think population restriction is something like the fourth most important problem. For many poor countries, population restriction is crucial. For India, for example, it's very important. For China, it's useful. For countries like the United States and Japan, it's merely nice. It may or may not be good for a country. It's just not equally important for all countries.

KURTZ: So in your view, ten billion people by the year 2020 is not a disaster?

KAHN: Not a disaster by middle-class standards.

KURTZ: And you think ten billion is likely by 2020?

KAHN: Ten to fifteen billion is a fairly reasonable number for 2020 or 2025, given the expected tapering off of growth rates.

KURTZ: Although population is a major world problem, you don't consider it as the first problem. What is then?

NUCLEAR WAR

KAHN: The first problem facing the world has been with us for some time now. It is the issue of war or peace. This problem seemed to recede in the sixties. We generally felt that the world was relatively safe then, regardless of what governments did. The risk of serious war is now starting to go up again, precisely because people are not worrying about the problem.

KURTZ: Now, what about efforts toward disarmament? Do you think that this is an illusion? What about the SALT talks?

KAHN: The SALT talks were both good and bad. They were what we call a fair-weather policy. The policy will work very well if it is not challenged and things go well. It's not a hedge against problems, and it helps to create the problems it's supposed to be a hedge against. But it also helps to create the fair-weather atmosphere. So it's hard to say. Some of the things agreed to were crazy from both the Soviet and the American point of view.

KURTZ: Senator Jackson, who was extremely critical of Nixon's policies concerning the Soviet Union, has often seemed to be the only one in this country aware of that.

KAHN: Everyone would be aware of it if they understood it. Take the number-one point of the SALT talks, the number of missiles each side has.

We don't even know if the negotiators knew what the Russians had. At no point did the Russians agree to any statement of ours as to what they had. We say it had been limited to so many missiles. We would start by saying, "You now have three hundred missiles." They would say, "That's a very interesting number." They didn't agree it was true. Even in the final agreement the Soviet Union made no statement of how many missiles they had.

KURTZ: Then, in your judgment, we don't know what they have for sure.

KAHN: We probably do know; but it's crazy to sign any agreement that in principle doesn't require open—

KURTZ: Inspection?

KAHN: Not even inspection. Just verification of what the number is. I'm willing to trust their word for it, but they haven't given their word. Throughout the entire agreement there is no admission by the Russians of what they have. Thus, if we accused them of building new silos, they could claim that they were old silos that the United States just never noticed before. You're practically asking them to cheat. This is the worst kind of agreement we can have—one that breeds suspicion.

KURTZ: Do you think then that the ideological crisis that we lived through in the fifties and sixties will emerge again in the future?

KAHN: No, I think it's winding down. The so-called domino theory is basically correct even in reverse. The defeat of Communism in Vietnam and the détente between the United States and the Soviet Union has made Communism everywhere in the world a defeated ideology. There's no place in the world where the Communists have high morale, even though a good deal of the world is hostile to the United States. Look at Latin America; Communist ideology is the prevailing ideology if you except Brazil, Mexico, and Colombia. Nevertheless, there's no active movement to rally around. There's no radical ideology with any kind of dynamism. Castroism is dead; Maoism is dead; Russian Stalinism is dead. However, it's possible to write scenarios for the revival of Communist morale.

KURTZ: Well, does this suggest a decline of Communist ideology over the next ten to twenty years?

KAHN: We don't know. But we do know that at the moment there are no left-wing Communist movements with high morale anywhere.

KURTZ: But then why do you think the problem of war and peace is still crucial?

KAHN: One, the nuclear weapons are becoming easier to buy. Technology is producing some very dangerous products here. Two, the kind of balance achieved by World War II is gradually weakening.

KURTZ: Your reputation suffered during the days of the Rand Corporation when you were "thinking the unthinkable," and you came under heavy personal attack.

KAHN: Our study on this is now a standard textbook at dozens of universities. As far as I know, there are no serious errors that wreck any part of its argument.

KURTZ: So you think that it was a kind of moralism in your critics when they reacted so bitterly to what you were doing?

KAHN: Nuclear weapons are extraordinarily unpleasant things and most people didn't want to talk about them. Unless you believe in unilateral disarmament, however, and are willing to accept the consequences of this policy, you have to consider the problem. If you believe in unilateral disarmament, you can say, "To hell with the Bomb, I don't want to talk about it." As far as I'm concerned, I think we're just lucky that we didn't have a war during the 1950s. We maintained our strength, and we prevented accidental wars without really knowing what we were doing.

KURTZ: But what about the 1970s and 1980s?

KAHN: As I said, I think that the probability of war will rise, in part because people don't take it seriously.

KURTZ: Does the China-Russia situation bother you?

KAHN: If I had to guess where the Bomb would first be used, I guess it would be Japan versus China. That's the most serious danger. The next would be China versus Russia. Of course, the Japanese and Chinese may succeed in avoiding war, but the problem is basically that Japan and China are going to compete for Asia. And Japan has the edge. Yet it's hard to imagine the Chinese taking a second place to Japan.

MEANING AND PURPOSE

KURTZ: Now what do you think is the next major problem facing the world?

KAHN: If the first problem is nuclear war and the second is the problem of accelerated growth, the next problem is the lack of a sense of meaning and purpose. Low morale is and will be a problem for the United States and the developed world. There is the whole question of what kind of character structure you want, the issue of what you mean by humanism, the problem of values for the United States. There's a terrible split between what I call "high culture" and "middle cultures." People in the "high culture" simply do not understand the value structure of the middle class. The next split is associated with the meaning and purpose of life.

KURTZ: In your view is the emergence of the humanist left also part of the problem?

KAHN: The humanist left is the most characteristic symptom of the problem.

KURTZ: Is not the humanist left a response to this loss of meaning and purpose?

KAHN: It is a response that only exacerbates the problem. It is many things—a symptom of the problem, a part of the problem, and a response to the problem.

KURTZ: You think the basic question is that of intellectual ideals, goals, and purposes?

KAHN: Yes, but I think the American president is in a position to do something to alter the basic attitudes and self-images of Americans, even if such action does not normally fall within the president's domain.

KURTZ: This is a larger issue than the political one?

KAHN: Yes. Once in a while you have a situation in history where a gimmick makes a night-and-day difference. The bicameral legislature in the early days of the Republic was basically a gimmick, but without it you never would have gotten the Constitution accepted. No gimmick—no Constitution. I think there's a gimmick that can can be used to fix up the country, which is the Bicentennial celebration in 1976.

KURTZ: Do we need a reassessment of purpose?

KAHN: Yes, a reassessment. Let me describe it in terms of the Hudson Institute program, which is broader than this. We did a study we called "The Prospects of Mankind." We make much stronger statements than anyone else has made. We claim that with current technology we can support a worldwide population of twenty billion people with twenty thousand dollars per capita. That's a surprise. The most surprising part is that we require no faith in the continued improvement of technology on a worldwide basis. We can do it with what we have now. That's the point we want to make. We had thought it would take improvements in technology.

KURTZ: We can do this with current technology and with the use of resources?

KAHN: That's right. Now, it's clear that improved technology is going to make things even better. It should be easy, not hard. The Hudson Institute believes that we can support twenty billion people at twenty thousand dollars per capita.

KURTZ: This will be a startling study when it's completed.

KAHN: The general public should be made aware of this, and the 1976 Bicentennial should be the means by which these prospects are made known. Now in the Bicentennial, the President has the right to look back two hundred years, and he has the right to look ahead to the year 2000—which is only twenty-five years ahead. When you look at the United States on that time scale, things look very good. In twenty-five years you can fix every problem in America—pollution, growth, traffic, housing—you name it.

KURTZ: You are a buoyant optimist.

KAHN: No. This is sober realism. There's no problem you can't fix in twenty-five years. What upsets people is the fact that you can't solve problems in five to ten years.

KURTZ: Your trademark is that you've got great confidence. Every problem can be solved.

KAHN: No, I don't say that about fundamental human problems. But remember the problems people are talking about—they're screaming about the slums, the roads, pollution, you name it. They are material problems. They can all be solved. It just takes money and appropriate planning. All of the country's material problems, as we currently worry about them, can be solved by middle-class standards. And the President has a right to make this observation at the Bicentennial. But he can't make it any earlier, because many would think him dumb, credulous, or deceptive. "Twenty-five years from now! Whom are you kidding?" But during a Bicentennial such "visionary" thinking is acceptable, if not required. He can make the second observation that worldwide poverty problems, except for that of the hard-core poor, will be mostly solved, and quickly, mainly because of the rapid growth of the United States and Japan.

KURTZ: On a worldwide basis?

KAHN: Yes, on a worldwide basis. The employment data is that everybody should have at least about five thousand dollars per capita, by current American and European standards, and everybody should have it by the end of the twenty-first century. It might even be much higher. Now, there will be a few exceptions—mainly those people who don't want it or are feckless. Okay, I can't help that. So that's the picture. There are ecologists who picture those people who "drop out" as doing God's work: they are not polluting or using up resources. They then portray those people who work in industry as doing the Devil's work by making the world uninhabitable. These ecologists are not helping things. They hold up a project, they prevent refineries from being built, and they see this as God's work.

KURTZ: These are moralist ecologists?

KAHN: Yes, and the point is, they are morally wrong and their opponents should *say* that they are morally wrong.

KURTZ: And the morally right position should be to try to get rid of poverty and to continue growth?

KAHN: Continue growth. That's absolutely right. Now, I'm not saying that growth is without problems. Remember the technological crisis of 1985 —if there is terrible growth, it will cause all kinds of terrible problems.

KURTZ: Not to grow would be a greater disaster?

KAHN: Yes. The main point is that you don't have to stop growing; you have a choice. The mechanism is there; you've just got to steer it.

PART

IMAGES OF HUMAN PROGRESS

Since positive images of the future speak to another and better world in a coming time, they must enkindle the belief that what the images promise is good and that progress toward what is promised is possible. However, "progress" and "progress toward" are notions for which no universal agreement exists. The following essays discuss different images of the future, each of which is based on a particular view of what progress means for the human race. Some of the images discussed already command the fervor of many adherents, while other images reflect what the authors feel are important for the future.

Manfred Stanley

Beyond Progress: Three Post-Political Futures

With modernization has come a spiritual malaise deeply affecting our sense of the significance of politics. In the process, faith in a benign historical Providence has been replaced by abstract models of alternative futures. Stanley describes three possible futures. Despite their secular-scientific gloss, each has retained an eschatological flavor promising to free the human condition from politics itself.

It is by now a Sunday-supplement commonplace that the social, economic, and technological modernization of the world is accompanied by a spiritual malaise that has come to be called alienation. At its most fundamental level, the diagnosis of alienation is based on the view that modernization forces upon us a world that, although baptized as real by science, is denuded of all humanly recognizable qualities: beauty and ugliness, love and hate, passion

This article first appeared in *The Humanist*, November-December 1973.

115

and fulfillment, salvation and damnation. It is not, of course, being claimed that such matters are not part of the existential realities of human life. It is rather that the scientific world view makes it illegitimate to speak of them as being "objectively" part of the world, forcing us instead to define such evaluation and such emotional experiences as "merely subjective" projections of people's "inner" lives.

The modern world view, in other words, forces upon our consciousness a disjunction between "private" and "public" that partly parallels, on the sociopolitical level, the post-Cartesian disjunction between the notions of "subjective" and "objective." All things that men and women tend to consider most central to their sense of humanity gradually come to be defined as private and subjective, while only the calculable, the utilitarian, and the predictable elements of life are allowed the status of objectivity. The world, once an "enchanted garden," to use Max Weber's memorable phrase, has now become disenchanted, deprived of purpose and direction, bereft—in these senses—of "life" itself. All that which is allegedly basic to the specifically human status in nature comes to be forced back upon the precincts of the "subjective," which, in turn, is pushed by the modern scientific view ever more into the province of dreams and illusions.

All this has deeply affected our modern sense of the significance of politics. Once sanctified by its connections with men's and women's collective efforts to build the good society according to one or another version of what was thought to be natural law, politics becomes, with modernization, an exercise in organized theatrics, having little resonance for what is now experienced as the "inner" lives of persons. The single most compelling claim to the moral significance of modern politics is that it represents the human version of a species' struggle in nature for collective survival. Looked at this way, the political life of humans does not always compare favorably with the efficiency of ant colonies.

Given this ambivalent attitude toward modernization among intellectuals, it should surprise no one that some modern evolutionary sociologies have retained, despite their secular scientific gloss, the eschatological flavor of movements that once unabashedly promised eventual freedom from the historical vanities of politics. Here I shall outline three such post-political eschatological themes. My purpose is not to attack or defend them but to demonstrate the eschatological character of some current modes of "futurizing," as evidenced in their promise to free the human condition from politics itself. Since politics has always been part of human history, these exercises in "futurology" are efforts to envision a new world at the end of secular time.

THE SECULAR-SOCIOLOGICAL VIEW OF HISTORY

Before turning directly to our themes, we must examine briefly what, until very recently, a secular-sociological view of history was thought to entail.

During the nineteenth century there emerged what was considered to be a scientific evolutionary perspective on history that is commonly referred to now as developmentalism. Sometimes combining elements of older philosophies of history with the new Darwinian biology, developmentalism in its various forms portrayed historical change as a series of stages arising progressively out of the dynamics of previous stages. Henri de Saint-Simon, Auguste Comte, Herbert Spencer, and Karl Marx were all major formulators of such developmental theories. One of the important features of such theories, as far as our discussion is concerned, is that nineteenth-century developmentalism was both a moral and a scientific analysis of history. The unfolding quality of history was usually considered a phenomenon of a moral, as well as a social and temporal, progression. Because of this, people were deeply attracted to these theories. This is understandable. Once we have a historical Archimedean point from which both the scientific and moral dimensions of events can be viewed in a single manner, the problematic relations between a person as subject and a person as object are theoretically solved. Subjectivity becomes understood as an aspect of the developmental history of the objective social world, and the inner life finds its fulfillment by identification, through action, with these developmental laws.

Efforts to reconcile the subjective and objective lives of people have become associated with some of the great totalitarian episodes of the twentieth century, but the humanistic appeal inherent in developmentalism should not be obscured by this identification. When people make themselves agents of developmental visions, they do not usually do so with a sense of sacrificing precious subjective freedom. They do it rather with a sense of desperate hope and often with a sense of relief from what they experience as the anxieties of ungrounded subjectivity. In a sense, modern developmental totalism is a form of secularized religious experience, in which man sees himself as "losing his life in order to gain it," a "second birth" into the truth that gives his life transcendental meaning. One does not have to know these laws in order to make oneself their agent any more than the medieval peasant had to understand the subtleties of the Trinity in order to go to church and obey his priest; one has only to have faith in their reality.

Faith in the inevitability of unilinear progressive development has been considerably undermined in the West by now. It has been replaced by abstract models of alternative futures thought to have been made possible by developmental sequences that have already occurred. Changes in philosophical approaches to scientific methodology, not to speak of the calamitous history of our century, have forced upon us a sharp cleavage between scientific and moral perspectives on the historical process. Present-day Western thinkers, deprived of a plausible faith in a benign historical Providence, find themselves hoping that a degree of choice or collective "free will" exists, by means of which we may choose from among a number of varying possible futures. Even the austere secularity of "policy analysis" is based on the assumption that some such freedom exists. Three alternative futures in particular have found favor among many contemporary intellectuals and their brightest students. These futures are quite different and appeal to different audiences. But they are alike in their eschatological significance as post-political worlds, and because of this their similarities are far more important than their diversities.

NEO-PLATONIC FUNCTIONALISM

The original Platonic vision of society was organized around the assumption that nature was divided into reality and that which was mere appearance. Reality was hierarchically arranged according to ascending levels of purity and form, or the Good. Apprehension of these levels was not simply an act of intellectual cognition but was an experience of inner conversion as well. The Platonic Republic was stratified according to people's diverse capacities for relating to these truths, and justice was defined in terms of the degree to which persons were functionally ordered and treated according to these capacities. It was a society designed for stability, and, because its focus was a timeless truth, the vision was static.

The modern mind does not believe in Platonic truths; but it still generates Platonic visions of social organization. The stable point of reference is not Plato's hierarchy of forms but rather a social hierarchy reflecting the requirements of an achieved (or about-to-be-achieved) stage of societal evolution. In this sense, Saint-Simonist technocracy can be thought of as a form of societal Platonism. According to this perspective, it is the technologized world itself—its institutions and dynamics, man's "second nature"—that is the criterion of stability according to which society should be organized. Production is the moral reference point. Without production all is chaos; but if enough can be produced, eventually all humanity's goals will be satisfied. It is a humanistic vision because technology is here viewed as the humanization of an indifferent nature that can be molded to our will. As in the Platonic Republic, people are defined in terms of their capacities to relate to a stable point of moral reference. Their attitudes, aspirations, and skills are collectively defined as their merits, according to which they will be functionally stratified in what has come to be called a "meritocracy." Modern schools are seen, like Platonic dormitories, as institutions that function to reorient the person from his parochial loyalties and provincial angles of vision to the societal functions it is deemed necessary for him or her to perform. (This, in essence, is what the concept of technologically rational manpower allocation is all about.) Like the original, the neo-Platonic Republic has its elite—not the philosopher-king, but the cybernetic systems engineer.

This vision was inherent in the work of Saint-Simon and was elaborated by Comte, the man who coined the term "sociology." Although Comte considered himself a fully secular development theorist, he believed that "positivism" (as a mode of consciousness as well as a methodology) was the final stage of history, the millennium toward which all things moved. For Comte, as for Saint-Simon, the salvation for ungrounded individualism was "function" in a productive sociotechnic engine that benefited everyone. There was nothing indirect about the religious significance of all this for Comte. Sociologists were originally meant to be the new priests of his Church of Humanity!

This neo-Platonic vision has received new relevance now that automation and electronics increasingly take the place of human capital, opening the way for more free time and hence subjective freedoms for large masses of people. A recent contribution to this modern Platonist vision is Zbigniew Brzezinski's notion of the "technetronic" society. He envisions a society split into two levels: a knowledge-possessing technocratic elite working full time to maintain the system and a mass population freed by technetronics from labor for the leisured pursuit of everything from humanistic play to hedonistic gratifications. Like the Platonic elite, the modern elite is, in principle, open to penetration by those with the requisite aspirations and skills; the modern version of the myth of the metals being Brzezinski's "meritocratic democracy." In a more detailed picture of such a society, Donald Michael reveals the mystic element of neo-Platonic elitehood when, in discussing the man-machine relationship experienced by his "cyberneticians," he says that they:

> ... will be a small, almost separate society of people in rapport with the advanced computers. These cyberneticians will have established a relationship with their machines that cannot be shared with the average man any more

than the average man today can understand the problems of molecular biology, nuclear physics or neuro-psychiatry. Indeed, many scholars will not have the capacity to share their knowledge or feeling about this new man-machine relationship. Those with the talent for the work will probably have to develop it from childhood and will be trained as intensively as the classical ballerina.[1]

The contemporary neo-Platonic resolution of alienation provides for many persons, especially those with technocratic inclinations, the most effective humanistic balance between usefulness and freedom. It is also eminently practical, in the sense that it does promise empirically to be the most likely outcome of present developmental trends. It appears to assure, without recourse to revolution, the millennium of public organization for productivity, combined with valued private freedoms. It does so, however, at a price. Some elements of that price are the seeming Platonic permanence of the gap between a powerful elite and a powerless mass, of freedom without power, and control of the private self at the expense of the public self. Another cost is the indefinite prolongation of present-day world-distribution patterns. Brzezinski is quite direct about this, setting forth for our reflection a future moral dichotomy for best defining who is the truer repository of that indefinable quality we call human. Is he "the technologically dominant and conditioned technetron, increasingly trained to adjust to leisure, or the more 'natural' and backward agrarian, more and more dominated by racial passions and continuously exhorted to work harder, even as his goal of the good life becomes more elusive?"[2]

There are those who would consider the global institutionalization of such a choice a cure worse than the present affliction.

REVOLUTIONARY MILLENNIALISM

A second way of thinking about developmentalism is to regard it as the history of sociological determinism itself and to posit beyond it a post-developmental state of freedom to be achieved once the progressive dynamic has run its course. This view of empirical history as the prehistory of freedom can be called developmental millennialism. Its major modern exemplar was Karl Marx.

In this perspective, based on a complex sociology and social psychology of Hegelian inspiration, the primary definition of alienation as a moral problem is the social organization of mankind's creative powers into a reified object-world of property systems, social roles, money, and ideologues posing as theorists. In orthodox Marxism, the developmental progression is itself the path to liberation, culminating in a final revolution beyond which a new history of freedom begins, one whose outlines cannot be discerned by those still on the alienated periphery of the promised land.

Given the revolutionary turmoil of the present century, many persons of this persuasion find themselves in the position of sectarians awaiting the intervention of their god while Armageddon is already raging about them. Leninism reflects the urge to pick up the weapons dropped by enemies and help the secularized Providence of History do its work of liberation through the efforts of human will and discipline. The results have been tragic, as measured by the original dream. Nonetheless, such a faith, still operative today for millions throughout the world, is a powerful engine of social change. Revolutionary millennialism forges the subjective consciousness into an instrument of future-creation by organizing a symbolic dream of liberation and treating it as objective law. Yet the humanistic element is especially stressed through the notion that the objective laws of history are themselves temporary. Although socially determined, men are nonetheless midwives of a freedom in which subjective consciousness itself will be liberated into awareness of its role in the creation of what are now falsely reified gods of the object-world. This humanistic aura has legitimatized iron discipline and unquestioning obedience under the allegedly objective necessities of revolutionary praxis. Such a vision is indeed a lever of social change, but it is one that runs on the fuel of promises. Broken promises, unlike mere spent fuel, will not only bring the journey to a halt but may also cause the engineer to throw away his worthless map and scuttle the whole engine in despair.

NEO-PRIMITIVISM

Of all the eschatological perspectives thrown up in the modernist context, there is one that sets itself in direct opposition to the modern consciousness. It is the neo-primitivist perspective, whose point of departure is what its proponents see as the antihumanistic effects of civilization as such.

Aside from the more obvious influences stemming from Rousseau, Nietzsche, and many romantic philosophers and artists, this view has derived some profound philosophical impetus from the writings of Martin Heidegger, the great German undertaker of Western metaphysics. Herbert Marcuse and Norman O. Brown are obliquely associated with a sort of utopian neo-primitivism too. But its most recent and popular formulation appears in two books by Theodore Roszak, *The Making of a Counter Culture* (1969) and *Where the Wasteland Ends* (1972). Roszak does not mince words about the allegedly destructive influence of the "myth of objective consciousness." Neo-primitivism's presence in secular social science is best represented by the anthropologist Stanley Diamond.[3] The whole oppressive structure of the contemporary state, of the law, and of modern social problems is intelligible, to Diamond, in terms of a neo-primitivist critique of modern civilization.

In its more popular forms neo-primitivism today is not a theory of social organization, nor is it directly a model for social reconstruction. It is rather a mood and an attitude toward the quality of modern consciousness itself. In its more theoretical form, it stresses the subject-object dissociation as an important cultural cause of what the neo-primitivist sees as our modern inability to understand our environment on its own terms. From this diagnosis follow various conclusions about the state of modern consciousness, in whose context attempts at purely social reform are largely fruitless. Neo-primitivism is a drastically antitechnological perspective that sees no compromise between the technical-utilitarian mode of relating to nature and the receptive openness that neo-primitivists define as the only stance toward reality capable of apprehending truth. In its more sociological form, the stress is in favor of the values and norms of custom and community over the hierarchial, legalistic, and socially complex forms of authority and specialization found in large civilizations.

Reversing modern evolutionary-progress doctrines, neo-primitivism looks to primitive societies for its standards of cognition; this is made very clear in Roszak's celebration of the "shamanistic world view." Only by this sort of return to the foundations of cognitive innocence, it is held, can people put aside their artificial object "pictures" of the world and open themselves once again to respectful communion with "things as they are." This vision should not be confused with the nihilistic notion that there is a different objective reality for every subjective consciousness. Neo-primitivism rests on a kind of faith that there are dimensions of the world that are closed to modern minds because of our intellectual, reductionist, and control-oriented mode of relating to the world. Thus, proponents of this critique charge that our modern notion of objectivity is, in reality, collectively subjective because it is based on a cultural motive, namely technological control over nature.

Unlike the Marxist approach to alienation, which stresses the mutilation of the modern subjective consciousness by capitalist institutions, neo-primitivists place their emphasis on how much of the world is concealed by an arrogant and rampant technologized subjectivity. In the hands of its most intelligent exponents, neo-primitivism has too much to say to be laughed off by educated moderns. Indeed, in its more technical form, important hypotheses contained in neo-primitivist analyses are of great relevance to cultural history and the sociology of knowledge. For example, much of Heidegger's work is a developmental theory of ideas applied to the structure of Western philosophy since Plato. The notion of the internal exhaustion of Western metaphysics that he propounds is vitally important for historians of culture, whatever one's reaction to his gnostic response to this history. (Naturally, Heidegger himself would consider these remarks an example of technicist appropriation of his ideas, since for him the scientific enterprise itself was part of the historical itinerary of the technological ego.)

In its polemic form, however, neo-primitivism has about it a noncompromising quality, a kind of either-or stance that seems based on what must strike many of the unconvinced as an unacceptable failure of nerve about the role of the intellect itself. Neo-primitivism seems to be a heavily deterministic orientation, in that the structure of civilization and its correlated technological and abstract consciousness is viewed as so destructive of other modes of consciousness as to be virtually unintegratable into a humanistic range of awareness. Certainly, careful readers of Heidegger and Roszak, for example, are inevitably led to wonder if these thinkers wish to leave any place at all for the notion of science as a mode of knowledge or for technology as one valid form of activity for man in nature. Indeed, neo-primitivism in its polemic form has about it a conflict orientation reminiscent of the early gnostic movements, with their disdain for empirically experienced reality and their consequent claims of radical dualism between false and true (but hidden) knowledge.

CONCLUSION

We have reviewed three eschatological styles of futurizing. Each looks toward the end of secular history insofar as this history is political. Each has its proponents within the social sciences, thus demonstrating that eschatology is not a hoary topic reserved for archivists of Biblical and medieval history. I shall not indulge in polemics regarding eschatological influences in "futurology." However, it is worth pointing out that there is a note of despair implicit in all three of these perspectives.

The neo-Platonic orientation seems to say that our primary problem is *adaptation* to technology, since it is the engine of social development itself. The revolutionary millennialists find hope in the developmental process for an eventual apocalyptic *transcendence* over social determinism itself. Thus they trivialize the hard-won freedoms already achieved within the confines of political history. And the neo-primitivists pay such extreme homage to deterministic developmentalism that they preach a near-total *resistance* to the accomplishments of centuries of Western intellect. In all these stances we find everything except confidence that human beings will prove rational enough to develop a politics capable of *disciplining* human powers for humane purposes.

NOTES

1. Donald M. Michael," Cybernation: The Silent Conquest," in *Automation,* ed. Morris Philipson (New York: Vintage Books, 1962), p. 123.

2. Zbigniew Brzezinski, "America in the Technetronic Age," *Encounter* 30 (January 1968), pp. 16-25.

3. Stanley Diamond, "Introduction: Uses of the Primitive," in *Primitive Views of the World,* ed. Stanley Diamond (New York: Columbia University Press, 1964); see also his "The Rule of Law Versus the Order of Custom," *Social Research* 38 (1971), pp. 42-72.

Robert T. Francoeur

Human Nature and Human Relations

Francoeur believes that there is general disillusionment with the utopian promises of medicine, technology, and science. Apocalyptic discontinuity is breeding a dangerous paralysis. Yet either we decide to choose our future or we perish. Two fundamental questions must be asked: What do we want to mean by human? *What kind of human relations do we want?*

Fred Polak has stated in exquisite detail and logic a sociological and scientific echo of an ancient biblical proverb that I paraphrase as follows: When your children cease to dream dreams and lose their vision of the future, your nation will perish.

Frankly I cannot agree more with Polak's basic thesis about the creative and survival role played by positive eschatological and utopian images in

This article first appeared in *The Humanist*, November-December 1973.

the evolution and growth of societies and cultures. I agree also that our culture is in serious trouble because of its near-total lack of positive images of the future.

Every culture, it seems to me, must consciously situate itself on the needlepoint of the present. But for this point in existence to have any meaning, it must be consciously seen within the dialectics of time. Life—an individual's life, a culture's life, a civilization's life—is a process. And when it involves conscious human beings, there must be a general awareness of the dialectics of the life process, dynamically balanced in the present moment between the thrust of its realized, historical roots that brought it to this point in development and the attraction of the future—an ideal, as yet unrealized goal. Without this dynamic orientation, the existence of any individual and of any society is doomed to a rootless vacuum, a purposeless Nirvana.

I am afraid Polak is right in concluding that for the first time in history Western civilization suffers from an absence of positive and generally accepted images of the future. There is a general disillusionment with the utopian promises of medicine, technology, and science. To the popular mind these have all created more problems than they have solved. Twenty-five or even ten years ago, medicine promised to cure all. Instead, in recent years, by extending life expectancy and reducing births—both laudable purposes— medicine has threatened to create a very unbalanced population, with increasing numbers in the more conservative and psychologically inflexible upper age brackets. What happens to a population when its percentage of adaptable, creative, venturesome youth is reduced below the critical number needed to keep the culture developing?

Medicine and technology together have created the problem of leisure, forcing men and women to face the prospect of an ever earlier retirement age, which some predict will be down to thirty-five or forty by the turn of the century. What does *homo faber* do when he has only twenty or twenty-five years of income-producing work and then thirty or forty more years of retirement?

Technology itself, in the popular mind, has turned the sweetness of luxury and comfort sour with the specters of pollution, dwindling natural resources, and a seemingly inevitable economic inversion in our standard of living. Even the sacred cow science is giving sour milk these days. To the general public, its positive implications for our future are far outweighed by the negative ones: eugenics and genetic engineering, reproductive technology, biological and nuclear warfare, the ubiquitous carcinogenic food additives, and the prospect of humans increasingly dependent on behavior- and personality-modifying drugs.

It hardly matters to the public that small groups of professionals in the health sciences, industry, technology, and science find much to hope for and work toward. Alvin Toffler made a mistake in entitling his best seller *Future Shock* (New York: Bantam Books, 1971). He could have much more appropriately entitled it "Present Shock." For most people the changes that loom on our horizon are so psychologically traumatic that there is an often expressed wish to not even hear, let alone think, about what may lie ahead. Better to live on the pointless needle, thinking neither of our past nor of our future, than to consider the variety of possible futures and decide which one we want to work toward. To the lay person the choices appear too serious, too imminent, too unsolvable, with too many unknown, unpredictable consequences. Better to live in one's own little world, better to ignore change, better not to plan for tomorrow, better not to decide.

Polak rightly labels this attitude a "failure of nerve." It certainly is that. But it is more. For those in the Judeo-Christian tradition, and especially for those who profess a practicing faith, this failure of nerve is also, more damningly, a failure of faith. It amounts to a radical lack of faith in the divine on-going creation, a refusal to participate in that co-creation, and a denial of the universal vocation of Abraham—the calling to leave one's comfortable homeland and plunge into the desert, believing firmly in the promised land. But for any human being, this failure of nerve is a basic denial of our human nature. Understandable as it may be, this paralysis of present shock marks a very critical threshold for humankind and Western civilization. Either we decide to go ahead—to choose our future and work toward it—or we perish.

I do not think anyone honestly can disagree with this either-or analysis of the problem, no matter how uncomfortable it might be for them to recognize and admit our dilemma. However, admitting the dilemma is *not* the problem as I see it. To more than one hundred twenty lectures I have given in the past five years on college campuses around the country, the pattern of response has been consistent. A crippling pessimism boils to the surface *after* people admit that we must go ahead, that we must choose and work. The paralysis comes when people are confronted with an encyclopedia of perplexing problems that all revolve around the key questions: Where do we go, and how do we choose? Trying to answer these questions causes paralysis, because people feel as if they have been tossed into a maelstrom, caught in a deluge without an umbrella. Answering this swarming galaxy of questions requires the accumulation of more technical and specialized information than most people can handle, at least in its present form. But I maintain that the information can be presented intelligibly and palpably for public consumption if we try. However, even if the information is absorbed, it often causes enormous emotional upset and absolute paralysis of decisional efforts because it points to such radical changes in our life-style and in our conceptions of what it means to be human that people shudder in horror and turn away from decision making.

TWO KEY QUESTIONS

Perhaps the questions we will have to answer within the next decade, the questions some try to answer in a few days or weeks, cannot even be fully itemized until the decade is over. This incapacity is not a bad thing. In fact, I am convinced that the paralysis resulting from informational and decisional overload may be therapeutic and useful. Hopefully, what Polak calls the "loss of nerve," combined with our overload of information and the admission nevertheless that we must choose now, will force us to simplify the encyclopedia of our problems to manageable proportions. This means focusing on the two most basic and urgent questions, which are fundamental in any list put together by futurists. They are the two questions we can and must focus on now. All the others are their second- and third-generation specialized progeny. They can be dealt with without causing paralysis, though they will produce much angry controversy and painful groping. Neither of these two questions has a once-and-for-all answer. They will have to be asked continually, with each tentative answer constantly modified, as we learn more about our abilities and become more adept as futurists and realistic dreamers.

Question One: Faced with the prospects of genetic engineering, reproductive technology, cryogenic suspension of life, behavior- and personality-modifying drugs, organ transplants and artificial organs, and even the hybridization of human and infrahuman tissues and organisms, we must decide what we really mean, viscerally and cerebrally, by the word human. Since we are already modifying humanhood indirectly and haphazardly, we must decide which indicators of humanhood we want to promote and which ones we want to reduce or eliminate as we move into the era of the designed human.

Question Two: Again, viscerally as well as cerebrally, with our synergic technological developments, we are radically changing the environmental niche humans occupy as social persons. Technology has always modified human life-styles and hence human relations. Thus we must ask: What kind of basic modifications are likely to spring up in human relations? In our images of male and female? In the elemental one-to-one pair-bonding of humans? In the family? In the quest for intimacy and belonging?

Briefly, what do we want to mean by *human*, and what kind of human relations do we want? These are the two central questions. All others are only orbiting satellites of these two issues.

CHOOSING TOMORROW'S HUMAN

With rapid medical advances in the area of human disease, we have unconsciously been answering that first question: What is human and what do we want humanhood to be in the future? Our medicine has unwittingly reduced the natural interaction of our genetic constitution and our environment. Natural selection is no longer the effective sieve it once was; often it is we, rather than nature, who do the selecting—and usually by default, inadvertently, blindly. When we taxpayers agree to certain priorities in allocating monies for medical research, it may well be for cancer, not alcoholism, or for sickle-cell anemia, not care of the aged. And a hospital chooses who among a dozen needy patients will benefit from its solitary kidney machine. Let us be honest. We are already selecting the human of the future and designing his genetic constitution by supplanting the forces of natural selection. It no longer is— and perhaps never was—a question of our not intervening in the process of natural selection and not contributing to the on-going process of human evolution. The questions are: How fast are the changes to come upon us, and how radical are they to be?

In recent years remedial medicine and science, predominantly but not exclusively, have become creative and manipulative of human nature.

Ernst Mayr of Harvard, one of the giants in evolutionary thought and in zoology, once pointed out that the "replacement of typological thinking by population thinking is perhaps the greatest conceptual revolution that has taken place in biology."[1] For the typologist, the type (*eidos*), the image, the model is real, and individual variations are only an illusion. For the populationist, the type or model (average) is an abstraction and only the variations are real. As Mayr concluded, "No two ways of looking at nature could be more different."[2]

What, then, about human nature? Our model of what it means to be human? And how will we define "human" tomorrow, or twenty years from now, when we can manipulate, engineer, and hybridize the human genome? Our very nature may change as much during the next fifty to one hundred years as it has since the days of the first Australopithecine eight million years ago, or even of Ramapithecus, an Indian ape, our remotest ancestor from fifteen to twenty million years ago. In this framework of compacted time one can hardly continue to speak of an eternal human nature.

At least one thinker has begun to look seriously toward clarifying what we mean by a true *human* being. Dr. Joseph Fletcher, professor of biomedical ethics at the University of Virginia School of Medicine, recently attempted an actual inventory profile of humanhood—an exploratory, tentative profile of man—which is an essential first step.[3] Because this fundamental question has been ignored, there have been all kinds of fruitless and disheartening disputes. When do individual organisms take that magical step into full status as human (the abortion dispute)? When does one leave that state (the euthanasia and organ-transplant debates)? Who is human and to what degree? Which organisms are human, and why are they considered so? What makes me human and you not so human?

Fletcher's profile was not some futile attempt to offer a precise definition of humans in terms of body and soul, substantial form and prime matter, or any other traditional typological image rooted in the fixed philosophy of nature that we inherited from the Greeks. Rather he took a process, populational approach, which raises many more questions in subsequent practical application than the neat definitions of past generations. But that is our burden as creatures of time, who realize that we are passengers in a temporal world.

Dr. Fletcher's tentative profile included the following positive criteria of a human image: an IQ of at least 20, self-awareness, self-control, a sense of time, a sense of futurity, a sense of the past, the capacity to relate to others, concern for others, communication, the ability to control existence, curiosity, changeability, a balance of rationality and feeling, and idiosyncrasy. His human criteria also caused him to reject the dichotomy of the natural versus the artificial: an individual is not subhuman or nonhuman just because he or she is the product of frozen sperm, artificial insemination, gestation in an artificial womb or a bovine surrogate mother, or even asexual cloning. He also maintained that parenthood and sexuality are not essential to humanhood.

Dr. Fletcher cautions us about how tentative his profile is; nevertheless he is doing something other than talk about developing a process profile of humanhood before he plunges into the morass of practical and futuristic questions, about designing the human of tomorrow. At least with Fletcher's profile in hand, one can ask the fundamental question we too often ignore in debates about the man-made man or woman and our playing God.

But we have to go beyond Fletcher's profile, develop what he boldly initiated, and popularize it in dialogue with the general public. Then, hopefully, we might have a working operational answer to our first basic question.

HUMAN RELATIONS TOMORROW

Twelve thousand years ago man discovered agriculture and created the city. The result was a radical change in human relations: the segregation of the sexes, emergence of the solitary male ruler, sex-role stereotyping, and some modifications of the tribal bonds of the earlier nomadic cultures. The Industrial Revolution and further urbanization had enormous impact on the structure of the family and on human relations, just as the automobile later destroyed the American extended family and the contraceptive pill produced the deliberately childless couple and reduced the woman's commitment to motherhood.

Our epoch is marked by a number of things: mobility—the average American moves every five years or oftener; the leisure of early retirement, now in the early sixties and creeping downward; a work week reduced to four or even three days; contraceptive controls—24 per cent of college students want no children after marriage; the emergence of educated women in business and politics; a divorce rate of one out of every three marriages; and predictions that within a few years four out of every five men and two out of every three women will have extramarital relations after several years of marriage. It is small wonder people panic and lose their nerve when they view these compounding revolutions in human relations and consequently in the central thread of our social structure. Modify the male-female relationship and you automatically send waves through all the other facets of our society, especially the economic and political. It may be that it is not the political and economic implications that upset people as much as the fact that a considerable number of people have accepted a pattern of life different from the traditional life-long, sexually exclusive monogamy.

I am convinced that people too often panic and lose their nerve because they get all tied up in practical and isolated problems: for example, the pros and cons of communes, gay unions, single parents, and nonmarital cohabitation.

The solution, to repeat my thesis, seems to be the ability to confront the primary issue: How do we survive as persons in our mobile, technological, fragmented world? How do we relate? How do we structure and satisfy our need for intimacy and security?

Several provocative concepts have been offered by the specialists in the future of human relations. British gerontologist Alex Comfort has written an essay, "Sexuality in a Zero Growth Society," for the Center for the Study of Democratic Institutions (*The Center Report,* December 1972). While suggesting that Western society has already virtually institutionalized adultery, he envisions a society in which pair-bonds are still central, though initially less permanent. He sees childbearing as a special responsibility involving a special life-style and settled couples engaging openly in a wide range of intimate and sexual relations with friends, other couples, and third parties "as an expression of social intimacy without prejudice to the primacy of their own relationship."

Another idea that has had tremendous impact on the public imagination was presented in the best seller *Open Marriage* (New York: M. Evans, 1972), by anthropologists Nena and George O'Neill. Their image of the marriage of the future is "an honest and open relationship between two people, based on equal freedom and identity of both partners." The late Abraham Maslow often spoke of the need to abolish the current cultural norms that severely limit the number and nature of meaningful relationships among adults. He argued for the development of a eupsychian culture, which would encourage individuals to develop a cluster of overlapping and simultaneous intimate relationships.

Finally, among the most widely disseminated influences provoking the public to develop new images for human relations have been the utopian writings of Robert H. Rimmer. In *The Harrad Experiment* (Los Angeles: Sherbourne Press, 1966) Rimmer dealt with the college cohabitation experience and group marriage long before many were willing to admit their existence. In *The Rebellion of Yale Marratt* (New York: Avon Books, 1971) he made the three-party marriage seem quite feasible and functional. In *Proposition Thirty-One* (New York: New American Library, 1971) he developed a type of corporate family by joining two mature families. And more recently, in *Thursday, My Love* (New York: New American Library, 1972), he explored what I think will become a dominant form in human relations in the near future: a type of open marriage with structured, institutionally recognized comarital or satellite relations. Family sociologist Oscar Eggers, in a review of *Thursday, My Love* (*The Futurist,* April 1973), praised Rimmer as a prophet "proclaiming the doom of narrow and empathyless relationships . . . [and] foretelling . . . the next phase of human development . . . [as] the development of the human potential for significant encounter, unburdened by jealousy or possessiveness."

PESSIMISM OR OPTIMISM

Polak's appraisal appears somewhat biased on the pessimistic side. Perhaps this is a valid perspective. Only the future of our culture will tell. I much prefer Margaret Mead's label for our age of apocalyptic discontinuity; she characterizes our culture as "prefigurative." Her emphasis is on a beginning rather than an end. Chaos? Certainly. But in one perspective, we are experiencing the birth pangs of a new creation, to borrow another optimistic bias from the visionary realist Teilhard de Chardin.

If we are indeed, *pre*figurative and painfully moving into a new social structure—some sort of "metahumanity"—then the role of models, images, and ideals becomes even more critical than it was in past cultures. Until recently, images of the future were really images of the past, images of some golden age man sought to recapture. However eschatological or utopian these images were, they were, in reality, archetypes into which man was to mold himself. Looking ahead, and recalling the contrast I made between fixed and process philosophies of nature, I can only accept as functional and creative the insecurity of the "flexible and dynamic working models" suggested by Ludwig von Bertalanffy, the late developmental biologist and founder of systems-theory analysis.[4] Von Bertalanffy's models would be constantly evolving, serving as guidelines for our use rather than as set molds to which we must conform. The visionary's world, be it eschatalogical or utopian, must lie out there ahead of us and not in the nostalgic past. It must be seminal, like a lodestone pulling us into the desert. For, however we tend to view man, his nature is that of a pilgrim, a diasporic wanderer.

If we have no generally accepted positive images of the future, it is because too few people want to think creatively and with faith about the future. The solution, I believe, is to focus on the two central questions: What do we want to mean by human? And what kind of human relations do we want? The discussion, controversy, and exploration that would result in the public sphere might very well bring to life some of the positive images already conceived by small circles of scientists, philosophers, theologians, sociologists, futurists, and specialists of other varieties.

There is hope, *but only if we learn to see*. Teilhard de Chardin once described the history of the living world as "the elaboration of ever more perfect eyes within a cosmos in which there is always something more to be seen."[5] Our task is an attempt to see and to make others see what happens to man, to us, when we situate ourselves dynamically at the interface of our past and our future.

NOTES

1. Ernst Mayr, *Animal Species and Evolution.* (Cambridge, Mass.: Harvard University, Belknap Press, 1963), pp. 5-6.

2. Ibid.

3. Joseph Fletcher, "Indicators of Humanhood: A Tentative Profile of Man," *The Hastings Center Report* 2, no. 5 (November 1972): 1-4; and "Four Indicators of Humanhood—The Enquiry Matures," *The Hastings Center Report* 4, no. 6 (December 1974): 4-7.

4. Ludwig von Bertalanffy, *Modern Theories of Development* (New York: Harper & Row, 1960), *Robots, Men and Minds* (New York: Braziller, 1967), and *Organismic Psychology and Systems Theory* (Barre, Mass.: Heinz Werner Lecture Series, 1968).

5. Pierre Teilhard de Chardin, *The Phenomenon of Man* (New York: Harper & Row, 1959), p. 31.

Robert Jungk

Toward an Experimental Society

There has been an enormous increase in social imagination and experimentation during the last decade, says Jungk. This change has not been perceived, because the human revolution cannot be measured by industrial yardsticks. He suggests some possibilities for humankind that could follow from normative goals based on the values emerging from the most influential sector of our youth.

Critics of the Club of Rome's *The Limits to Growth* (Donella Meadows et al., New York: Universe Books, 1972) have rightly pointed out that one important variable—probably the most important one—is missing in the world model developed by the Club, namely, man—man, the problem solver; man, the unpredictable; man, the unquantifiable. My image of the future is based on the hope and the possibilities for human development, badly neglected in

This article first appeared in *The Humanist*, November-December 1973.

the past decades, devoted to the perfection of technological tools and the conquest of outer worlds.

THE GUERRILLAS OF INDUSTRIAL SOCIETY

When Fred Polak first published *The Image of the Future* in 1955 (Dutch edition; the first American edition was translated by Elise Boulding and issued by Oceana Publications, Dobbs Ferry, N.Y., 1961), his analysis was correct that our capacity to develop pertinent visions of desirable futures was diminishing. Since then, in a worldwide search for alternative ideas and solutions, I have found that attitudes and capabilities have begun to change. All over the globe, not only in the Western world but to a lesser degree also in the communist countries, there is an enormous increase in social imagination and experimentation. The profound importance of this vast movement of ideas has not yet been perceived, partly because of the narrow outlook that the "new breed" has criticized. The human revolution cannot be measured in statistics as can the output of the Industrial Revolution. The beginning of a change of values or a budding alteration of attitudes cannot be assessed in the same precise way as can changes in the stock market.

Another reason for underestimating the depth and strength of the new currents may lie in our captivity to the standard of "success." The fact that the so-called Movement has been defeated in its first assault on the alienation and inhumanity of our present society is seen by many as the early end of an unrealistic dream. My own evaluation is quite different: the groundswell has not subsided; it has been partly integrated and used for superficial changes, but it continues to gnaw at the foundations of present order not only from the outside but also from within. There are more and more guerrillas to be found in the structures of corporate managements and undemocratic governments. Sometimes they are ferreted out, but new ones take their places. They know that the Zeitgeist is with them.

Where do they come from? Very often from "new" schools. A growing number of young people have learned to use critical analysis and have been led to the discovery of their own inner resources. Some of them also have been taught to conceptualize, to use their imaginations, and to progress from diagnosis to proposals for therapy, from analysis to vision and model building. A worldwide survey of the impact of the new pedagogies, such as that made by Professor Hayward of the Organization for Economic Cooperation and Development a few years ago, would give a rough idea of the forces for change liberated in hundreds of thousands of youngsters. The fact that they are still a small minority numerically should not be taken too seriously. In the old-fashioned but still prevailing language of our quantitatively oriented society, one might equate one active "changer" with thousands of passive "containers," as Paulo Freire has called them.

As a futurist I try to base my image of tomorrow, at least in part, on signs and trends as perceived today. Human forecasting, based on man's changed attitudes and new capacities, in my view has to supplement and influence technological and social forecasting.

An exploratory forecast, extrapolated from emerging values and attitudes in the most influential sector of today's youth, would have to take into account the desire for creativity as opposed to acquired knowledge, for cooperation as opposed to competition, for simplicity as opposed to affluence, for participation as opposed to "being told," for an enhancement of the emotions as opposed to cold rationality. A normative forecast, to which I subscribe, building on such feelings and turning them into aims, will attempt to design and plan for a future that could open to man the following possibilities, among many others.

CREATIVITY FOR EVERY MAN

Most people, as Jonathan Kozol has pointed out, meet "death at an early age." Future man should be able to stay alive mentally as long as physically. Much is already being done in preschool education to liberate and strengthen children's imagination. In the schools, original ideas, questions, and creative thinking will be valued more highly than the intake of the already known. Younger children will be asked from time to time to teach the older ones and their teachers, who will turn into Socratic "midwives." Children will no longer be secluded and kept away from the real world. Part of their education will consist of active participation in many areas of the work of older ones.

Today young people leaving progressive schools often feel frustrated by the life- and work-styles of adults. Neither the ethics nor the attitudes they have learned seem to apply to the real world. But this real world will have to "give." The right to a challenging and interesting workplace, where the worker is no longer a cog in a machine but a creator and mover in his own right, will be as important as salary, rank, and social security. Lifelong creation will be part of lifelong learning.

Such a tapping of creativity buried in every man must and will profoundly change the economic, as well as the administrative, structures. It will also remold technology as we know it today. Technology will not be abolished by the human revolution, but it will be greatly changed. I can see three avenues to the technology of the future.

First, there will be a tamed technology. This will aim, through technology assessment and technology control, to prevent dehumanizing and dangerous impacts of industrial developments through a continuing decision-making and designing process, which would at every stage be open and transparent to trusted delegates of all parts of the population. A special "advocate of the unborn" would always be present to defend the interests of those whose present (our future) too often has been occupied and colonized by earlier generations.

Second, there will be a soft technology. Parts of the community would go back to simpler forms of technology. They would live on the land, using natural energy sources and natural materials, planting and eating their own natural food. This model cannot and should not be enforced, but it could be encouraged.

Third, we will have a responsive technology. Cybernetics and electronics have made possible the invention and design of machines that respond to their operators in a way not yet known. Pioneering work by Gordon Pask, Warren Brodey, Avery Johnson, Nicholas Negroponte, Sean Wellesley-Miller, and Simon Papert in Great Britain and the United States may pave the way for instruments that can become cooperative, highly responsive partners in man-machine systems. Such a technology, dubbed "dialectic technology" by Belgian philosopher Henri van Lier, will try to bridge the gap between living and artificial creatures; its blueprint to a large extent will be influenced by patterns discovered in biology. Decentralization of industrial plants brought down to a human scale will then be made possible by a dense tissue of electronic networks. Such a technology would be similar to the machinery in the human body—one can forget it as long as it functions well and in an unobtrusive way.

HUMAN GROWTH

In the age of technology, human sensibility has greatly diminished. We have become sensual and mental cripples assisted by ever more powerful prostheses. Enhancement of the human senses of hearing, touching, smelling, tasting, and seeing would be part of the future I like to imagine. We would hear sounds and combinations of sounds that have been drowned out by the noises of the present. We would increase our erotic sophistication and maybe begin to create great tactile works of art. We would redevelop ways to be "led by the nose," which animals and some primitive tribes still possess. We would give gastronomy the high standard that it has begun to lose, even in France, and we would learn at last how to see in a way that has been only the privilege of great painters. The widening of our intellectual abilities would uncover a whole universe of low signals that we have blocked out and deep emotions that have been suppressed because we could not cope with them. I am not advocating some kind of superman but the self-fulfillment of under-developed man.

REAL DEMOCRACY

Today's "democracy of analphabetism," where the citizen must express his choices in rather inarticulate ways—such as pulling a lever or marking a ballot—will grow into real democracy through the education of critical, imaginative, active citizens and the development of institutions worthy of them. Today, voters are asked to take part in the political process only after the most important decisions have been made by a small group of men. In the future I envision there would be a new kind of town hall in the center of every community. There, all interested citizens would be able to express their ideas of the kind of future they want to build, and they could discuss their different visions of the future. Image forming for the future should no longer be the prerogative of intellectuals nor the monopoly of the political establishment.

How could this be done? Here, I would like to mention the experiments with workshops for "future creating" that I have conducted for a number of years in Europe. They are a kind of brainstorming devoted to social invention. In the first stage all participants critically evaluate the matter at hand—work, school, private life, and so forth. The next phase is given over to the invention of desirable designs and models. In the third phase, the imaginative planners are confronted with experts, who evaluate the proposals in the light of feasibility. And in the fourth round the dreamers and the realists decide how and if the new ideas could become reality.

The most interesting result of these exercises in creative social planning has been the opening up of citizens who have never had a chance to develop ideas of their own. In fact, we have in our society an additional social barrier as solid and high as caste or wealth: qualification through knowledge, often highly specialized knowledge. In a future, more democratic society, this disenfranchisement of the "unqualified" citizen will no longer be acceptable.

His needs and wishes, be they primitive or naive, will be heard and made into political realities with the understanding and help of experts who are there to listen and explain, rather than to dominate.

SUPPORT FOR SOCIAL EXPERIMENTS

These ideas may be discounted as utopian, and that will be that. But in this time of crisis new ideas must be welcomed. Therefore I would like to make two proposals that might inject alternative thinking into the so-called real world.

First, a medium of communication and evaluation devoted to a growing number of social experiments is badly needed. Such experiments not only try out new life-styles but also new methods of administration, new systems of health care, new modes of transportation, different styles of teaching and learning, innovations in communication, and so forth. People usually know only one facet of that vast and growing picture. The situation is similar to that in the natural sciences before scientific journals were founded. Therefore, a yearbook of social inventions and experiments might be very helpful. It would improve the ways such experiments are being started, observed, and evaluated. It would help the mutual learning of all people interested in new societal forms.

Second, a society that aims at a more human future should begin to devise, finance, and conduct, on a restricted but representative scale, both simulated and live social experiments—new towns, schools, and factories, more equal distribution of economic power and rewards, and so forth—to test new images of the future. Such experiments would not and could not have the stringency of natural-science experiments, but they are useful and necessary as heuristic devices. Today they could be tried more easily than at any earlier stage of history, because our capacity to observe and to record, correlate, and store data has increased tremendously and will increase even more.

The experts may say, "It cannot be done." And we missionaries will quietly have to tell them, "You have said this many times before, but you were often proved wrong by those who dared to imagine the new and the different." In the difficult times ahead, we need imagination more than ever before.

PART **5**

NONMALE AND NONWHITE IMAGES OF SOCIAL RECONSTRUCTION

A civilization is a complex tangle of public images of the future. While certain images will dominate—in the sense that they are the core guiding images —there will always be a pluralism of images that reflect the world views, histories, and expectations of various subgroups. The following essays explore images of the future from a nonmale and nonwhite orientation. What makes them particularly important is that they offer a social analysis, as well as ideas about humanly fulfilling images of the future that most white, male thinkers probably could not have written. They also demonstrate quite well the extent to which white, male intellectuals and professional managers have monopolized the imaging process in Western civilization.

Elaine Morgan

Women and the Future

Morgan makes a prediction that the status of women in their own eyes and in the eyes of men will reach parity. Then, any social, legal, and economic disabilities directly attributable to race or sex will be eliminated. New scientific techniques will offer women control over their own biological destinies so that, essentially, the future of women will be no more and no less than the future of people.

One way of looking into the future is to analyze existing trends and extrapolate them. Economists are doing this when they say, "By the year 2000 the demand for x (fuel, color television sets, PRO's) will have increased by y percent." This is, roughly speaking, the Herman Kahn approach.

The other way of looking into the future is to evaluate an existing situation and, where it is felt to be intolerable, to determine that it must be modified or reversed. This method has the disadvantage that it cannot be farmed out to a computer; it has to be carried out by individual and fallible human beings arguing with, fighting, reasoning with, entreating, negotiating with, or throwing things at other human beings. Nevertheless, on balance, predictions made by this method are more likely to be fulfilled.

In the case of sexual equality, this process is well under way. The status of women in their own eyes and in the esteem of men will continue to improve until it reaches parity, just as the status of non-whites will follow the same path. Wherever these demands for equity are being resisted by whites or males, they are being resisted with increasing shrillness and decreasing confidence. This is similar to the posture of an animal aware that it has strayed into another animal's territory. It is morally handicapped, and seeks to retreat with a minimal loss of face. It is fairly safe then to predict that when parity of esteem has been achieved, any social, legal, and economic disabilities directly attributable to race or sex will be eliminated.

THE BIOLOGICAL PROBLEM

Women, however, have one problem apart from all these—the biological one. For millennia this has seemed to be insuperable, but it is now diminishing with considerable speed all over the world. There is, for example, every reason to believe that improvements in contraceptive techniques will advance to a stage where simple 100 percent effective protection against unwanted pregnancy will be taken for granted as unquestioningly as we now take the provision of running water in the West. (Running water may become a lot more expensive by that time, but that's a separate issue.) The debate about abortion will thus be not so much resolved as rendered obsolete, except in rare cases, as for instance where prenatal tests determine that the fetus of a wanted child is deformed. In these cases it should be easy to arrive at a consensus.

In gangster movies the slang expression "old equalizer" was often used to refer to the revolver, because it could compensate for any differences in human size and strength. For women, chemical "equalizers" are now coming thick and fast. For example, there is no reason why, in the future, menstruation should not be as optional as pregnancy. (Not that all women will want to avoid it. For a great many it is a troublefree process; on balance it causes less inconvenience than other physiological necessities all of us are heir to.) However, any woman will have a psychological advantage when her male colleagues have learned to regard menstruation as optional or obsolete. It will put an end to the male's assumption that whereas his moments of irritability are attributable to irritating circumstances, or maybe to a perfectly normal hangover, the female's are invariably due to some irrational emotional cycle linked to menstruation that renders her unfit for promotion to a position of power or responsibility. This will mark the collapse of the penultimate, pseudoreasonable argument against equal opportunity.

MOTHERHOOD

We are left with the final argument against equal opportunity: motherhood. In the past, there has been a tendency for some women to regard this as yet one more millstone, the explanation of past subjection, and a stumbling block on the road to equality. This attitude was natural and justified as long as many, if not most, pregnancies were unplanned. But in the future we're going to be in a whole new ball game.

Babies there will have to be; no one in charge of human affairs is ever going to challenge that proposition. However little commitment some people may have to the abstract idea of human survival, they will not want to face their own old age and death in a world where there are no younger hands to keep them supplied with food, warmth, company, attention, and hope. In connection with babies three major problems will arise: How many? Who bears them? And who rears them?

I grew up, in Britain in the thirties, in a society where demographic alarm notes were being sounded; but then people were concerned that the birthrate was too low. (In those prenuclear days nation-states used to worry a lot about where the soldiers were going to come from.) Since then, the problem of overpopulation has been put forward as our number-one headache, as world population graphs have followed those of the Western nations into an explosive growth curve.

This problem will undoubtedly remain somewhere among the top ten for another generation—perhaps two. But, like the converse panic of the thirties, it is a temporary one. The birthrate is dropping everywhere, especially in the cities and suburbs. Awareness of the dangers of too crowded a planet is increasing and will continue to increase until the graph levels off; all studies of overcrowding in animal societies suggest that in the end it does level off, even without rational propaganda and scientific techniques to aid it. Meanwhile here and there, in countries where the economic equality of women is most widely recognized—Sweden and the USSR, for instance—the old worries are beginning to return. Is the reproduction rate dropping too steeply? Where will it all end? How will the economy cope with a top-heavy proportion of aging and retired persons? Where will we get the people to fill all that empty space east of the Urals?

Before the twenty-first century is over, these questions are going to be more widely canvassed (beginning as before in the more industrialized nations), and the answer, as *never* before, is going to have to come from women. It will begin to dawn on the world that babies are the one natural resource as essential to our survival as food (far more essential than oil); that woman, the archetypal primary producer, has monopoly control over this resource; and that she, like the Arabs, has recently waked up to the fact that she has the power to restrict or even to cease production.

If any sizable proportion of women choose to exercise this option, the effect will be, as in the case of oil, that the value placed on this commodity (human progeny) will rocket, and the producers of it will be treated with the utmost diplomacy and offered higher inducements than ever before in an effort to prevent the supply from drying up altogether. For, whatever level of population our descendants decide to stabilize at, Zero Population Decline will then be as necessary as Zero Population Growth. From the infant's point of view, and the mother's also, this change of attitude is a consummation devoutly to be wished for.

Here we have to assess the possibility that (as with other scarce resources) an orthodox attempt will be made to find an alternative source of supply, namely, the old futuristic dream (nightmare?) of test-tube babies brought into the world without benefit of womb. The scientific problems could be resolved if the will were there, and doubtless we should be capable, after a period of agonizing debates and ethical upheaval, of accustoming ourselves to the idea. It would have some fringe advantages besides the obvious one of sparing women the certainty of a few uncomfortable months and the possibility of a few painful hours. In a perfectly controlled prenatal environment not only could malformed or premature births be altogether eliminated, but the prenatal period might conceivably be extended to ten months or even longer, unless there is some genetic instruction we know nothing about imprinted in the fetus itself, which would lead it to rebel in some way against this delay.

We presently assume that the timing of the ejection lies in the mother's biology rather than the baby's and that most of the unborn would be quite happy about an extension of their tenure. Some people have taken a very optimistic view of the possible results, since this is precisely the direction in which homo sapiens has been driven over millions of years by the forces of evolution. These forces, having run up against the barrier of the incompatibility between the size of the female pelvis and the skull size of an infant demanding a longer and longer gestation period, countered ingeniously by inventing the fontanelle, but since then have been able to progress no further.

But babies growing in a man-made environment would not need to enter the world through such a narrow gate: they might be able to go on perfecting themselves. In practice, however, the outcome of this would be somewhat short of revolutionary. The infants would certainly be larger and heavier before taking their first breath, and their skins would certainly be smooth and creamy rather than red and wrinkled. More than a few weeks' delay, though, would be counterproductive, as the need for new sensory impressions and experiences would be paramount, to ensure normal mental development. I fear that George Bernard Shaw's far-future fantasy in *Back to Methuselah* —that we shall ultimately emerge from the egg as fully vocal and well-educated young adults—will remain only an allegory.

I should like to add one peripheral comment here, because it is of urgent significance to the care of premature babies now. After all, what we are doing is in effect transferring them to a test tube for the last stages of their prenatal existence. If they are to be kept psychologically as well as physically healthy, we must ensure a closer imitation of the habitat they have been deprived of, where they were not only warmed and fed but held close and constantly rocked and caressed and given tactile stimulation by the movements of their mothers' bodies. The usual practice in too many hospitals today places them in traumatically empty space on a motionless plane surface.

Is the laboratory, then, likely to become the seedbed of the human race? It is, I suppose, a possibility, far ahead in the unforeseeable future. But we are not nearly as close to it as many science-fiction scenarios suggest. For one thing, the popular vision of power-mad dictators ordering scientists to provide them with serried (probably cloned) ranks of docile human cannon fodder ignores one simple fact: that while it takes nine months to produce a baby, it takes many long patient years of constant tending to turn him into a creature that is of any use to anyone except himself. And this job has to be done by hand, by human beings and, if the end-product is to be an asset to society rather than a liability, it ought to be done with love.

This kind of service is at present willingly (at least as a rule, more or less willingly) rendered by women to their own individual children. The cost to the state of hiring such labor on behalf of mass-produced, future assembly-line attendants or soldiers would price the project right out of the market. Robots will always be cheaper, besides being much easier to control and repair.

There is no doubt that a technique for extrauterine gestation will be developed, for the classic reason that it is too fascinating and possible an experiment to remain forever untried. But unless it should result in some spectacular, and highly improbable, increase in the capacity of the children thus produced (such as was once prematurely claimed for babies born after "decompression" treatment of their mothers), the experiments are likely to remain just that—isolated experiments—for both social and psychological reasons.

The social reason is that certainly over the next couple of generations, until we have taught ourselves some far less destructive and exploitative methods of coming to terms with our environment, the economic climate— and the ethical one—is going to be increasingly opposed to any new, expensive, artificial way of doing anything that has hitherto been done naturally, and free.

I believe we shall solve our ecological problems in due course. Human reason is not currently our most trendy attribute. But I still have enough faith in it to be confident that it will combine with our instinct for self-preservation to somehow steer us away from the cliff's edge that our present habits are leading us to. By the time we have solved these problems—indeed, as an integral part of the solution—the population bulge will have peaked and gone into decline. And to the extent that women have attained full control over their biological destiny and discovered less laborious paths to self-fulfillment, the decline may prove a lot harder to arrest than it was to initiate.

CHILD REARING

The more successful we are in building a good society, the more varied and exciting and fulfilling will be the options open to all citizens, both male and female. Those women who then choose to devote a portion of their lives to bearing and rearing children are likely to comprise a smaller proportion than at present (even though the attitude of society will have become far more supportive than it is now).

By the same token women are likely to be more highly motivated, and it is quite likely that they might go for the complete package—pregnancy, lactation, and the lot—rather than pressing to have the whole thing mechanized. For the maternal instinct is quite as subtle and complex an affair as the sexual one (though currently less fashionable as a field for human-behavior research), and a mother-child relationship may be as badly handicapped as a male-female one by feelings of fear or revulsion concerning the physical processes involved.

When I suggested, in *The Descent of Woman*, that one consequence of the liberation of women and the end of unplanned parenthood could be that women with less maternal drive will, in evolutionary terms, select themselves out and cease to reappear in succeeding generations, this forecast was regarded in some quarters as sexist and obscurely reactionary. I hold it to be neither; though even if it were both it would not necessarily affect the likelihood of its coming true.

I even heard expressions of a fear that to have a human race descended from the kind of women who positively *like* children would be dysgenic. "Those women are kind of bovine, aren't they? And timid, and you know, not really very bright." The answer to this, of course, is "rubbish." All that most mothers have been, up to now, is underprivileged. There is no biological connection between maternity and ineffectiveness. Ask any matriarch. Ask any she-wolf. And to link philoprogenitiveness with low IQ is to out-Eysenck Hans J. Eysenck.

As for the prospect being reactionary, surely the essence of the concept of progress is a concern for the future of humanity, and humanity's future is represented now, as it has always been, by a screaming, incontinent, egocentric, ludicrously vulnerable, totally unreasonable, voraciously demanding little biped with its umbilical cord still dangling. Until recently, like other human subdivisions such as slaves or women, the infant has been regarded as a chattel or possession of more powerful human beings, but when all other civil rights have been granted, its demands will be as vociferous as ever and will one day have to be met. Every man-hour or woman-hour expended on meeting them properly will pay for itself over and over again by drastic reductions in the apparatus presently devoted to coping with crime, delinquency, mental disorders, and general social inadequacy.

So who rears the infant? A basic need of the infant is to be raised by some person or persons who love and enjoy him or her and are prepared to stick around long enough to give the baby a sense of security and continuity. There is no reason why men should not choose to be involved in it; probably many of them will, as the social pressures on them to enact a "tough" masculine role are eased. Certainly the work will not be in short supply since, if it is to be enjoyed, it must be adequately remunerated and adequately buttressed by ancillary services, and in the most strenuous (toddler) stage there should be a higher than one-to-one adult-child ratio.

I have used these impersonal terms because in a rapidly changing world no one can forecast with any confidence the precise future of marriage or the nuclear family over more than a few generations. The current Western trend favoring the non-stick spouse shows no sign of abating, but so far it affects only about half of the human race. The infant's needs, on the other hand, remain constant. We may safely predict that they will not have changed perceptibly by the year 20,000, let alone 2000.

I have put it in these terms also because, after much thought and argument about the complex tangles of alimony, maintenance, custody, maternity benefits, dependants' allowances, and all the other anachronistic problems that will continue to bedevil the relationships between men and women if the nuclear-family ties continue to slacken, I have concluded that the only way of cutting through all this is to regard everyone as a legal and economic unit in his or her own right, *including children*.

The final answer may well be pensions for babies, on the same humane grounds as for any other human beings temporarily or permanently unable to look after themselves. Such pensions could be administered on their behalf by a Children's Tribune. They would need to be fairly high, sufficient for them to afford a full-time attendance allowance, for the very young are even more helpless than the very old.

I have little doubt that the allowance would go in most cases, in the future as in the past, to the mother, as long as she and the baby were both happy about the arrangement. For one thing, if she did not wish to take on this work, it is hard to imagine why she would bother to initiate the creation at all. We cannot endure forever the system by which a woman is able to produce a chattel-child and maintain legal rights over it even if she neglects it, or ill treats it, or hires, to bring it up for her, a less privileged woman, who acquires no job security and may be sacked at will. This is no more justifiable or durable than the system that once granted a husband legal rights over his wife.

For another thing, once child rearing is divorced from the poverty, harrassment, isolation, squalor, and exhaustion that have too often accompanied it, there will be few more rewarding occupations. It cannot always be regarded as a mindless and degrading chore simply because historically it was an undervalued one performed by an undervalued sex. That would be as though, because the Romans once employed Greek slaves to read and write for them, I should now take umbrage at being asked to stoop to the servile task of writing this article.

Apart from this one factor, the future of women will be no more or no less than the future of people; for once they have attained economic equality and parity of esteem, what else will there be to distinguish them from the complementary half of humanity?

There's sex, of course. But as far as the future of sex is concerned, I've got nothing to add to the answer once given, I believe, by Miss Hermione Gingold: "I think it's here to stay."

Mary Lee Bundy

A Nonmale Image of the Future

The Male Attitude, explains Bundy, is the archetype of the oppressor in all oppressive relationships. Men cannot envision women's freedom, because of their personal stake in domination. Similarly, advantaged white men have a deep investment in racism and class privilege. To exploited peoples, the ending of a civilization that protects white, male privilege is a victory. The future of the people will be one in which there are no oppressors.

Since I have been asked to supply a nonmale image of the future, I shall of course describe the ending of the oppression of women. I shall present a picture of a future in which women are no longer victimized and exploited. I shall also explain why futurists are unable to support the most crucial human imperative, the ending of oppression in all its forms.

First, however, I wish to deal with why it is necessary for a woman to express the liberation goals of women in a book on the future published in the United States in 1975. Most men in this country cannot envision the freedom of women, because such a prospect is nearly intolerable to them. Men have too heavy a personal stake and too great a material and psychological investment in the status quo. This also holds true for the advantaged white man's stake in racism and class advantage. The Male Attitude, presented here, is that of the oppressor in all oppressive relationships. The relation of men to women reveals its most fundamental form.

THE MALE STAKE IN OPPRESSION

Male Privilege. Because of their sex men enjoy a range of advantages in this country. They prefer to think of those advantages as rights because this is one way to justify and hold on to them, just as white people deny that what they enjoy comes from having white skins.

Very few men are prepared to concede that they may not have been the best-qualified persons for obtaining a position or a promotion. Many men did not get into college on their own merits; some did not earn their fellowships. Nor did all of our most illustrious men earn their prizes for writing the best novels or making the greatest scientific advances. White men in this country have never competed fairly for what they have achieved. They won their positions, their awards, and their prestige, even in the system they created and control, by first eliminating from the competition over half the population—women—along with almost all the people of other races. Male privilege got them what they call achievements—besides giving them, if they are married, someone to wait on them, keep house for them, and take care of their children without the expense of paying that someone a salary.

Men go to any lengths to justify male privilege. Having profited from the dehumanization of women (their being forced to repress their human hopes and aspirations and to act out grotesque mockeries of themselves), men point to the results to justify their right to dehumanize them in the first place. (Women are dumb, stupid, ignorant, silly, vain, foolish.) Men have had, however, to bear the consequence, which, as in all oppressed-oppressor relationships, is that they cannot trust one single thing any woman says to them. Men do not want honest relationships with women; they do not have them.

Male Dependency. Men cling to their sexism because they have much to lose materially and because they doubt their ability to function on their own.

The particular plight of oppressed people in their relations with those who oppress them is that they have to *act* inferior and that, for lack of a formal education, they do not have some essential technical knowledge that can be gained no other way. Some oppressed people—women in particular, for lack of a cultural life apart from men—develop their relations with their oppressor as their central personality, or they misdirect their hate against one another or themselves. But those in oppressor positions, on the other hand, are poorly prepared to deal with a world that does not provide them with unfair advantages and with props to support their illusions of themselves as superior. Because others do for them, they do not know how to perform essential tasks. In survival terms, they *are* inferior.

Women, like others in the oppressed role, develop the skill of predicting what men will do, based on accurate observations of them. Men, on the other hand, have been able to depend on the reactions of women to conform to their expectations of them; therefore, they have not developed any real understanding of women or of themselves. In fact they rigidify and further fortify their false beliefs because of a continual reinforcement. This is why the rising consciousness of women leaves men behind and threatened.

Their male-supremacy beliefs have firmly convinced them that women, talking about liberation, must want what men have and want to be what men are. Domination is so engrained in them as a necessary and positive value that they cannot fathom any other roles between people. Because men define manhood as masterhood, they do not know who they are any longer. In material terms they have a great deal to lose by women's liberation; in psychological terms, they are already bereft.

A NONSEXIST SOCIETY

Women and Poverty. In the future working-class women will no longer be relegated to marginal, inferior jobs with low pay, no security, no opportunity for advancement, and the poorest of working conditions. We shall see the end of the welfare system, whereby the state (acting out the dominant-male role) keeps women from working (confining them to the home, "where women belong"), forces them to live on a less than subsistence level and circumscribes their personal relationships as a condition for getting support. Women in prison will no longer be subjected to dehumanized conditions or to the particular degradations practiced on women. The economic deprivation that forces women, in order to survive, to go into prostitution will end, along with the laws that penalize them for doing so.

Women as Sex Objects. The personal worth of women will no longer be defined in terms of their sexual attractiveness to men, and they will not play this less-than-human role. They will no longer pretend to be not very bright lest they seem unwomanly. These and other subterfuges that allow men to excel will be ended. Women will not be treated as existing for male pleasure. They will be free people.

Women as Mothers. The role of mother in the future will not be so different from the role of father. Women will no longer be forced to take on an unfair and demeaning share of the responsibilities and burdens of parenthood. They will not have their entire lives shaped by the fact that they are the childbearers, which after all takes at most six to eight years of their lives. By having fathers assume parenthood, the present excessive and lifelong dependence of the male child on women will end. Child-rearing habits will be changed so that children will no longer undergo the present excessive period of nurturing and domination at home.

I am saying that men will no longer keep their "superior" role by preventing their wives from working, or even going to school, lest they acquire some independence. Women of the future *may* choose to play the traditional role of homemaker; but they will not do so because their situation kept them from having any other choice. The socially necessary tasks in the home will not be done solely by women for no pay so that men can control the purse strings, that is, "be a man."

Equal Opportunity. The discriminatory barriers that today keep women from getting the educations to qualify them for entrance to male-dominated occupations and professions, and from advancement in them, will no longer exist. A woman's sex will no longer cost her a job or an education; maleness will not be worth an added four thousand dollars a year in the marketplace. There will no longer be the double standard whereby a woman must be twice as qualified as a man to get the same job. Men will no longer be able to hire women merely because they will play a nonchallenging role. Whereas in the past, professional women have let themselves be considered an exception ("she's smart for a woman"), the woman of the future will take no favors; she will no longer play the male-superiority game. She will have her rights.

White men will no longer pit white women against black people for the 20 percent of jobs that white men are prepared to yield—while they keep 80 percent of the rewards of the system. Women not only will refuse to be relegated to the present work roles assigned to women—clerical, domestic worker, nurse, librarian, and so forth—but they also will end the domination of these fields by men's holding all the top positions. They will end altogether those jobs that are by their very nature demeaning.

Women will take advantage of the removal of these barriers to achieve financial independence and to gain opportunities for personal fulfillment in work. Women dedicated to the liberation of women will enter the professions to ensure that they begin to cater to the distinctive needs of women; they will end the myths by which psychology and other male-dominated fields have perpetuated sexism in this culture. Women will learn technologies, so as to harness them for positive social ends. Women will be fully involved as participants in the political affairs of this country.

Woman as Rape Victim. Women will no longer take the blame for having been raped, that is, they will no longer need to prove resistance, their virtue, or the fact that they did not somehow invite the attack. The myth of the "good" woman, the possession of one man, will be forever dispelled, and it will no longer be used to rationalize bestiality toward women who do not fall into this category. Women will have the right to withhold consent to any man at any time. The laws that penalize the woman and leave the rapist to go free to rape another woman will be changed. Ultimately, there will be a society where women do not have to be constantly on guard against sexual molestation.

Man as Child. The "other" child, the husband, will no longer be babied at home or at work. The fantasies catered to by wife and secretary to prop up the fragile male ego will be shattered. The male's illusion of himself as man—calm, intelligent, completely in control at all times—will be dispelled. Men will no longer be allowed to be weak, selfish, and destructive—or noble. Men will no longer label women as emotional, intuitive, or any of the other labels they apply when they judge women by the male standard (considered universal and desirable) and find them deficient, that is, not male. Women will no longer have to act passive and submissive, less able and capable than they are; they will no longer have to slow up for fear they will outdo and outpace men.

The Heritage of Women. Women will no longer be kept from learning their heritage as women. The myths of the past will be replaced by a truer history of women. Women will not accept the role models of the passive woman and the helpmate of man offered them by men. Women will learn about the women of the past who fought for the liberation of women and about the important part women and women's groups played in positive social movements in this country. The storybooks and textbooks that perpetuate sexist values so as to acculturate another generation of children will be removed from schools and from the shelves of libraries.

THE FUTURE OF THE WOMEN'S MOVEMENT

I have spoken of the goals of women about which, among progressive women, there could be no serious question, and I have described the condition of women in the United States, showing the reality that while all women are oppressed, the oppression is not distributed equally. The full weight of institutionalized oppression falls upon women if and because they are poor and/or black.

While in principle women may subscribe to these goals, it does not mean there is any real unity that would hold up under the test of reality. Race and class interests effectively preclude the participation of the majority of white, middle-class women in the struggles to end class and race oppression in the United States. The liberation struggle of women is likely to continue within their social-class groupings. White, advantaged women may achieve greater status among men of their own class and race, but they will take more than enough at the expense of those this country victimizes the most viciously.

THE FINAL ANALYSIS

The inability of white male futurists to align themselves with women on the issue of women's liberation is illustrative of how they bring their vital interests into their intellectual endeavors. Knowingly or unknowingly, they are protecting race and class as well as sex privilege. Under the guise of "thinking for everyone" and taking a so-called world view, they are protecting their vested interests.

Futurists now say that we have a world crisis, because they can see coming events that are threatening to their interests. Yet, for the exploited people of this planet there has surely been a desperate crisis for generations. The ending of the civilization that controls and exploits them can only be viewed by them as a victory, not a catastrophe.

The appeal to reason is a false appeal, because it cloaks these vested interests. The search for an ultimate rationality, for the enlightenment of "man," avoids the central facts about oppression, its nature, and its extent. Millions of people today lead hopeless lives and are threatened with total destruction as a people. The interests that exploit them are not going to yield anything. What is rational for people who hold power, trying to keep what they have and to get more, is not rational for the people it is being taken from.

Listening to an appeal to rationality could be harmful for people because it would keep them from coming together to develop the collective strength needed to overthrow their oppressor. For people to be deprived of their struggle, in the realist sense, is to be deprived of their freedom. It is a fact of logic and the human experience that freedom can never be given; it must be taken.

Ivan Illich provides an example of the fallacies and dangers of this type of thinking. He openly and blatantly believes in women's continuing in social servitude. He speaks about equality, and yet to oppressed readers his words have the same hollow mockery as always when they come from those who have complicity in the oppression. He says there is an overuse of power tools, which is harmful and has made "us" dependent. He is effectively ignoring (because he does not see people *not* like himself as mattering) that the majority of people never had these advantages or had to pay a cruel price to get them. Now, when they are within their grasp, he says they are not good for them. Tied to the system that keeps him in privilege, he is making a futile appeal to people in power to see reason.

The future of equality that he talks about cannot come about in this way. Equality will be achieved by the direct, planned actions of the masses of the people, who will overthrow their oppressors. Mr. Illich, your fears are groundless. When you superimpose or force a culture on people, you may addict some of them. But when people freely choose, as they shall, they will not thus entrap themselves. You do not need to prescribe for them; you and people like you have never needed to.

What is the compelling vision of the future? Freedom. The only question is what is freedom. Thomas Jefferson's version of freedom, passed along in the American social system, exploited the labor of people and denied a whole race and a whole sex of people opportunities for growth as human beings and rationalized this exploitation on the grounds that the people thus disenfranchised and victimized were innately inferior.

In contrast, the future of the people will finally be one of liberty and equality because they will be *no* oppressors. There will be an economic system where the few do not exploit the many, a political system where the people decide, and a social system where people care and sacrifice for one another.

White, advantaged men (a world minority of less than five percent) should begin to prepare themselves for a future in which people like themselves will have lost their race, sex, and class privileges. This is a compelling vision of the future now for millions of people; it can be equally so for as many more as commit themselves to bringing it about.

Vine Deloria, Jr.

The Future of Racial Minorities
in American Society

Deloria feels that the era of power development by minority groups is nearly over. During this period the racial minorities leveled the old concepts of social reality, which had given all Americans their sense of national identity. The present task is one of reconciliation—to begin building a new sense of personal, group, and finally national identity once again.

In the past two decades the public has become aware of the status and condition of racial minorities in American society. Beginning with the civil-rights movement and continuing onward through the recent outbreaks by Indians and Chicanos, the racial minorities have each had their time to strut upon the stage of American consciousness. In the process of arriving at their spot in the sun, the racial minorities have traversed the road from demands of complete integration to goals of complete separatism and cultural integrity, and the process appears to be continuing in one form or another in spite of the recent determination by the communications media to deemphasize the role and place of racial minorities in the news.

The militant attitude still runs deep among blacks, Indians, and Chicanos, but it has recently taken a different and more ominous direction. The veterans of the early stages of social movement in each of the three groups have now aged, and with their maturity has come a series of new opportunities to solve problems within the existing institutional structures of American society. The younger people in each of the groups, however, have adopted the old war cry "You can't work through the system" as a truism, even though the vast majority of them have had little or no relationship with the system. With the traditional American catering to the wishes and wisdom of youth, this attitude displayed by many younger members of racial minorities has effectively boxed the respective groups into a rhetorical universe in which little if any substantial progress can be made.

The irony of this generation gap, which exists in the three minority groups that have been most affected by the social movements of the past, is that the present younger generation of blacks, Indians, and Chicanos has had opportunities that few of their older brothers and sisters would have dreamed possible two decades ago. What had been an experienced reflection of frustrations even five years ago has now become a dominating theme by which younger people in the racial minorities now interpret the universe with which they are confronted. It matters not, therefore, that solutions might be possible. The simple fact seems to be that people are no longer looking for solutions, because they have defined the world as being incapable of realizing solutions.

The situation is far from hopeless, but it entails a deeper and more profound analysis of American social reality than anyone, white or nonwhite, has been willing to undertake. One cannot be sure that even the parameters of the problem can be described accurately, but the time has certainly come when people must venture to project solutions and analyses with the hope that such offerings will invoke a desire in people to examine their situation with more serious concern than has been shown thus far.

RECENT EXPERIENCES OF RACIAL MINORITIES

We should perhaps begin an analysis of our current situation with a review of the experience of the three major racial minorities in past decades of American history. Universally, the groups experienced discrimination because they were racially different from peoples of Western European backgrounds. This discrimination seemed to be practiced in the United States more than in other nations of similar cultural and racial background because the United States was, in a real sense, attempting to deal with the problem of creating a society and advancing that society up the scale of national identity until it had achieved parity with older and more established countries.

Racial discrimination in the United States has been an overt doctrine of social reality because the universe of meaning in which social reality was determined projected a pattern of behavior in which Anglo-Saxon norms were uncritically accepted as archetypes of civilized and universally realized humanity. American racial minorities were thus short of the mark and were discriminated against because they could not, by definition, become full citizens or complete human beings. In those areas in which members of minority groups adjusted to political and economic norms, discrimination was less real, and when those members had the good fortune to blend social conformity and the political and economic adjustments that they had made, discrimination was not an important aspect of their lives.

The great rebellion of the past two decades, while clothed in specific complaints against institutional practices of racial discrimination, was more than a rebellion against patterns of behavior. Rather it was a revolution, largely successful, against the conceptions of social and anthropological reality that had been uncritically foisted upon Americans of all racial backgrounds. The initial stages of domestic social movement in the 1950s saw a determined effort by blacks and their allies to force the issue of equal citizenship, which was, by all counts, a superficial problem compared to the philosophical problem lying beneath its tangible manifestations—the philosophical problem of American identity.

When the Indians and Chicanos began to emerge in the national consciousness as an alternative to the civil-rights struggle, it was in conjunction with the power movement in the black community. Indians and Chicanos uncritically accepted the rhetorical world of the Black Panthers, which projected a universal rebellion of peoples who shared an oppressive status determined largely by the old criteria. As the power movements developed in the nativistic minority communities, peripheral problems of culture, language, tradition, and geography came to dominate their concerns. Neither Indians nor Chicanos were successful in making the transitions from the rural and cultural worlds in which they originated to the urban and largely homogenized world in which civil rights had its natural philosophical base.

The shift from equal citizenship and legal rights to cultural awareness and reclamation of group integrity completed the destruction of the old conception of both American citizenship and American anthropology. The natural result of the power movements was the admission of the more aggressive members of the three minority groups to the positions of power that had been forged in the institutional structure of American society. A new industry—consumption of minority-group culture—was created, and was fed largely on the irrationality of emotions that were running rampant in the. groups. Whites became virtually helpless to protest the destruction of criteria by the racial minorities, because they had foolishly accepted uncritically the rhetorical conception of the world advocated by the more militant members of the racial minorities.

Protests had become a form of entertainment; they were based largely on the recitation of examples of discrimination taken from American history that conflicted with the traditional American view of the world. By pitting past realities of discrimination against past fantasies of social reality, militants had the best of all possible worlds and posed problems insoluble at best and debilitating in their impact on present problem-solving movements. In the process, the racial minorities leveled the old concepts of social reality that had given all Americans their sense of national identity. It remained only for Richard Nixon and his people to prove that the cherished values of the old America were never respected for the present gloom to spread across the American landscape.

THE CURRENT CONCEPTUAL POVERTY

Today many members of minority groups are secretly longing for a path back to some conception of what it means to be an American, but no leverage exists on the conceptual stage through which either whites or racial minorities can find their way. People cannot accept the old definitions of American social reality, but neither can they find a point at which new realities can originate. No area of American existence today has shown itself capable of generating a reconciling set of concepts that will allow people to confront the meaning of their lives that corresponds to their immediate past experiences of having been members of a group at odds either with the majority of other people or with the pace of social movement. Changes have been experienced, but they have not been understood, nor have they been digested and become objects of reflection and analysis.

The generation of a new conception of social reality must become a dominating theme of our present society, but the chances of such a movement appear to be increasingly bleak. We are dominated by electronic media that is controlled by a select group of people who are motivated by the unfortunate combination of novelty and economics. The latest thing, whether of substance or not, is also the most profitable thing in terms of immediate income generation, and when the communications media is viewed more properly as an intellectual cancer of no mean dimension, the state of our confusion becomes clear. We cannot advocate substantial change, because we have leveled the conceptual landscape to such a point that truisms about our condition now pass for mature and reflective judgments on the state of our condition.

The question of American identity is becoming less and less important in the practical operation of our lives, but it has not yet been purged from tools of analysis through which we understand the world. Too many of us are still yearning for a cohesive social unity that can be described in terms of citizenship, equality, humanity, and "Americanism," while we fail to realize that we have long since destroyed the world in which that type of analysis made sense. Descriptions of conditions and proposed solutions still vibrate between the twin poles of liberalism and conservatism, and these terms have long since come to describe attitudes about experience, and not philosophical persuasions.

THE BASES FOR NEW SOLUTIONS

Our concern should be one of understanding the experience of having been alive and part of a group that has undergone severe dislocation as part of a historical process that has become known collectively as American history. The clarifications of historical reality that have become so prominent a feature of recent social movements should now form the boundaries of the conceptual world from which we move toward a new center of understanding. We must recognize that, with the forces of social, political, and economic change unleashed centuries before the discovery of this continent, things probably would not have been much different even had the most atrocious events of American history been avoided. In so doing we can gain a new view of the concepts and movements that have passed unnoticed in our understanding of historical reality.

In clashes between peoples and cultures and in the rush for economic security in an ever increasing technological movement of the mind, causes and effects of unsuspected dimensions have come into play and have created not a history of America so much as a series of interconnecting experiences that bind us together in the present. American intellectuals of all racial and cultural backgrounds apparently do not find the strength to understand or.

the necessity for understanding the scope of experiences that have characterized existence in America. The seeming inevitability of certain developments
in law, transportation, literature, science, and economics would appear to be
more important than conceptions of American history as the unfolding of a
single political, economic, or social idea whose time had come.

American history has, in a real sense, been a history of the efforts of a
diverse mixture of people to create an institutional reality. Many of the old
goals of American life have been defined as institutional participation rather
than as a more flexible sense of having realized the potential of particular
human beings. In almost every time and place in American history individuals of different groups have come to terms with their differences and found
some kind of reconciliation. It is this process of reconciliation that we are
beginning to experience, yet are rhetorically obligated to deny.

Institutions may not appear to work today because many of the problems that are posed for institutional solution are actually incapable of institutional solution. Rather, many of today's problems require a new sense of
commitment and determination combined with an awareness of the changes
that have already been wrought in our society. As one sees the generations of racial minorities merge into various niches of American society and
come to grips with structural problems of adjustment and meaning, the old
cry of obtaining "power" for specific groups in society becomes less frantic. Few members of racial minorities will admit it, but the push for group
integrity has brought about integration in our society in a more profound
manner than the civil-rights movement of a decade ago. Once this movement
is recognized, admitted, and understood, we will be in a position to begin
building a new sense of personal, group, and finally national identity once
again.

It is difficult in these days to project an image of our society that can
attract any significant number of adherents. Yet we are daily achieving a
better perspective on the events of our times that allows us to recognize not
only successes but also failures and inconsistencies. Unless this reflective process is made more tangible and articulated in place of the defeatist slogans of
frustration, it is entirely possible that we shall fail as a society. Unfortunately,
we have been unable to open sufficient channels of articulation to allow concepts to flow freely across group boundaries. But where members of one
group have reflected on the values and beliefs of other groups and incorporated them into their thought patterns and universes of discourse, the process
of unification has begun.

Gary Snyder's poem about the deer infiltrating men excellently illustrates the process that must come into being if we are to find a means of stabilizing our future. It is this image of partaking of each other, which is presently distasteful to many, that will finally provide us with the analytical tools for understanding ourselves and our society. The recognition that men can change and experience each other without becoming an homogenous mass of anonymous citizens must finally dawn upon people in our society. Until this feeling supersedes the old rhetoric about racial minorities "contributing" things to American society, we will still feel a sense of alienation, betrayal, and deprivation. America holds together at present because it is simply too complicated to fall apart all at once. But it can be bound up with a new sense of human worth that can provide meaning for the future if current problems are faced with intellectual integrity and serious concern for truth.

The era of minority-group power development is nearly over. We may have a few sporadic gasps of protest, but in general the limited goals of the sixties have been accomplished and the beliefs and rhetorical truisms of those days have been surpassed. Within racial minorities stability of a kind already exists that was not possible in former times. Our opportunity today is to grasp this situation and demand from ourselves an honest though agonizing appraisal of conditions, so that from the pinnacle of two decades of accomplishment we can project a future free from doctrinal considerations. Humanity's experiences on the planet have been varied, torturous, and even glorious. But no one, after all, promised us a rose garden.

PART

RELIGIOUS IMAGINATION
AND THE FUTURE

The central images of the future of a civilization reveal the meanings people hold about the cosmos, the world, God, human beings, institutions, time and history—in short, the sacred values of the civilization. In this sense all images, whether eschatological or utopian, have a religious dimension, since they speak to things that have ultimate significance to the possessors of the images. The religious imagination of a civilization is thus a good indicator of potential for image renewal and development. These essays explore the religious imagination in the West from two quite different perspectives. The first summarizes some of the principal religious images found in contemporary society. The second probes the problem of and a possible solution to our severing of value controls from the use of our scientific technologies.

Elise Boulding

Religion, Futurism, and Models of Social Change

The ideal image of the future has eschatological and utopian elements. A delicate balance between the two is necessary if the optimum conditions for social change are to prevail. Recognizing the decline in utopian and eschato-logical images, Boulding considers the possibility of a "rebirth" of God. Four models of religious imaging of the future are presented. She believes the sociologist of religion can make important contributions to contemporary futurism.

While the imaging and forecasting of the future has always been one of the major preoccupations of Judaism and Christianity, and millennialism is in fact a religious concept, nevertheless the current millenarian fervor as we approach the year 2000 is exhibited not by religionists but by scientists. One looks in vain for the names of theologians in the numerous publications of the last fifteen years concerning the year 2000.

Why are religious conceptualizations so notably absent in contem-

This article first appeared in *The Humanist*, November-December 1973.

porary futurist thought? (I am not referring to traditional Christian futurism, which continues to operate within sectarian circles, but to what might be called "mainstream futurism," as reported in professional and popular literature.) The answer lies partly in institutionalized religion and partly in social science. The secular trend within the churches has created embarrassment about speaking outside church circles on such topics as "the kingdom," "last things," or the supernatural generally. Many regard their own traditional religious projections of the future and theological models of social change as irrelevant to the secular world. The result, for church-related intellectuals, is either an uneasy compartmentalization or outright rejection of traditional beliefs.

The social scientist, for his or her part, has become fascinated with religion as a product—and process—of socialization, and this has led him to a view of religious activity as a homeostatic process (viewed positively in the Durkheimian sense, or negatively in the Marxian). The idea that the processes involved in religious activity might be change processes, and not just equilibrium processes, does appear in Max Weber's concept of the interaction of material and ideal interests in shaping the conduct of human beings.[1] However, the Protestant-ethic hypothesis concerning the development of modern capitalism is an isolated example of a model of social change, rather than part of mainstream theorizing about social change.

One area in the sociology of religion that has scarcely been touched and which is relevant to a theory of social change is a study of religious encounter, of the act of relating to the unknown. Sociology has not yet had its William James. Thus far, sociologists have resisted studying an interaction in which they cannot make satisfactory observations on one party to the interaction. They label such interactions "mysticism," to be treated as a special case. However, it may be precisely in this sphere of interaction with the Other —and in the feedback system it involves—that some key developmental social processes take place.

One contemporary sociologist who has had the courage to deal with the dynamics of relating to the unknown is Fred Polak, whose work has produced a theory of social change that integrates human-to-human and human-to-supernatural interaction processes in one model.

IMAGING THE FUTURE AS A THEORY OF SOCIAL CHANGE

In Polak's theory of social change, images of the future generated by creative minorities in society act on the present to shape behaviors and institutions that will move society toward the desired future. The ideal typical image of the future has both eschatological and utopian elements. The eschatological element introduces the divine-human interaction into the social-change process. As I have noted elsewhere: "The eschatological, or transcendent, is the element which enables the visionary to breach the bonds of the cultural present and mentally encompass the possibility of totally other types of society, not dependent on what human beings are currently capable of realizing."[2] It has this effect because eschatology treats history as the unfolding of a divine plan that begins with creation and ends with the final redemption of the world.

The eschatological element is not the sole determinant of human beings' imaging capacity, but works with the utopian human-to-human element. The utopian, or immanent, element designates human beings as co-partners in shaping the Other in the here and now. In Polak's words, "Eschatology is the oratorium of religious fulfillment, and Utopia is the laboratorium of social process."[3]

The optimum conditions of social change involve a delicate balance between utopian and eschatological elements. The Judaic image of the future, Polak suggests, achieved that rare balance with its conception of the Covenant. The Covenant represents a unique bonding between human beings and the supernatural, in which humans are responsible for creating the new Zion—but here on earth and according to divine instructions.

This difficult immanence-transcendence balance was maintained by Jesus (in his role as a Jewish prophet), but it did not survive his death, in Polak's view. The past twenty centuries have seen the pendulum swing between the extremes of transcendence, with God in charge and nothing for humans to do, and of immanence, with everything left to humans.

The onset of the Industrial Revolution also ushered in the great age of utopianism, when man was sure he could do anything. The inevitable tendency in eschatological thinking to spiritualize the other reality and to conceive it as realizable only in the afterlife took over in Christian thinking at the very time when humanistic utopianism was coming into its own. The Second Coming was increasingly seen, not as a continually postponed end-state, but as something not for this world at all.

In response to this sterile spiritualization, theologians resorted to the drastic remedy of pensioning off God. In Nietzsche's time Europe was nearing the end of the tremendous surge of activist optimism that had flowed from the struggle in the Middle Ages between the chiliasts and the hydra-headed monster of caesaro-papism. The optimism was furthered by exploration in the laboratory and around the globe. The development of laboratory science made it possible to regard the natural world as something to be arranged and manipulated, and the voyages of exploration brought new ideas about how to pattern those arrangements. Polak points out that "most features of social design in contemporary western society were first figments of a utopia-writer's imagination."[4]

The decline of the creative imaging powers of the utopian with the onset of nationalism was paralleled by a fading of the notion of Christ's earthly reign and by a decline in the vitality of earlier experimental models of such a kingdom, as represented by monastic communities. Polak's main message to his contemporaries is that the decline in imaging capacity is serious but not necessarily fatal. Mankind, by taking thought, can reverse the trend.

While Polak himself, as a thoroughgoing humanist, does not actually propose a rebirth of God, the remainder of this essay will survey precisely this possibility. I will look, not at developments within the institutional church, but at thought about the future in the religious sphere as it relates to the rest of society. My analysis will be directed to the capacity of the contemporary religious imagination to conceptualize the future, as seen by a few selected sociologists, theologians, and modern writers on religion. In the process I hope to demonstrate that the sociologist of religion has important contributions to make to contemporary futurism that he or she is not making at present.

TRENDS IN RELIGIOUS IMAGING OF THE FUTURE

I have grouped the scholars I will discuss according to certain characteristics in their thinking about the religious imaging capacity of mankind. These characteristics in turn reflect the model of the religious dimensions of the world with which each operates. I shall categorize the models as follows: (1) the existential model, (2) the radical-Christian-secularist model, (3) the signals-of-transcendence model, and (4) the sacration model. (*Sacrate*, "to make holy," is used in this obsolete form since the word *sacralize* has specialized meanings in theology that may interfere with the meaning to be conveyed here.)

Following Polak's method of analysis, I will examine the imaging capacity associated with each model in terms of the following components relating to the eschatological strength of the image: (1) the time horizon, (2) the spatial horizon, (3) qualities of Otherness, (4) qualities of transcendence, and (5) optimism about the respective roles of God and man in the world.

THE EXISTENTIAL MODEL

The existential model covers a wide range of orientations from religious to atheist, activist to escapist, but the main orientation is set by Nietzsche's pronouncement on the death of God and Sartre's urging humans to forget God and, in the words of Martin Buber, to "recover the creative freedom which [man] once falsely ascribed to God."[5] For the existentialist, the only reality that exists is that which he or she creates by his own actions. Polak comments that this existential person "finds himself in a blind, indeterminate, unaware and soulless universe, in a chaos that knows no countering cosmos. Nothing more is expected or commanded of man than that he make pragmatic decisions and concrete choices . . . the farthest limit of being is not-being."[6]

The modern Christian existentialist who has a tremendous talent for transcendence can say with Dietrich Bonhoeffer, "The God who makes us live in this world without using him as a working hypothesis is the God before whom we are ever standing. Before God and with him we live without God."[7]

But most religious existentialists wind up like John A. Robinson, author of *Honest to God* (Philadelphia: Westminster Press, 1963). Having rejected the "rich aunt in Australia" hypothesis of God and the "cosmic Cheshire cat" hypothesis, Robinson concludes in Jungian fashion that there is something or other deep inside men and women. The image that this kind of language irresistibly conveys is of someone crawling into his or her own womb and assuming a fetal position as an ultimate affirmation of existence; it is certainly a travesty of Paul Tillich's "ground of being" concept, out of which it came in part. If there is an experience of transcendence to be had, Robinson complains, it is only open to those who "have an ear for it." Can he help it if he, and most of his fellow Christians, are tone-deaf?

The existentialist image of the future is of a prolonged Now. In both time and space it is limited to what humans can now touch, hear, and see. If there is an Other, there is no hope of human contact with it. Transcendence is not possible except in a purely mystical sense. While many existentialists are gloomy, there are also joyous ones. Popular reading on college campuses at the beginning of the seventies included William Schutz' *Joy: Expanding Human Awareness* (New York: Grove Press, 1967), which expresses one brand of joyous existentialism.

The dynamic for change in the existentialist model of the world consists of a strong commitment to act in the moment, stemming from the sense that there is no other reality than that which mankind shapes. Yet the future toward which men's and women's efforts are bent is unknown.

THE RADICAL-CHRISTIAN-SECULARIST MODEL

The radical-secularist view of the world arises out of the tension between the commitment to the concept of a divine plan for the world and a recognition of the massive social injustice and oppression found here. The Christian's dilemma is that an eschatological view of the world does not see the struggle against sin and injustice as completed in history, and yet it generates a readiness to participate in struggles for human liberation. A participant in the 1966 World Conference on Church and Society spoke of a continuation of the tradition of revolutionary Christianity from the days of the English Revolution. He might also have included the French Revolution. The social-gospel tradition in the church has had a long and stormy history, and the struggles of Swiss and German Christian socialists in the first decades of this century are not among the least of them.

The drive to enlist the church in social revolution is carried on fiercely within both Catholic and Protestant churches. But in what frame of reference shall the Christian revolutionary act? Munster University Professor of Theology H. D. Wendland suggests that, since God himself holds the door open for human history to go forward, Christians must join with others in taking advantage of divinely generated opportunities for shaping society. "Christians are not carrying out a Christian revolution; they are working with secular, human methods of justice and politics to reform society for the sake of man. Christians therefore remain within the limits imposed on them in this world. They do not set up any 'Christian' orders, systems, states, and societies . . . their task is to humanize secular orders, and the slightest real progress that can be attained there is more important than the most perfect Christian Utopia, because it guarantees real help to definite people of social groups." [8]

The paradox is that while the Christian must in a sense step outside his or her religious frame of reference to work in the world, nevertheless the secular revolutionary needs something from the Christian. He or she needs "resources of transcendence and transgression." The Christian, in short, in acting as a humanist must retain a capacity for transcendence.

What is the image of the future of this radical-Christian-secularist? "The long-term future is hidden from us," says the World Conference on Church and Society's official report published in 1967. Nevertheless, there is a program for action. The work of the Christian is to extend the concept of *koinonia* into the secular world, helping to build new types of communities to cut across ethnic, national, class, and other boundaries. At the same time, the usual churchly rhetoric is being ruthlessly stripped from the word *koinonia*. The church is being told very sharply to scrap the old church-centered concepts of parish and community and to pioneer in the reversal of the usual roles of teacher and taught; middle-class parishioners must learn from the poor, if meaningful reciprocity is to be achieved in human relationships.

At the action level, priests and even archbishops are joining guerrillas in various places. Archbishop Dom Helder Camara and Father Camilo Torres both embody this revolutionary commitment.[9] These trends represent a very small minority in the churches but an intensely active one.

The radical-secularist image of the future has a double time horizon. It provides for the realization of a drastically improved human society within historical time, but a small opening is left on the near horizon for vistas of eternity. Spatially, the planet is its province, again with the door to eternity left ever so slightly ajar. This double sense of space and time is what differentiates these Christians from the "world's people" with whom they work, and it enables them to contribute the sense of Otherness, the "resources of transcendence" that secular revolutionaries require.[10] Empirically, the radical-Christian-secularist renounces the transcendental aspect of his or her image of the future when entering secular movements.

The radical secularist's image of the future is optimistic. He or she can visualize a reconstructed society and a role in it. Furthermore, he or she is grateful to a secular society for relieving the church of responsibility for governing men and women. The dynamic in the radical-secularist model of the world lies in the conviction that secularization has liberated the church for its real business of translating the Gospel into a workable model of social interaction. The ambiguous role of Otherness and transcendence in the radical secularist's image of the future creates a three-way set of tensions between himself, the church, and society. At its best, this tension releases religious commitment into constructive social action, achieving the ideal balance that Polak envisaged between utopia and eschatology.

THE SIGNALS-OF-TRANSCENDENCE MODEL

A model of the religious dimension that appeals to social scientists is the signals-of-transcendence model presented by Peter Berger in *A Rumor of Angels*. He begins with human beings solidly grounded in the physical and social world. "If the religious projections of man correspond to a reality that is superhuman and supernatural, then it seems logical to look for traces of this reality in the projector himself."[11]

Berger identifies certain prototypical human gestures, which he calls "signals of transcendence." They are "phenomena that are to be found within the domain of our 'natural' reality but that appear to be beyond that reality."[12] The propensities for creating order, for play, for hope, for revulsion against evil, and for sensing the comic are universal human propensities that point to another reality. Harvey Cox in *The Feast of Fools* (Cambridge, Mass.: Harvard University Press, 1969) deals with the same theme, suggesting that the propensities to fantasize and to celebrate point to that which is fantasied and celebrated. Cox and Berger both present a scene in which mankind creates a world bit by bit (man's "plausibility structures") out of a passion for order, laughter, play, hope, and goodness, in response to invisible signals of which a person is only dimly aware. Both authors caution against placing too much emphasis on this back-door rediscovery of the supernatural but hint that there might, after all, be something out there to which men and women are responding. No images of the future are suggested by this approach, only the possibility that at some future time, when a person is more aware of what he or she is now rediscovering, images of the future might be generated.

This Noah's-ark view of the cosmos, with mankind shaping the world in response to nearly inaudible instructions, is bound in time and space to the immediate perceived environment, but it is boundless with reference to what a person may create in the future. The sense of the Other is there, the unknown from which a person wrests the order that comforts him, and transcendence is at least there as a "rumor of angels." The mood is one of cautious optimism. The dynamics of this vague signaling-from-somewhere, however, can at best produce equally vague images of the future.

THE SACRATION MODEL

We have looked at existential, radical-secular, and cautiously sacred models of reality. Of these three, only the radical-secular model has a clear-cut image of the future and an accompanying dynamic of change. The radical-secular model also has built-in instabilities owing to the tension between the utopian and eschatological elements and the danger (according to Polak's theory of images) of its adherents giving up the eschatological elements entirely.

The sacration model of the world stands in direct opposition to mainstream theories of secularization. Sacration theory, instead of speaking of the liberation of mankind from the bonds of the supernatural, speaks of the liberation of the physical world from the bonds of mechanism. Teilhard de Chardin, in *The Phenomenon of Man* (New York: Harper, 1959), saw *noogenesis* as a process of psychosocial evolution that drew the whole of the material world into a pulsing, aware relationship with the layer of human consciousness that he called the "noosphere." The scientist-priest witnessed daily during Mass a gigantic transubstantiation of the entire planet as it "became" the body of Christ.[13] His vision of the planet as a mystical extension of the body of Christ had practical daily correlates in the contributions of science and technology to weaving the strongly meshed web of the noosphere that binds mankind and planet to God. Ecologists, incidentally, find this a very acceptable perspective on the role and uses of technology.

Arnold Toynbee's reading of history has given him the same vision that Teilhard's reading of biology gave him: The earth as the Commonwealth of God is the only intelligible sphere of human action, and humans relate to humans and the planet over time as a "voluntary coadjuter of a God whose mastery of the situation gives a divine value and meaning to Man's otherwise paltry endeavors."[14]

The significance of Toynbee's view of the churches as a higher species of society is often missed by those who remember only that he says that great religions are born in the great spiritual voids between civilizations. Civilizations do not outgrow religion but are themselves the discarded husks of mankind's spiritual progression. In a magnificent synthesis of utopia and eschatology, Toynbee points out that the terrestrial communion of saints will come about as men strive to be good citizens of the City of God, succeeding "incidentally in saving the situation for social life in This World within the vastly larger framework of their own spiritual field of activity. Even a mundane law and order can be effectively established on Earth only on the model of a building that 'we have from God—a house not made with hands, eternal in the Heavens.'"[15]

Jürgen Moltmann, who has come to be known as the theologian of hope, creates a different synthesis of utopia and eschatology. A radical committed equally to dialogue with Marxists and non-Marxists and a founder of "political theology," Moltmann can't be grouped with the radical-Christian-secularists because he counters the God-is-dead thesis with the startling proclamation that God is *not yet*. *"God is* present in the way in which his future takes control over the present in real anticipations and prefigurations. But *God is not as yet* present in the form of his eternal presence. The dialectic between his being and his being-not-yet is the pain and power of history. Caught between the experiences of his presence and his absence, we are seeking his future, which will solve this ambiguity that the present cannot solve."[16]

Moltmann has no patience with intellectualized ameliorism. We are construction workers, he says, and the only place to begin advancing toward the God who is coming to meet us is at the point of our accumulated historical evils—with the poor and oppressed. The agony in the human heart finds its correspondence in the suffering within matter itself, as we painfully discover the direction of cosmic fulfillment.

Another passionate lover of God with a powerful sense of urgency about the radical reconstruction of society is Edward Carothers. His personal experience of God as both Pusher and Puller[17] —a pusher within the evolutionary process and a puller baptizing a thirsty world with grace—has led him to a serenely hectic life of social action.

All these thinkers belong in the Teilhardian community, in that they see the world as increasingly infused with the divine presence, while they also see, with a clarity perhaps even sharper than Teilhard's, the human toil that must be invested in this sacration process.

The vein of mysticism associated with these concepts of sacration is hard for the current generation of social scientists to accept. Observers of radical youth movements, however, point out that while theologians and sociologists are still speaking the language of secularization, students are "into" the sacred and the transcendent.[18] Arthur Waskow devotes a chapter of *Running Riot* (New York: Herder and Herder, 1970) to "The Religious Upswelling on the Left," which begins with an itemization of solemn public acts of religious ritual by the New Left. His *Bush Is Burning* (New York: Macmillan, 1971) makes of the life of radical political action an epiphany of the presence that led the Jews out of Egypt, pointing to a new Zion built on faith and hope. Many of us have observed—perhaps participated in—some of the politico-religious rituals of the New Left, but we tend to see each act as an isolated instance rather than as part of a genuine groundswell.

Waskow defines the religious sense as a feeling of urgency for reconnecting mind, body, and spirit, and he sees it not only as a moral response to dehumanization but also as a "politically liberating response to politically oppressive institutions." Like the guerrilla priests among the radical secularists, the communion-taking radicals in the New Left are a small but intensely active minority.

What image of the future emerges from the sacration model of the world? Teilhard, Toynbee, Moltmann, Carothers, and the mystically inclined radical activists all see a reconstructed earthly society as part of the realization of the divine potential in mankind. They all view human action as being inscribed on a much broader canvas than the here and now. The time horizon expands to geologic time scales, the spatial horizon to the cosmos, yet the action is here and now. The sense of the Other is strong, with openness to the idea of radically different social structures, brought about with the aid of human science and technology. Transcendence is the key characteristic of the sacration model—the world is suffused with the divine. Optimism is strong, since sacration is an evolutionary process. Mankind could stand in the way of this evolutionary process and thwart it—by refusing to wake up—and a man or woman does have to fight through all the ages against sin, being human and not divine. But if a person can be awakened to the vision of his or her possibilities, *he or she will want what God makes possible* and work for it.

While tensions are created in the radical-secularist model by an ambiguity about the role of transcendence in the image of the future, in the sacration model tensions grow from an ambiguity about the role of mankind. The secularists are tempted to abandon transcendence; the sacraters are tempted to abandon man. The sacration model tries to hold the balance Polak prescribes between utopia and eschatology.

THE RELIGIOUS IMAGE OF THE FUTURE
AND THE WILL TO TRANSCEND

This survey of religious models of the world and their associated imaging capacity has been incomplete, but perhaps it is suggestive. By looking at religious models that have some acceptance outside the church, we have identified some of the resources available to the larger society in its task of imaging the future. Polak has deplored the weakening of the eschatological element in religious images of the future as contributing to the weakening of mankind's will to make a breach in time. The existential image of the future, or non-image, does display this weakness. However, each of the other images, in varying degrees possesses some dynamic of transcendence. Judgments about the relative power of the various images are difficult, though this is an empirically researchable question.

In the meantime it is attractive to speculate about the extent to which these images and world views are generation-bound. Does the existentialist view belong to the older generation of intellectuals, the timid signals-of-transcendence view to the middle generation, and the sacration view mainly to youth? The radical-secularist view cannot be generation-bound in my opinion, but it is different from the others in being a phenomenon within the church. Born before World War I, it has been a powerful source of tension within the church throughout this century, but it is more in public view now than ever before. People of all ages can be found holding each of these images. Which are the key creative minorities? Which images will catch hold? Polak's theory needs more work before we can answer those questions.

Meanwhile, we may note that millennialism in the form of a "year 2000" fervor is notably absent among students of the religious image of the world. This is probably due to the vastly larger time perspectives with which religion usually deals, and this should serve as a corrective to the millennialism of professional futurists. It is one more argument for persuading professional futurists to look at the scientific study of religion in their exploration of the dimensions of that which is to come.

NOTES

1. See Max Weber, *The Protestant Ethic and the Spirit of Capitalism,* trans. Talcott Parsons (New York: Charles Scribner's Sons, 1958).
2. Elise Boulding, "Futuristics and the Imaging Capacity of the West," in *Human Futuristics,* ed. Magoroh Maruyama and James Dator (Honolulu: University of Hawaii Press, 1971[?]), pp. 2-3.
3. Fred L. Polak, *The Image of the Future,* trans. Elise Boulding (New York, Oceana Publications, 1961), vol. 1, p. 438.
4. Boulding, "Futuristics," p. 32.
5. Martin Buber, *Eclipse of God: Studies in the Relation Between Religion and Philosophy,* trans. Maurice Friedman et al. (New York: Harper, 1952), p. 67.
6. Polak, *Image of the Future,* vol. 1, p. 159.
7. Dietrich Bonhoeffer, *Letters and Papers from Prison,* trans. Reginald H. Fuller, ed. Eberhard Bethge (New York: Macmillan, 1962).
8. World Conference on Church and Society, *Christians in the Technical and Social Revolutions of Our Time* (Geneva: World Council of Churches, 1967), p. 24.
9. See Dom Helder Camara, *Revolution Through Peace,* trans. Ampara McLean, ed. Ruth N. Anshen (New York: Harper, 1971); Camilo Torres, *Revolutionary Writings* (New York: Harper, 1972); *Camilo Torres: His Life and His Message,* trans. V. M. O'Grady (Springfield, Ill.: Templegate Publishers, 1968); also, Francine D. Gray, *Divine Disobedience: Profiles in Catholic Radicalism* (New York: Knopf, 1970).
10. Whether secular revolutionaries have independent resources of transcendence or are dependent on the church for this is discussed in Boulding, "Futuristics."
11. Peter Berger, *A Rumor of Angels: Modern Society and the Rediscovery of the Supernatural* (New York: Doubleday, 1969), p. 59.
12. Ibid.

13. See Pierre Teilhard de Chardin, *Hymn of the Universe,* trans. Simon Bartholomew (New York: Harper, 1965).

14. Arnold Toynbee, *A Study of History, Vol. 7B—Universal Churches* (New York: Oxford University Press, 1963), pp. 513-14.

15. Ibid., p. 523.

16. Jürgen Moltmann, *Religion, Revolution and the Future*, trans. M. Douglass Meeks (New York: Charles Scribner's Sons, 1969), p. 209.

17. See J. Edward Carothers, *The Pusher and the Puller: A Concept of God* (Nashville: Abingdon Press, 1968).

18. See Donald L. Rogan, *Campus Apocalypse: The Student Search Today* (New York, Seabury Press, 1969), pp. 66-67.

Ralph Wendell Burhoe

A Cosmic Perspective on Man's Future

Earthlings are now in the position of the sorcerer's apprentice. New scientific procedures provide vast powers for human use. But religions, which transmit ultimate values, have remained encoded in ancient myths that are no longer credible. This cultural split has severed humankind's value controls from our scientific technology, thus permitting its unchecked growth. What are the prospects for the future? Burhoe examines these prospects, by means of an interesting story technique.

Modern science and technology constitute the most radical breakthrough in human cultural evolution since the origin of language, and those not familiar with the new perspectives remain confined in the other of C. P. Snow's two cultures. The basic crisis of our times is this split in our culture, a massive schizophrenia of the noosphere or thought-world of Homo sapiens. In one compartment of this thought-world is confined the subculture of science and technology, uninformed by the values that are essential or sacred for human life, with the result that people run wild with dangerous if not lethal new powers given them by various technologies. In the other is the subculture of

This is a revision of a portion of a paper the author gave at Syracuse University in 1974.

182

human values, clothed in such ancient literary, mythical, and logical forms that they are fast becoming ineffective in motivating people whose world views are shaped by the new subculture of science-technology.

This split of facts from values in our culture threatens the future not only of humankind but also of other precious elements of life in the earth's ecosystem, which has been several billion years in the building and which gives this point in earth's history something of a cosmic significance. From the vantage point of one who has been working with many others in both the sciences and the humanities on the problem of human values in the light of the sciences, I will try to present the problem and a saving solution in a cosmic perspective provided by recent scientific images.

A COSMIC VIEW OF MAN—FROM PLANET X

On my way across the campus a few days ago, I saw an unidentified flying saucer. I went up to it, found no one there, but noticed something like a tape recorder. I took the tapes and went immediately to the university computer lab. The tapes appear to contain the briefing of an interstellar expedition to investigate Earth. Here is the translation.

We creatures on Planet X of Star Y, who know something about the operations of the sovereign and indivisible, evolving cosmic ecosystem—the system that we call God, which we understand generates and orders all that happens in all times and places, apart from which nothing is, and yet whose laws of operation remain invariant forever—we have been exploring the nature and will of God here on X and in other parts of the universe.

One of our interests has been a planet called Earth, one of those rather rare and interesting planets that has created life like ours. Of course, we know that the sovereign cosmic system in many places has created these fantastic and marvelous, evolving cybernetic systems of great complexity that are able to maintain semistable or metastable patterns of energy flow far from thermodynamic equilibrium. But we of Planet X have not been able to find, visit, and study many of them. The following analysis of the Earth situation is given as background information for our Tenth Field Expedition.

THE EARTH SITUATION

These evolving patterns of life on Earth have followed the sequences of evolutionary stages corresponding to ours. We have empirical observations for the same general sequence of stages on both planets, and both historical sequences correspond to the computations from our theory. According to our theory, the initial given conditions on both planets would yield the same succession of emerging properties on various levels, from simple molecules to thinking minds and civilizations.

As in the case of our ancestors on Planet X, the selective processes on Earth are selecting, in Homo's cultural evolution, certain types of symbolic systems that orient Homo to the superior powers sovereign in his ecosystem, the sources that gave rise to or created Homo and that currently sustain him.

In Earth's evolution, as anywhere else in the cosmos, living creatures (metastable dissipative flow systems) are created by the variations of matter and energy that constitute a search which from time to time results in the finding of new levels of metastable dynamic patterns. Progress from one level to another takes place when there are discovered boundary conditions or memory systems that can keep their shape for aeons with only gradual modifications, which permit the building up of a hierarchy of dynamic operations corresponding to the hierarchy of memories. The top of the hierarchy of boundary conditions or memory is always a reflection or image of the total habitat or ecosystem, which is of course cosmic in scope.

On Earth, DNA served for more than a billion years as the primary memory system, orienting the flow patterns in ways that are viable in Earth's particular habitats. As we would expect, when Homo appeared with a new type of memory called culture, the orientation toward the ultimate sources of being took patterns in the noosphere as they did in our earlier history on X. Like us, Homo in the past worshiped or oriented himself to the sacred conditions and definers of life symbolized in both Earth and Sun and in various other subsidiary phenomena such as Light, Thunder, Wind, Rain, Mountains, Trees, Beasts, and special symbols pertaining directly to Homo himself—all as deities generative of and sovereign over Homo's being and destiny. Also Homo has properly integrated all these diverse agencies under a single rubric of universal extent in time and space, essentially representing the cosmic ecosystem, or God.

The present expedition to Earth is being sent because we are concerned about some new problems. Earth is one of the relatively few planets we have come across in our region of the Milky Way that have thus far created a second stage of memory codes for shaping the dynamics of life: cultural symbols. And we understand Earth is now on the verge of the third or postbiological stage of evolution of life systems, which we ourselves only reached approximately a thousand years ago.

We are particularly concerned about Earth and Homo for two reasons.

First, our reports indicate that Homo is in dire trouble and may need help. We know that it is God's law that even relatively distant and strange forms of life must involve themselves in the welfare of God's total system, including less-advanced creatures and even preliving forms of the elements of nature or God's substance. We therefore recognize as our duty and privilege to be of any service we can to this distant fellow creature, Homo.

Second, our worry stems from reports from Earth that Homo actually has, or at least believes that he has, taken charge of his own evolution. If Homo believes that and is mistaken, then he certainly is in trouble; for all of our knowledge thus far tells us that if any creature fails to adapt to some potential ecological niche where it exists—established by God's initial boundary conditions of the habitat and by the consequent historical events produced by the operation of God's universal laws—then that creature is an unstable or inviable pattern of dissipative energy flow and disappears from the scene. If, on the other hand, Homo has in fact taken charge of his own evolution, he has indeed become God and does incarnate the complete wisdom of cosmic evolution. This is, of course, in our view very improbable. But if it were true, then our theology would have to be revised. We should then be required to either worship Homo as God incarnate or, at least, concede that the space-time solid of the cosmos we know contains powers that are independent of it.

While each of these hypotheses seems incredible, our long history of scientific theology requires us to investigate this situation on earth and correct our theology accordingly. If the truth is that Homo mistakenly supposes he is God, then our expedition should seek to learn what strange circumstances or hubris of Homo led to such a self-destructive myth, and we should serve as agents of the true God's grace in communicating correct information to Homo about what is truly sacred for guiding his future behavior. God's extremely costly, several-billion-year effort to bring life to a stage on Earth that is so close to ours on Planet X should be redeemed if it is possible.

On earth, Homo is the only creature who significantly possesses the cultural level of divine information to structure his behavior. Nevertheless, we have reports that Homo has in the past century been observed to succumb to such disorderly, entropic forces as planet-round (1) suicidal actions in which use is made of recently found atomic-weapon technology, (2) pollution of the ecosystem on which his life depends, (3) cancerous growth of his own population along with depletion of its ecological support base, (4) psychosocial disruptions and disorientations consequent to planet-round dissolution of the former cultural institutions that had reasonably well transmitted Homo's values, purposes, duties, and proper hopes for evolving creatures within the divine cosmic order. Recently we have observed some of Homo take their first trips away from the Earth to its small satellite, and we have wondered if they are preparing to escape the holocausts threatening on Earth, and if this may be a contemporary acting-out of one of their earlier myths about an ark to save them from a great flood.

HOMO'S CULTURAL EVOLUTION

Life on Earth, as on Planet X, was made in the image of God. Among the millions of kinds of creatures that God created by the operations of his invariant cosmic laws within the initial conditions he had created on Earth was the genus Homo, beginning only some 10^6 years ago. In Homo there emerged a new level in the evolutionary mechanisms of Earth as different from the selection of genetic symbols as was the process of "natural selection" of genotypes from the cruder feedback systems and boundary conditions in chemical evolution prior to the symbiosis of nucleic and amino acids. All creatures before Homo were shaped into God's image by two sets of molds: (1) the patterns of the external environment, and (2) the genetic pattern that was an image or remembered symbol of successful prior learning of God's image for a particular ecological niche. In Homo, a third input of information for molding him in the image of God was added: the cultural pattern or culture-type. The evolution of culturally transmitted molds has made Homo different from all other creatures on the Earth. Cultural patterns, as we have long known on Planet X, are a naturally expected, emergent mechanism when an evolving ecosystem reaches the point that puts a premium upon a capacity to learn God's will about higher-level complex systems at a much faster rate than such learning can take place in the relatively slow sorting of random mutations in the gene pool of a species.

Cultural information is designed in hierarchical structures consisting of adjustable units at different levels akin to genetic information's hierarchical structuring. In cultural memory, information to guide proper behavior operates by means of facilitated or reinforced neurological channels between simple symbols and organic states. These have been ordered in various culture-types to yield more or less coherent and implicitly logical operating patterns of symbols within the brain that correspond reasonably well with the actual events in the habitat or cosmic scheme.

The dissemination of culture is quite different from that of genetic information, and is not confined to random mutations or random bilateral pairings, in radiating linear phylogenies. Rather, when any Homo opens his or her mouth a particular culture-type is spewed abroad to the whole community or species of potential receivers. A single TV voice may almost instantaneously alter some element of the culture-type in some 10^8 or 10^9 brains of Homo, such as the announcement of an act of warfare that will mobilize in reoriented behavioral patterns that huge number of individuals; and the same genesis may be undone or reversed at another moment. Nothing like that could happen to the gene pool of any species. The pool of cultural information has been structured to integrate with the products of genetic information in the brains of the same population in order to produce these effects.

In general, the patterns of the various cultures have also been integrated to produce viable living patterns in their respective total habitats and ecological niches, to such an extent that the societies are viable. They are viable because of information that genetic codes by themselves in general cannot bring about because their "learning" rate is too slow and too confined to a single individual instead of being dispersed in multiple, mutually cooperating forms of immense complexity in a large population of individuals, such as the kind of technological or scientific research program that made possible Homo's trip to the moon within a decade of the time that the project was undertaken. This compares with the millions of years of genetic learning required for insects or birds to learn to fly.

The culture-types also have the advantage that they can be stored outside the brains and bodies of the populations they serve; the cultural equivalents of DNA genotypes are found recorded in books, films, tapes, and other artifacts. As we have long known on Planet X, culture-types can also come alive outside of biological systems entirely.

As our theory would require, the development of the new cultural level of dissemination of information (or what the Lord requires for a living system) means that there must be a delicate integration of genetic and cultural information if the system is to be viable at all, since the two systems are symbionts. There is clear evidence that the symbiosis of Homo's cultures and genotypes during the past 10^6 years has led to simultaneous modifications in both these systems of recording patterns of life. The more viable patterns have been selected by the nature of the greater ecosystem, or God. Likewise, millions of costly errors have been eliminated by God in this period of history.

Since genetic information in Homo is still basic to his very being and cultural information is merely a superficial modification—albeit now a major and vital one—our evolutionary theory suggests there must have arisen in Homo cultural institutions for collecting and transferring accumulated wisdom for integrating behavior to fulfill the implicit goals and program of the total living system, or ecosystem. This would include Homo's necessary restraints or taboos in his relations with the various elements of the ecosystem that may be relevant for his life. In other words, Homo's cultural mechanisms must have had to communicate the most general and ultimate goals or values and motivating mechanism for behaving so as to adapt to those overall requirements for human life prescribed by God.

As is expected from this theory God did create and select for this function basic cultural institutions—religious institutions—by providing the opportunity for various mutations and then selecting those he approves. On Earth it is estimated that during the past 10^5 years there have evolved some 10^5 cultural species of religion. As in the case of genetically structured species, these religious species—which are necessarily structured jointly by cosmic, genetic, and cultural information—are selected or rejected by the immediate agencies of God on Earth, the sacred laws of the Earth's ecosystem. As in the case of evolutionary processes in general, only a small portion of this large number of religious species remain in being at the present.

However, it is a new trend in the history of Homo that even the religious institutions, whose function it is to transmit the ultimate values of the Homo system, either are in a stage of rapid metamorphosis or evolution that is hard to discern or else are in fact dying. If the latter is true, Homo's cultural systems will shortly be uninformed by the values or purposes they serve, and Homo will not be adequately motivated to adapt to conditions that God has set for his life under the new possibilities that seem to be at hand as a result of the recent scientific-technological revolution.

THE SPLIT IN HOMO'S CULTURAL INFORMATION

The problem is put before us by the fact that, in cultural evolution on Earth during the past two millennia, and especially during the past two centuries, Homo has split his cultural information into two separate and largely disconnected parts. His new scientific procedures for accumulating valid knowledge have given him the power to unlock the secrets of atoms or travel to other planets in the solar system or even to change his own genetic code of information. But at the same time his religions—which have kept him

oriented to the ultimate and supreme powers that govern his destiny and reminded him of his duties and given him hope when he is forced to suffer
under the Lord's extravagantly costly and sacrificial ways of increasing valid
information—have remained encoded in ancient myths that Homo no longer
finds credible. As a result his religions have become ineffective, even though
the gist of their messages, in some cases at least, is as valid and true as ever.

But if Homo's religious or value culture is now ineffective because of
some logical incompatibilities between the religious symbols of his ultimate
goals or values and his scientific symbols of what is true or factual, then it
would appear that Homo is seriously wounded by such a split in his culture.
The remaining integrity of Homo's gene pool becomes irrelevant, since for
Homo his culture-type has become essential for his viability. It is possible
that the most recent dramatic stages of the evolution of human culture,
which severs the value controls from the now unbridled growth of scientific
technology, may be lethal, cancerous mutations for Homo.

But there are some among us on Planet X who are also worried about
the implications posed by the case of Homo for the validity of our thousand-
year-old doctrine that the Lord of the cosmos rules all history everywhere—
not only on Planet X—and that nothing can escape the rule and judgment of
his eternally invariant and omnipresent power or will that generates all
behavioral sequences in the cosmos. A thousand years ago our cultural
evolution was at the stage where Homo is today, but when we passed through
the stages where science and scientific technology emerged, we did not suffer
the severance of the patterns and institutions of sacred values from our other
technologies. Nor have we observed such a splitting of the vital integrity of
values from other facts in cultures on any other planets. Hence the present
condition of Homo is our first case in the cosmos that even suggests that there
can be any viable creature whose values are not adapted to the requirements
of the sovereign Lord of cosmic history as specified in the local ecosystem.
Homo, as a test case of cosmic significance, must be carefully studied.

Particular examination should be made of that sacred symbol-system
called Christianity, since it was in its midst that the cultural mutations of
modern science and modern scientific technology appear to have originated.
Actually, this Christianity was in part a product of a somewhat earlier mutation that took place in the eastern end of the Mediterranean basin some two
or three thousand years ago. The Mediterranean culture had advanced to the
point of building cultural symbol-systems—models, myths, theories, philosophies, and so forth, but some of the first signs of the present problem of
Homo also appeared: the failure of the symbols of his sacred, long-range

religious values to keep up with the rapid evolution of his other symbols.

More than a thousand years later the second major mutation producing modern science occurred in Homo. In the seventeenth century some of Homo's intellectual explorers began to insist that the empirical evidence of actual historical or empirical experience be applied to test the validity of the still-prevailing ancient theories and to insist that an imaginative search for better models or theories to fit the facts be made.

At first the new sciences were religiously exhilarating and even made some of the pioneers religiously ecstatic. Johannes Kepler and Isaac Newton, for example, saw visions of the beauty and reasonable structure of God's nature, from their perceptions, behind the confusions of sensory experience. But within a couple of centuries, the growing differences between these new scientific symbols and traditional religious symbol-systems became so great that very few in that society could manage to correlate one symbol-system with the other.

To help understand this situation, we may note that the sciences were again the kind of evolutionary mutation or breakthrough in cultural evolution that we might expect, since the God of evolutionary history operates by ecological stress patterns to encourage mutations and new patterns of adaptation in new ecological niches.

Homo is now becoming more fully aware of the costs of evolutionary advance and of his responsibility as an agent of God to act consciously to advance God's kingdom on Earth. At least, that is the long-range implication of what seems to be happening.

A BLEAK, SHORT-RANGE VIEW

But, for the short range the picture is bleak, for Homo may be becoming inviable—unless the remote possibility is true that in Homo we have living evidence that God does not completely rule the cosmos, that there are forces that are actually independent of the cosmic ecosystem or nature.

The truths about the sovereign Lord, whose will and nature control all destiny in the cosmos, have been lost to modern Homo as his religious institutions have become custodians of symbol-systems and myths that are no longer credible or effective for moving the hearts of men and women in ways effective in the past. The new scientific myths are potentially destructive for all the religious cultures of the Earth, from the most advanced species to the most primitive, and not merely for the Christian system in which they arose. The Planet X Expedition to Earth must inquire into this problem. It may be a problem of greater magnitude than that faced by Homo a few hundred thousand years ago when this present *sapiens* species was selected to replace earlier species of Homo.

What makes matters worse is that, while in our history on Planet X the arrival of scientific technology was an opportunity for *transcending* our previous stage of cultural evolution, for Homo, lacking a sense of his need to bow before the transcendent sovereign reality determining his destiny, the new powers of scientific technology may shortly doom him. He has come to assume that the powers God gave him by grace of his prior evolution are somehow independent of that history and its present reality. Homo has tended to take a more existential view of himself, as a given without a long history and destiny utterly dependent upon the realities of an essentially infinite space-time of the cosmic ecosystem.

Scientific technology did not arise on Earth to give Homo significant powers until about a century ago. It was at about this time that his religious cultures began to wither from their inability to maintain credibility or beliefs in the reality of the gods, and thus to shape Homo's behavior in fitting ways to that reality. As a result, the new applications of blossoming scientific myths in new technologies to fulfill man's unsacralized wants have so transformed the Earth that the total ecosystem may become inviable, not only for Homo, but for any forms of life that are found there now. Moreover, it is these new powers of application of scientific knowledge in technology that have sold science to countless groups of Homo who use the technologies with little capacity to restrain themselves to the proper uses of its magical powers that are ordained by the cosmic ecosystem as it operates in Earth's societies. Thus, earthlings are in the situation of the sorcerer's apprentice, who does not know the proper words to stop the machinery he has set in motion.

Homo has discarded his traditional religious wisdom and failed to see that the new sciences give him the same general message: Homo is a complex creature who did not make himself, but was made by a sovereign, omnipotent, universal, dynamic, evolving system in which Homo is privileged to play his interesting role as long as he continues to incorporate the general plans laid down by the total system. He cannot afford to forget past revelations of these plans and must eternally seek new revelations adapted to new stages of life. Furthermore, he must live these revelations as well as understand them, since both past and new revelations do not produce life until acted out.

Apparently there are some among Homo who seem to be aware of the real tragedy in supposing Homo to be in charge of his own destiny, in supposing that he no longer is required to adapt to the ultimate realities underlying Earth's ecosystem and cosmic laws, which have, according to our theory, structured his behaviors, perceptions, and societies as well as the behaviors of the world around him.

Of course, we of Planet X could be wrong, and hence the Expedition to Earth must examine the hypothesis that Homo has indeed freed himself from control by the cosmic God in which we believe. This improbable hypothesis we must test, for in that case we on X would have to have a new vision of what is ultimately sovereign, and we should want to adapt to that.

PART 7

IMAGES OF
EDUCATION AND LEARNING

If we are to dream new dreams that help inspire confidence in the future and give us the collective strength to deal aggressively and humanistically with our many problems, what role can formal education play? History tells us two things in this regard. First, the sources of new dreams are the "mutants" who break away from the status quo. Second, formal education in every culture serves to perpetuate the status quo. It would seem then that formal education has little to offer in our quest for new visions of the future. And yet, in an age of discontinuity, might not the exhaustion of existing models of formal education be the seedbed for the mutants? And might not a radical restructuring of education become possible as the structures of our civilization radically change? The first essay discusses in quantitative terms where formal education is likely to go if current growth trends continue. The second explores in qualitative terms where a discontinuity might take us. The resulting gap is enormous, but suggestions for a few connecting bridges do emerge.

W. Timothy Weaver

Growth, Distribution, and the Professional Frame of Reference

Weaver shows that reducing the dropout rate below grade twelve will not contribute to overall growth in educational attainment. Since this goal of growth is likely to continue, the shifting of funds to post-secondary education will mean that those at the lowest socioeconomic level will not complete the minimum schooling necessary for entering post-secondary education. The same pattern is occurring in modernizing nations. The difference is that stabilizing growth in educational attainment at the lowest socioeconomic level in poorer countries will cut off a majority of the world's people.

While three-quarters of the world struggles with basic literacy, the United States and the other industrial countries struggle to meet the rising aspirations for schooling beyond the twelfth year. It appears that the industrialized nations, especially the United States, have become, in effect, an image of the future for developing countries.

In G. Z. Bereday's view, not only will the less advanced, industrialized nations follow the image created by the United States, Japan, Canada, and the USSR, countries Bereday refers to as the "club," but also the impoverished, modernizing countries seem to be following the well-charted course. They are expanding the benefits of schooling in such a way as to satisfy the needs of the elite, a pattern very much like that found in the early history of the industrialized countries. These countries resemble a salamander slithering through time, with the club countries at the head and the modernizing countries at the tail. Where the head is today, the tail will be tomorrow.

ATTAINMENT AND THE DISTRIBUTION OF BENEFITS

What is to be expected beyond quantitative growth? James Coleman speculated that education systems, particularly those in the Western hemisphere, seem to evolve in phases. First, they grow quantitatively, then change qualitatively and structurally. The structural changes tend toward flexibility, and qualitative changes toward redistribution. Such a pattern does seem to characterize the schools in the United States. The very serious questions of distribution of educational resources and benefits in the 1950s and 1960s followed an intensive period of quantitative growth that goes back to the turn of the century but which accelerated during the years following World War II.

Because the United States in many respects appears to be at the front extremity of the salamander, a picture of what might be expected in other countries, after quantitative growth has occurred, can be seen taking shape now in the United States.

As the rich and poor nations resemble a salamander, so too does the distribution of educational attainment within the United States. Those at the tail pass the level only previously passed by those at the head. Social and economic status determine who will be at the head and who will be at the tail. The overall process would eventually benefit everyone up to some minimum level if left alone to play itself out. However, it is now becoming evident that the final group in the procession, those Thomas F. Green refers to as the "group of last entry," may not successfully complete the process. They may not because their needs, as perceived within the professional frame of reference, differ from those of their predecessors to such a degree that new forms of education are required, together with massive increases in funds. Neither the will to provide the funds nor the wisdom to create alternative forms of education appear to be emerging. The prospects are very real for a halt in the procession before everyone has passed a minimum level of attainment. This prospect seems likely not only for the United States but for the other nations in the industrialized northern hemisphere as well. If this prospect is real for the rich nations, the implications for the modernizing world are enormous, particularly in view of worldwide inflation.

What this could mean is that growth in educational attainment would be stabilized just at the lowest socioeconomic level, effectively cutting off persons at that level from further benefits, while at higher socioeconomic levels attainment would continue to rise. In industrialized countries, those so cut off represent a minority. However, it is significant that in modernizing nations those cut off represent a *majority*.

By way of illustration: In the United States what this could result in is a more or less permanent pattern of growth, as witnessed during the decade from 1961 to 1971. During that time the education-attainment level in the lowest income quintile rose by 6 percent but remained well below the completion of the first year of high school for heads of households. For those in the second quintile, attainment rose by 21 percent, reaching near high-school completion for heads of households. At the highest level of income, attainment rose by 10 percent, reaching close to college completion for heads of households. The education-attainment gap between richest and poorest stretched from nearly six years to nearly seven years from 1961 to 1971.

The most startling change observed in these data during the past decade in the United States occurred among the lower-middle class, those in the next to the lowest fifth of income distribution. In one decade lower-middle-class heads of households have moved up from bare completion of grade school to completion of high school in large numbers. The lower-middle-income group, as have all groups above it, has arrived at the necessary attainment level to now reach for postsecondary education in large numbers in order to maintain upward social mobility. The enormous accomplishment of the lower-middle class has left a large gap in educational attainment between itself and the lowest fifth on the ladder of economic status. That gap widened an astonishing 136 percent over the past decade.

There is a peculiar irony to this issue. On the average, the disparity in educational attainment throughout the population is diminishing in the United States. According to data prepared by Christopher Jencks, it can be shown that since 1900 the average difference between individuals with regard to the number of years of schooling attained has declined approximately 31 percent. But while the disparity among individuals has decreased, it is clear that the disparity between certain social groups is increasing significantly. And not only is the disparity between social groups increasing with regard to education but also the disparity in income between richest and poorest has increased considerably since World War II.

The process feeds upon itself. As the wealthy accumulate more and more years of schooling, they use up an increasingly greater proportion of educational resources. For example, taking into account that children from rich families stay in school longer and that their schools spend on the national average about 20 percent more than schools attended by the poor, the United States spends about twice as much at the elementary-secondary level on the children of the rich as on the children of the poor. By the time they reach the age when most would have completed their studies, those who benefit most by education have consumed about twice their share of educational resources, while those who benefit least have received about one-half of their share.

The expected pressure from the lower-middle class to expand post-secondary educational opportunities to accommodate their needs during the coming decade may result in a shift of historical proportions in the funds allocated to higher education in the United States. If that shift becomes a reality, the attainment level of the middle class as a whole could rise to four-teen or even sixteen years. One of the most certain consequences of that reality would be to deny sufficient funds to those at the lowest level, whose needs are yet to be met in elementary and secondary schools. Such a transfer of funds from one level of the system to the other would advance the interests of the lower-middle class while blocking attainment of the lowest group at a point below the minimum required for ever entering post-secondary education. The latter group would be forced out of the schools at a point that would effectively deny them any further educational benefits, a situation that prompted Jencks to suggest that school dropouts be given some alternative social benefit, such as subsidized housing or tax rebates.

COMPETING AGENDAS

In the United States three types of educational reform create different and conflicting educational agendas. The agenda of educational growth is most clearly an agenda of higher education. It would mean a continuation of the historical rise in aggregate educational attainment, which now stands at 12.6 years of schooling completed. The agenda of qualitative reform is an agenda of need among the urban schools—but one they cannot afford. Qualitative reform would focus on correcting imbalances in achievement that stem from the social and psychological backgrounds of the child. The agenda of structural change is an agenda only the affluent suburbs can afford to discuss. It would mean more choice within and between schools but would have little effect on distribution.

Historically and presently, the only way for attainment level to rise in the nation as a whole is for more people to attend school or for those in school to remain longer. However, because more than three-quarters of those who now enter school eventually receive a high-school diploma or its equivalent, to further reduce school failure below grade twelve will no longer contribute much to overall growth in educational attainment. If the agenda of growth is to be continued, most of the future expansion that takes place in the average number of years of school completed must take place among persons who have already completed high school. If the agenda of reducing school failure is to be pursued further, there must be a reduction in the educational disadvantages that separate children of different social backgrounds early in their school experience. While the first agenda serves those who have already completed high school, the second agenda serves those who have not—and in all likelihood will not. What we see is the prospect for a serious discontinuity of purpose in the two parts of the educational system.

Meeting both of these agendas, as they are now defined, will mean, at least for the foreseeable future, an increase in funds devoted to each of the two parts of the system. But to accomplish one is no longer to accomplish the other, and unless funds are diverted from some other national priority, the real prospect is for resolving neither the financial crisis in higher education nor the crisis in the classroom. The only alternative may be to accomplish one at the expense of the other. What this could mean, for example, is that we would be willing to tolerate a dropout rate of 20 percent while aggregate attainment continued to rise. It would simply mean that more high-school graduates would enter and complete more years of college.

If the goal of growth is to continue as this country's top priority during the remainder of this century in education, then the following considerations become critically important. First, expansion will occur mostly above Grade 12, benefitting only those who can successfully make it to that level; costs will rise proportionately as more of the age cohort enter and remain in postsecondary education for longer periods of time. Second, almost one-quarter of those who enter school do not successfully use the elementary and secondary schools, dropping out before completing high school. Further help for that one-quarter will have little effect on overall educational attainment, and the costs of helping that last one-quarter will rise faster than previous costs because of the specialized programs required to meet their needs.

Third, the problems of imbalance eventually will shift to the post-secondary level, as a larger percentage of the population with learning deficiencies successfully enters postsecondary education. Right now, an increasing amount of the educational resources at the community-college level and at urban universities such as the City University of New York is diverted to remediation. As growth continues, the problem of disparity in achievement due to social inequities will permeate the entire educational system. There is evidence that the process is well at work now.

However, the decline in enrollment at the elementary-secondary level presents in theory what amounts to a surplus of funds at that level. Given the historic rate of expenditure increases for elementary and high schools, there will be a residual of about 12.5 percent in these school budgets. That residual just about equals the amount required at the postsecondary level if the colleges are to continue to expand to meet demand.

The more important question is one of priorities. Dale Tussing and James Byrnes of the Educational Policy Research Center at Syracuse University proposed in *Financial Crisis in Higher Education* (1971) that the dividend be used to expand higher education to accommodate pressures for growth. The consequences of choosing postsecondary over elementary-secondary needs would be to increase student years of schooling completed at a rate of about 3.8 percent annually among persons of college age to 1975. However, the other consequence of this choice is to lock more children into school failure by ensuring that our success in curbing the dropout rate slows down to about one-half its historic pace. Since school failure is concentrated mostly among the lowest socioeconomic group in this society, this kind of trade-off will alter the long-term distribution of educational benefits along class lines. Expansion of postsecondary opportunities will mostly benefit those in the lower-middle class who are now in a position to seek advanced education in large numbers. The provision of such opportunities is an admirable goal of this society, but unfortunately it may be implemented at the expense of those at the very bottom of the social hierarchy.

CHOOSING THE QUALITATIVE AGENDA: THE PROFESSIONAL FRAME OF REFERENCE

What if the Byrnes and Tussing proposal were reversed, that is, what if we chose elementary and secondary schools as targets of first priority during the remainder of this century? Would it be possible to correct imbalances in educational achievement that now mark urban schools in particular?

In order to answer the last question, it will be necessary to consider two kinds of condition: first, the scope of the problem and the cost of correcting it, and second, the willingness and understanding required to cope with the problem. I shall consider these conditions within the frame of reference of the professional educator. There may be other more appropriate frames of reference; indeed, there *are* other more appropriate frames of reference but they are beyond the scope of this paper.

What percentage of children need help, as defined by professional educators? The data in this area are scanty and inconsistent because we lack uniform definitions of need. Nonetheless, professionals who work with children in the schools perceive some general indicators of the size of the problem. Using several rough indicators, I have estimated that the elementary-secondary schools, by professional definition of need, could have absorbed an additional $10 billion in 1970.

Can we afford such costs? Given professional definitions and assumptions regarding the nature, size, and cost of the problems confronting the elementary and high schools, the residual forecasted for the elementary- and high-school budget will have disappeared, and in fact will have turned into a deficit of -6.5 percent by 1975. The assumptions expressed here deal with minimals. In many urban areas the dropout rate exceeds 40 percent of the school-age population and is, in fact, not precisely known.

Perhaps the more important question is: Will we choose to assume these costs?

There are at a minimum two necessary conditions. First, there must be a public acceptance of distribution of educational resources according to need. Second, educators must be able to demonstrate that they know how to reduce disadvantages originating in the social and psychological backgrounds of children. In my judgment neither of these conditions is likely to be met anytime soon.

The first condition, distribution of resources according to need, goes beyond the concept of equal educational opportunity. Equal educational opportunity holds that each child be treated exactly alike. What is proposed here, as we now define the professional services of education, is that in order to reduce inequities in achievement, each child would have to be treated not alike but according to his or her specific learning needs. Thus, the requirement is for compensation or compensatory opportunity, rather than equal opportunity, if the problem is to be addressed successfully. Treating all children alike will simply mean that some will continue to fail.

The goal of compensatory opportunity is not absolute equality among individuals. The goal is to ensure that every child achieve some minimum standard of learning required for successful participation in society, as that standard is defined by professionals. If that standard can only be measured in terms of years of schooling, then no child should be forced out of school before reaching that point that enables others to enter the mainstream of the society and its economy.

Unless the society intervenes and severs completely the tie between parent and child, the consequence is that differences that characterize parents, be they rich or poor, will characterize the children of the rich and the poor and their institutions. Since some amount of inequality is bound to occur in a free society, the question is not one of eliminating inequality among individuals. The question is how serious the inequality must be and whether the inequalities inordinately penalize particular social groups.

Whether compensatory opportunity succeeds rests largely on what might be called the principle of hospitalization. Hospital insurance is based on the premise that the healthy will subsidize the sick. All pay the same rates but health resources theoretically are distributed according to need. Of course, the fact is that medical resources are not distributed according to need but according to the needs of the advantaged. Nonetheless, we accept in principle that physical affliction should be treated in a compensatory fashion. In a sense, the needs of the handicapped are so treated in the schools. On a per capita basis, the nation as a whole spends about twice as many dollars on the child in special education as it does on the average child. Thus, one might argue that, in principle at least, the public has already accepted the notion of distribution of educational resources according to need. What this suggests is that there seems to be a general principle of acceptance if the affliction meets one important test: it can theoretically happen to anyone. Disease is no respecter of status, so the old saying goes. Any parent can have a handicapped child. Insofar as compensatory opportunities are provided in these cases, any person may stand to benefit and those who do are more or less selected by fate.

To the extent that special learning problems of children are defined as stochastic in nature, there will probably be support for compensatory education. We are talking, of course, about special learning disabilities that are somewhat or entirely a manifestation of some organic disfunction. It is an entirely different matter to talk of a condition in which children of approximately the same potential ability are widely separated by achievement results. It is clear that there is general resistance if compensatory education is proposed (1) when the problem is so concentrated among particular social groups that these groups reap all or most of the benefits at the expense of others or (2) when the social benefit from compensatory education exceeds some limit in cost, regardless of who benefits.

Even when there is public acceptance, compensatory education has not been successful to any large extent. First, educators cannot control the total learning environment of the child, and it is quite clear now that the portion of the environment outside of school is more significant than the portion in school. Second, some parents denied the correction of disadvantages for their children in school will offset this situation by providing more supplements outside of school. These are conditions that can only be controlled by exposing the disadvantaged child to the school curriculum for longer periods of time than the advantaged—a solution obnoxious to many who see the schools as the debilitating factor in the first place. I will return to this point.

In terms of what educators can do to alter the curriculum and pedagogy, there are four basic elements that can be considered: (1) time, defined here as length of exposure to the curriculum, (2) instructional resources, (3) aptitude and intelligence of the child, and (4) the child's pace in mastery of the curriculum. All of these can be altered except the child's aptitude and intelligence. In order to so arrange these elements that compensatory opportunities would succeed, one of three strategies would be necessary: (1) a disproportionate allocation to the disadvantaged of learning time which is sufficient to offset supplementary efforts outside of school; (2) a disproportionate allocation of learning resources sufficient to offset supplementary efforts outside of school; or (3) a pedagogy that would help the disadvantaged but have no particular benefit for the advantaged; or, if both were exposed to it equally, the disadvantaged would benefit more than the advantaged.

Creating such arrangements appears to entail formidable costs as well as resistance. A large sector of even this supposedly egalitarian society is not yet ready to accept equal treatment for all, let alone compensatory treatment. Furthermore, because school is now fixed by both time and age constraints and because children *under ideal conditions* will master the curriculum at different rates, the ultimate success of this approach cannot be measured in terms of bringing about equal achievement, but rather in terms of reducing the number of children who fall below some minimum condition or critical level of achievement. Since such standards are nonexistent, the task of convincing taxpayers by hard data and precise results is made very difficult.

If we were to take mastery learning seriously, we would discover that ideally the achievement of children would cease to correlate with aptitude, but it would also be true that achievement would have a high correlation with time. Benjamin S. Bloom and his associates have discovered that as a rule of thumb it takes the slowest child above five times as long to master a body of knowledge as it takes the fastest. The trick is to discover what prevents a particular child from learning and then tailor the curriculum to his unique learning needs. The problem with this trick is twofold: discovering models that actually do what is proposed, and the expense. But it must be kept in mind that if the time factor is held constant, mastery learning would widen the gap between certain learners, even though fewer of them would fail ultimately.

Compensatory education, as an ideal model, would have to entail at least the following general principles:

1. allocation of learning resources and time according to each child's learning needs;

2. curriculum strategies tailored to each child's unique learning style and aptitude;

3. responsive learning environment;

4. separation of the child for significant periods of time from debilitating influences outside the learning environment.

It seems preposterous to imagine that this kind of educational model will find widespread acceptance and financial support except in a few isolated instances, where very wealthy communities can afford to experiment with compensatory education. Nonetheless, if we do not do something like this, we are then denying prima facie evidence: although certain children obviously need help, the public refuses to pay the cost.

Where we arrive in this analysis is the point of exhaustion of the potential of the professional frame of reference. Since the educational system is now defined and controlled by professionals, the only solution to learning problems confronting the society is seen as more professional services. First it is suggested that class size be reduced (adding more professionals); next that a one-to-one ratio of pupils to teachers is the ideal; and now it is being seriously proposed that what is needed is a multidisciplined, diagnostic team (several professionals per child). This is an impossible model for developing countries. Indeed, it is an impossible model for the United States.

In the professional frame of reference, the best hope for a solution to distribution problems seems to lie both in tinkering (but not too radically) with the curriculum and in lengthening exposure to the curriculum, particularly for children in the lower socioeconomic groups and for all children with learning disabilities. The data on equality do seem to show a consistent correlation between the length of time spent in school and achievement. One is left to conclude that equalizing the amount of schooling each person gets would do a lot to equalize achievement. But the deck is stacked. Without exposure to the professionally defined curriculum, one cannot achieve. To fail to achieve is to fail to receive certification that one has learned. Without certified learning one cannot advance in the system. To fail to advance is to fail to receive a credential. Future social benefits are tied to these credentials. The professional solution is thus more for those who now have little.

CONCLUSIONS: DISMAL SCENARIO

Apart from the impoverishment of the professional model, it is my judgment that three powerful factors make it very unlikely that the postsecondary-growth agenda will give way anytime soon to the qualitative-reform agenda in the United States. (Or at least it is my judgment that the quantitative expansion of the system will not give way to goals of redistribution until the needs of the advantaged are satisfied.) These factors are, first, ingrained attitudes toward the disadvantaged that linger on from nineteenth-century notions regarding individualism and independence. Second, a form of tyranny of the majority seems to have emerged: once a majority of the population benefits from a social subsidy—in this case, schooling—the incentive to expand it further is reduced significantly. This is particularly true if the costs of expanding it compete with other benefits desired by the majority. And, third, the costs entailed would rise at a proportionately faster rate than at any previous time, while the results may be meager and certainly would contribute little to the overall goal of raising aggregate education-attainment levels.

What are the implications for modernizing nations?

The inflationary spiral in the costs of general services worldwide, of which education is a part, place universal or mass education out of the realm of possibility for living generations (and in all probability, for several generations yet unborn) in most modernizing countries. Equal educational opportunity, not to mention compensatory education, if the pattern in the United States holds, would not be feasible until at least a majority of the advantaged population succeeds in using the schools. This is a condition that even most industrialized nations outside the "club" countries have not yet reached. Thus, for the developing countries this condition would not be reached until well into the next century.

If the least-advantaged peoples of the world are to have access to formal education anytime soon, a very radical alteration of the arrangements for schooling will be required—and that too seems very unlikely.

Roy P. Fairfield

Learning: Rivers and Nets!

Fairfield explores the kinds of imaging in education and learning that are needed for the future and concludes that we need exponentially expanded imagery. The most meaningful constructs are those that suggest flowing, networks, human linkages and horizons. This means, among other things, that humanist-teachers-learners must move toward openness, fallibility, daring, ambiguity, and a profound appreciation of paradox, irony, and humor.

The little red schoolhouse, so vivid an image of the American educational past, has practically vanished. It seems reasonably safe to predict that the sterile, factorylike school buildings that have filled cornfields and surburban edges since World War II will practically vanish by the year 2000 or at least by 2050. Rather, learning will be more identified with rivers in the mind, networks that extend around the world and into the already extant planet-girdling cameras from which we may see ourselves ever more clearly.

When I sat down to the prospectus for this volume—namely, to think in global terms, to connect education with my humanism, and to relate all this to humanity's critical problems—my initial response was to doodle. So I scribbled on one page of a yellow notepad the following fragments:

PROCESS (?) IMAGES

Rivers in the mind
  flowing streams - melting icebergs
  music - transitory - ephemeral
learning without walls
    plains   open spaces
    seas   places to move
    far-off horizons   Bucky Fuller
                      John Portman
                      geodesic forms
    mobility & flexibility
      (pens, portable elec. type.
      teawagon with anchor
      bus - field trip)
  mazes to master
    with minimum energy
    Zuckerkandl syndrome (becoming
    unconscious of the conscious)
icebergs (pumping air into their bases -
  unconsciousness
space relationships
  (Hidden Dimensions; more awareness of . . .)
language as *portal* rather than *closed* room
fourth ear
  hearing more dimensions of *noise*
    (connotation - denotation)
  hearing psychic messages
    psychological - conscious
                  unconscious
    linguistic
convert linear thought relationships to gestalts
  lateral thinking
the *world* as school
all *insight* as growth
accepting and rejecting - experience of a moment as real
convert *what* questions into when, how, why, who questions
computer to calculate
  paradox - irony - humor
  verbal statement of a question (run it through
    ten times rather than once to exploit all its

```
            meanings and possibilities)
         put all propositions into computer sets to double-
            check every combination
         model—metaphor
         converting—converter
         wave - wavicle - wire - interconnection
                        communication
```

During the course of this doodling, I also scribbled two grooks, in the spirit of Piet Hein, the Danish engineer-artist-poet:

```
Images static            Avoiding pictures
if picture's frozen      frozen in mind
accept what happens      chew sour lemons
if you're dozin'!        way down to rind.
```

And it occurred to me at the time that perhaps I should have stopped right there, encouraging the reader to use these thoughts as his or her springboards or thresholds to the future. And even as I write the first draft of this *now*, I question whether these images, in "outline" form, will "put across" my fundamental point. I happen to believe profoundly that Piet Hein's grook form, as well as Japanese haiku, are incredibly valuable searchlights for expanding and sharpening awareness and insight. Hence, as I scribbled that evening, riding from one formal learning session to another, I looked out the jet window in Montreal to perceive:

```
            Black delta winging
            into velvet night leaving
            jewel rugs behind.
```

Perhaps I should have stopped at the first line of doodling where I questioned the question itself? To find a single image such as "spaceship school" for instance and use that as the harbinger of the future might even block the further imaging that seems so imperative if we are to catch the spirit of learning for the future. If we are to survive as a global people, we need to develop images that facilitate imaging; for instance, a kind of Rorschach blob might become clouds that become elephants that become circuses that carry human achievement—fantasy, creativity, and stability— toward the horizons (*educare* in Latin meant "to draw out" a child); we do not require images that freeze into solid clay the unsoarable. And note my

concern for the "frozen" in the two grooks as a kind of conscious-uncon-
scious image; for I write most such grooks in an existential mood/mode,
letting the pen lead me as much as catch my antennae of awareness.

IMAGING AND EDUCATION

Hence, imaging in the educational/learning fields seems to *demand* constructs that suggest *flowing:*

> rivers rather than ponds
> seas rather than bogs
> wheat-waving fields rather than calm meadows
> kinesthetics rather than statics
> calculus and exponential relationships
>   rather than arithematics
> impressions as well as concepts
> dynamic daring and risk taking rather than
>   cool securities
> enthusiasms and hot sweats rather than cold logic
> manifestos under constant revision rather than
>   credoes as eternal verities
> networks expanding and contrasting, available to
>   all the world's people, rather than cages
>   to entrap mind and body ... TV, radio and
>   human resource networks, not ropes, wires
>   and handcuffs
> language revisions that carefully scrutinize
>   such connectives as "rather than" and "as
>   well as" as limiting and expanding perceptions

Alluding to the fact that language shapes perception, I am reminded
of an experience during a summer-school program on Long Island in the late
fifties. A young woman who had sat in my philosophy-and-education class,
·Education in a Free Society, for two days suddenly showed up outside my
office. She asked me to sign a "drop slip" so she could leave the course. I
casually inquired, "Why?" She took offense at my query, sputtering, "I don't
need any course about alternative ways of knowing. I teach art in the second
grade. I want my kids to see that sky's up and ground's down, sky's up,
ground's down. Sky's up and ground's down, that's the way it is and that's
the way it's going to be!"

As I looked into her somewhat agitated face, I pondered something
I've wondered about many times since, namely, how many of her second-

graders had their imaginations and curiosities stunted in her class? One wonders, too, "how on earth!" one can ever encourage such a teacher to subject herself to basic assumptions and cliché therapy? Also, one wonders about one's own assumptions and clichés, to wit:

As *both* a rationalist and an existential-phenomenological humanist, I *assume* that writing this very chapter may "make a difference" to some person or persons *working in the world*. Too, that images such as rivers, streams, and open spaces are literally metaphors with deep personal connotation for whoever is reading this. If my assumptions are accurate reflections of one piece of reality, then I may further *assume* that *anybody* coping with imaging can generate images that are human on their terms. Also, *assuming* for my own, Erich Fromm's notion that being human is the capacity to respond, once more I can contemplate without fear or guilt the possibility of stopping right here to let the reader evolve his or her own images applicable to learning futures because my continuing might "turn off" the very process I advocate!

But, a disclaimer or two: this is *not* to downgrade (at least, not completely!) systems-making as important imaging. There will always be room for idealistic (such as the Catholic), romantic (such as Rousseau's), pragmatic (such as John Dewey's or the scientific at its best) philosophies *if* one does not preempt or attempt to destroy the others. I say *attempt*, for I cherish human plenitude, stubbornness, and ingenuity, feeling reasonably certain that the human image, many human images, *will out*—even in the face of the most repressive politico-socio-economic system, to say nothing about prison, endurance, and fortitude. Viktor Frankl and others, writing about the Nazi concentration camps, and Alexander Solzhenitsyn, recounting the story of Soviet labor camps, reinforce that belief. This belief also serves as a kind of prophylactic against absorbing too completely whatever the current "in" fad is, whether team teaching, audio-visual magic, modular scheduling, competency-based teacher education, management by objectives, or any other panacea that becomes the official imagery of bureaucracy or ministries of education.

Nor am I opposed to computer imagery such as "input," "feedback," "printout," and so forth, words whose magic in proper mouths is supposed to impress, even if the problems at hand are of the foot-in-the-mud kind. Computers can be the servants of humankind, storing information more vastly and more "fastly" than the brain can comprehend. Employed *for* humans and not *against* individuals (psychology at its worst), computers not only can accomplish quantitatively what humans could not do "in a month of Sundays" but also can qualitatively expand human comprehension and appreciation of alternatives in ways not even yet imagined—*if* some complex problems (and I deliberately would feed paradox, irony, and humor into a computer) can be perceived in ways to carry human imagination beyond every known horizon. In short, systems, yes; System, no.

But back to rivers, streams, open spaces—and flowing!

EDUCATION TOMORROW

No doubt education throughout the world will continue to be locked into cubicles called schools, libraries, carrels, classrooms, and other such. Too, no doubt much learning in the name of education will be frozen into schedules, curricular, and time dimensions. Further, also no doubt, people known as professors, teachers, and administrators will continue to assume roles and to be perceived in those roles as persons who educate. And there is little doubt either that the major amount of funding for such places, persons, and times will be connected with what is perceived as "legitimate" and major learning endeavors. Nor is there any doubt that each nation's heritage will be perpetuated, each person's socialization effected, via these means. I would simply argue that learning is too important to be left to educators. We need expanded, exponentially expanded, imagery, in both qualitative and quantitative gestalts. We have *started* to evolve such imagery in using terms such as *facilitator*. The image "university without walls" *begins* to frame an arena in which learning can take place. The specialist as "resource" also suggests that the learner must extend his or her own efforts if he or she is to gain knowledge, skill, and understanding; in short, learning is an extension of learner *as well as* extension of teaching energy. Some institutions today are beginning to recognize "life experience" and hence are credentialing it; notions of "continuing education," "external degree programs," and "emeritus university" suggest learning as a lifelong program *in living*. So, we have *begun*.

I would contend, however, that we have not gone far enough. Even after recognizing some fundamental needs of humans for roots in places and in fixed times, even after admitting how difficult it is to motivate persons to move "from rhetoric to risk,"[1] even after looking at practical matters of cost and logistics in getting each person in the entire world to develop his or her own potential as a human, I would say that we have only scratched the surface. This is not to review the statistics of illiteracy (either functional or formal) on the globe, nor to attempt to measure the accuracy (let alone the poignancy) of Thoreau's view that most persons live lives of "quiet desperation," nor to expound upon relationships between formal education, poverty, gross national products and per capita incomes, sales of books and records, destructive exportation and importation of colonialist learning systems and/ or attitudes, and so forth. There are storehouses full of such empirical data.

Rather, this is to share some biases related to the rivers and streams, biases that may sound all too dogmatic when stated so briefly. I believe:

•that every waking *and sleeping* moment is a potential learning moment if we will but focus upon the *how* to make it such and that the *how* should move beyond mere gimmickry to fundamental questions of existence. Hence, it's a matter of learning that extends beyond increasing efficiency in adding two and two (however important that may be when scaling valuing) to recognizing, somewhat self-consciously, how one's mind, body, mind-body, unconsciousness, and so forth, work to make him or her a vital creature in every moment of time, place, and psyche, time-place-psyche. Dream logging, for instance, will reveal remarkable data about sleeping, a veritable gold and goal mine. Hence, the image of temporal and spatial and psychic rivers.

•that (as Carl Jung suggested) far too much perception is a projection: psychological, linguistic, conceptual. Query: How can we learn a means for breaking such vicious (because killing) cycles? If we are poor at linguistics and the way in which our language governs perception (as Sapir, Whorf, and Chomsky illustrate so well), then let us learn more about the silent languages of gesture, spatial relationships (proxemics), and the profound messages of silence itself.[2]

•that "what" questions may destroy more than we know. Especially if those asking them (Johnny, what is *your* name? What is the name of our first president? Who killed cock robin? What do *you* know?) know the answer and the questioned knows that the asker knows! If every teacher-facilitator-parent-administrator were to subject his or her questions to careful scrutiny, perhaps bombarding those questions with streams of doubt, uncertainty, and queries about querying, we could add an entirely new dimension to learnings, to interactions among learners, to relationships between persons ostensibly *in* authority and those *out* of it. Is it so difficult to convert "what" questions to why or when questions? Or perhaps to structure such an approach as a test of one's own ingenuity to cope with such querying about querying?

•that we *must* modify all current concepts and practices of "residency"! Residency connotes and denotes place. Hence, a college or university student must attend certain prescribed functions, be in certain spaces (courses) until the total of one hundred twenty hours (or its equivalent) is reached. This is too restricting; and, though those attempting to "credential" life-learning experiences are to be commended, the whole question of residency needs examination, analysis, restructuring in terms of the flowing stream of existence. This is not to say that one merely need exist to learn; it is to claim that learning need not be confined or even evaluated in terms of specific spaces conventionally perceived as "residency." Concepts of "course," "credits and hours," and even "credentialing" need exploding.

•that process is product and product may be learning process! In Western society and increasingly in *all* societies, there is a propensity to add, subtract, multiply, and divide everything, from apples, rice, and olives to minutes, hours, and seconds. Technology demands it. Our global village demands it—if we are to use Telstar efficiently, or at all! It may be part of the human propensity to codify even as we daydream. To think is to attempt escaping chaos. Educators in the modern world, invariably cognitive if neither effective nor affective, perpetuate the adding, substracting, multiplying, and dividing processes, more frequently measuring progress by product than process or by the student-in-process. But videotaping, the insights of the phenomenologists, and other such forces make it more acceptable (hence, credentiable, statusworthy) to accept and/or even encourage learners to perceive "process as product." In fact, it's okay to log any experience. So, let us sail on rivers of the mind and enjoy, enjoy.

•that the peoples of the world, regardless of nation-state, ethnic origin, or state of identity-seeking, must strive for functional literacy, taking from East or West, powerful or weak, elite or populist that which will further *their* human ends—not adopt or adapt that system which is thrust upon them, or seems to guarantee status, or whatever.

•that optimal human creativity is achieved when self-directed learning contexts are evolved, either formally or informally. We spend all too much of our lives doing that which somebody else decides is good for us. But how can one person or group decide what is good for another or others to learn? By what criteria? In what mode? We need to achieve competency-based *self-education*.

•that learners gain confidence and a greater sense of their own worth when they perceive their experiences as unique and significant. Hence, my own belief that dream-logging (both day and night dreams), letter-writing as a way to develop writing competence (being human is the capacity to respond), haiku and grook construction, picture-taking or picture-painting, carpentry—in fact any form of craftsmanship or artistry—will afford the individual a glimpse of the artist's place in the world.

•that symbolizing and imaging as well as craftsmanship and artistry are incredibly valuable self-healing processes. To wit: playing with words, punning, standing concepts on their heads, bending over to see the world between your legs (Thoreau's prescription for avoiding a kind of world-jaundice)—all are fun and constructive if not directed against others. Also, to wit: what's the harm in constructing a grand theory of cynicism about the kind of world in which we live? Or in perceiving the world as one in which creative schizophrenia is a norm (holding mutually exclusive value-systems in order to survive)? Or in taking a simple phrase, saying it backward, middleword, however, to develop the habit of seeing the world from odd angles of vision, turning it around in one's mouth, one's ears, one's fingers, one's nose, one's dreams, one's eyes, until one *sees* with every sense? Or in constructive daydreaming, for instance, imagining what life at thirty or forty or fifty would be like if one had two six-month vacations (or three four-month ones) per year, with pay? Or in so perceiving the world that full *un*employment rather than full employment were the norm? Or in imaging a world in which the right to eat were a human right and not contingent upon needs tests, the quality of sweat, or the nature of sycophancy? Or, or, or, or . . . ?

•that learning modes twenty-five and fifty years hence will consist more of networks than school buildings, networks with the home as the vital nodes; television and radio networks, extending current NET station power and impact exponentially, newspaper "course" networks (like that currently at the University of California at San Diego) multiplied a hundredfold; continuing education and consortial resource networks with more transfer values and opportunities than now available; legal, medical, and other professional-school networks, extending the university-without-walls concept in order that more and better services will be available; and hundreds of thousands of smaller human networks (running beyond friendship circles) that may be perceived as a re-tribing phenomenon (image), one compensating for the disadvantages of the nuclear family, disadvantages of senior-citizen compounds and villages. The major subset image for network will be linkage, human linkage. Better that learning be perceived in terms of learners linking with one another than persons occupying discrete chairs in discrete classrooms in discrete courses earning discrete hours and credits, K through the PhD. Better that transcripting, which may still be necessary, be perceived as creative writing, creative narrative of what learning was *done* rather than standardized descriptions of what some school or professor *might* do.

But enough biases in this shorthand form. I have elsewhere spelled out at some length my belief that humanist teacher-learners (co-learners) must move *toward* openness, *toward* fallibility, *toward* daring and ambiguity, *toward* relevance, *toward* affirmation and continuity, *toward* empathy and loving, *toward* human support and supporting, *toward* spontaneity, *toward* structuring nonstructure, in short, *toward* a profound appreciation of paradox, irony, and humor.[3] Also, in short, those who would develop their power of imaging humans toward the future might expand that power by keeping a kaleidoscope as well as a logic book handy. The evening news certainly provides that clue. The networks specialize in providing bits and pieces, fragments, quanta. Who can "make sense" out of the varieties of human experience the world over without turning his or her seeing, hearing, tasting, touching, feeling, and intuiting to the vast congeries (quanta) of human experiences, but especially to the contradictions, such as:

•a high American official gets a slap on the wrist for a major crime against his people, whereas a lower-class ethnic draws several years of incarceration for a misdemeanor;

•members of the upper classes and especially government officials the world over buy table-groaning banquets for others they want to buy or impress, while millions starve, literally, and both phenomena are available for TV viewing, sometimes on the same program;

•governments spend billions for national defense and in the process become less secure (some American air bases sport signs saying "Peace Is Our Business!");

•the greater the consumption of material goods, very often the sharper the hunger and decrease in satisfaction—and the larger the therapy bills;

•the more the world's "democrats" use totalitarian techniques (wiretapping, data-storage banks on individual "misdemeanors") to "contain" communism or fascism or to assure "national defense," the more they look like that and those which they fear most!

Such a list of contradictions and paradoxes is almost limitless. And awareness of the contradictions, too, seems to be rising like the tide. But is the learned competence for coping with it also rising? If there is little or no coping, and paradox and irony do not become part of a person's world-human view, what are the long-range consequences? Will laughter be internalized in vital, life-giving ways? Be little more than reflex or an acknowledged "Ah, ha!" as in responding to a first-rate cartoon? Degenerate into bitterness, corroding cynicism, or self-denigration? Can one, for instance, tolerate the seemingly endless Watergate images if he or she does not have a fairly well-internalized attitude toward the paradoxes, the ironies, and the resulting humor? For it has long since become clear that the average citizen. on whom such rhetoric is spent knows full well that he or she is engaged in the "dialogue of the deaf" and/or "an exercise in futility" if he or she tries, single-handedly, to be heard in his or her local capitol or nation's center.[4]

It is my bias that educators not only must encourage the imaging that this book applauds but also must work with any and every learner in both deep and shallow rivers of experience, must feed curiosity with querying, and must make humor central in human learning—wherever, whenever, whatever, whoever, whyever the opportunity, with every situation or setting (on jet, log, bench, phone, table, ad infinitum) perceived as a *natural* one. If educators are going to use mechanistic images, let them talk about gears of relevance meshing noiselessly. If they use philosophical language, let them encourage praxis. If they use fad images, they have much to learn from the streaker, getting down to the bare facts and with speed enough to stay out of jail. But if all the world's a school and we would link to one another humanly in it, let us eschew any image that suggests confined space and opt for the open-air images of horizons, rivers, seas, jet streams, and the most organic of flowings.

NOTES

1. For some discussion of this concept, see my essay "To Bury the Albatross?", *Journal of Research and Development in Education* 5, no. 3 (Spring 1972), pp. 107-118.

2. Works of Sapir, Whorf, and Chomsky are many and can be located in any reasonably good library. The concepts of "silent languages" and "hidden dimensions" appear in the work of Edward Hall.

3. See my book *For Humans Sake* (Fort Collins, Colo.: Shields Publishing Co., 1974), in which I discuss these concepts in the context of moving *toward* the qualities listed here.

4. These are concepts conceived by André Gide, but they have been taken into the language for everyday use.

Robert Bundy

Epilogue: A Summary and Some Notes on Finding a New Meaning for the Future

The reader who has carefully studied each of the essays included in the book will have been struck by the profound nature and importance of images of the future. From what appears at first to be a relatively simple concept, a most complex subject rapidly emerges. Integrating what has been said by our provocative contributors is a difficult task. Nevertheless it is a task that must be attempted in order to draw out the major ideas presented and to encourage and aid further study in this vital area.

In what follows I have organized a discussion of some of the pieces in a way—hopefully—that will both provide a sense of wholeness to our inquiry and identify points of major argeement and disagreement. Five topics serve as organizing themes: (1) the nature of images of the future, (2) the process of image development, (3) current images of the future in the West, (4) new images needed for the future, and (5) areas for further study. In discussing the first two topics I have spliced together the important statements made by our contributors. The result is a composite picture that provides a helpful perspective but which would not necessarily be agreed to in its entirety by all the authors. For the third and fourth topics I have distilled the key point of view from each essay and made some comparisons between the different points of view. In the discussion of topic five I have made some suggestions for deepening and extending this inquiry into images of the future. Finally, at the end, I offer my own observations in an effort to assist us to move toward a new meaning of the future in the decades ahead.

THE NATURE OF IMAGES OF THE FUTURE

Images of the future are those condensed and crystallized expectations prevailing among peoples in certain periods that are developed into systematic projections for the future. They may be eschatological or utopian, and either positive and optimistic or negative and pessimistic (Polak). Essentially, images of the future are mythological images of the past, and in a certain sense it is a case of them choosing us rather than of us choosing them. Since what is important to images is their meaning, not their truth, they are always grounded in our uses of the past, not in history (Green).

For an image of the future to have any real value, it must offer a way of life acceptable to society as a whole (Ellul). However, images cannot exert power in life or in history unless they can be rendered as a reasonable hope. But memory lies on the other side of hope. Without memory of concrete and specific events, of good things, there can be no hope; no belief in a world pregnant with good possibilities (Green) or a world capable of realizing solutions (Deloria). But hope cannot be founded merely on good luck. Hope requires the experience of having worth—the experience of competence—in ways that demand the witnessing and endorsement of other people. Inevitably then, hope brings us to the edge of community. Shared images of the future must always derive from memory, be grounded in our uses of the past, and involve the consciousness of some collective (Green).

Positive images tell of another and better world in a coming time. They infuse people with the foreknowledge of a destiny of happiness, and thus engender the courage to confront and solve the problems facing a civilization. Negative, pessimistic images work in the opposite way and may forecast a period of cultural decline and breakdown (Polak). Without a living image of the future a society can become doomed to a rootless vacuum (Francoeur) and condemned to disappear (Ellul). Negative images, however, can be important to learning what should be avoided (Ellul), and can serve as a healthy warning system (Squires).

The ideal typical image has both eschatological and utopian elements, and the optimum conditions for social change involve a delicate balance between the two (Boulding). At another level, there must be a balance between commitment and responsiveness, between relatively static, collective symbols (needed for social cohesiveness and action) and the shifting needs of a plurality of factions (Christiansen). However, not all positive and optimistic images are necessarily good or constructive images. For example, some positive images can discredit authentic human capabilities and accomplishments (Stanley), or lead to widespread human and environmental destruction (Squires).

Society can be viewed as a set of more or less shared expectations about the future and about behavior based on them. Humans are time travelers, who chart their courses through time with maps of the future (Bell). Images of the future thus form the primary driving force, the main generating process of the birth and growth of culture patterns. Moreover they help to explain the specific uniqueness of cultures or of separate culture-configurations. Images of the future tell the unfolding story of humankind and help illuminate the mysterious path of history (Polak). While in a strict sense there is no knowledge of the future, humans must act as if they know the future (Bell). Images of the future, therefore, prefigure the actual future of a civilization because, in calling for their own fulfillment, images give shape to and promote their realization. The promises contained in these visions make a purposeful choice between many possible futures, and they harness the elected potential future into active operation. Images, however, always have to be reevaluated to be adapted to the changing times, since each age has its own uniquely fitting images (Polak).

Therefore, images of the future are real and may summon forth a future reality (Bell) by being already at work and by challenging people to labor for their realization in advance of their becoming an apparent part of reality (Polak). What this theory of images of the future does not tell us in the present is who are the creative minorities and which images will catch hold in the future (Boulding).

THE PROCESS OF IMAGE DEVELOPMENT

How do images of the future arise and take root in the consciousness of a people? What are the conditions that must be met for an image to become a living faith? Again, our contributors have offered some crucial insights.

The search for the future has become basic to human behavior.

Human beings cannot become fully human if they cannot simultaneously elaborate and refine their mental picture of another world in a coming time (Polak). A failure to do this is a basic denial of our human nature (Francoeur). Spiritual leaders and visionary messengers emerge in various periods and evolve constructive images of the future. Through their emotional and aesthetic appeal, these images designed by the elite are communicated to the masses and arouse their enthusiasm and burning belief (Polak). More precisely, the images are planted. They take root, grow, and take possession of a people's consciousness (Green). In time new images emerge to replace the worn out, antiquated, or frustrated images of the past (Polak). During this process, however, unrealized images can sometimes leave groups skeptical and ambivalent toward new images (Ellul). In sum, human culture results from humankind's efforts to create the world in the image of the preceding and prevailing images of the future (Polak).

Yet it is only by the telling of stories about the past that images of the future are transmitted from generation to generation in the consciousness of a people—and their meaning grasped. We can invent the concrete details of stories but not what the stories are about. The stories provide a common mythological structure for belief, and the events recounted in the stories provide the grounds for real hope. The stories reflect the truths people know about themselves and their world, and they always have a basis in fact, though in detail they never happened (Green). Humankind's religions have been the custodians of symbol systems, and myths which have kept people oriented to ultimate powers and values, reminded them of their duties, and given them hope (Burhoe).

In traditional societies an image formed itself slowly by an accumulation of experiences, a synthesis of competing ideas and progressive elaborations going on sometimes for generations. Images of the future that are meaningful cannot be brought into existence by arbitrary or artificial means. Nor can they be the fruit of a single mind unless propaganda is used for indoctrination and domination (Ellul). Moreover, images of the future are not invented or made up with the intention of their becoming visions to be shared by large numbers of people (Green).

A story that takes root in the consciousness of people will never add to what they know except as it sums up what they already know, and it will not take root unless it sums up what they already find in their experience. Stories make memorable those truths that are so timeless and basic that they could not otherwise be easily taught or recalled (Green). For images to be efficacious, that is, able to give meaning and direction to a society, certain factors must be considered. (1) Existing social conditions in terms of experiences, desires, feelings, beliefs, and problems—in short, the reality as lived by the people—must be taken into account. (2) It is necessary to recognize the limits that reality imposes upon the collective imagination. People can imagine a future which, although it is lacking in particulars, is taken very seriously. But it is essential to remain inside the limits of the collective imagination. (3) It is necessary to take into account common values believed in and accepted by all as self-evident. If there are no common values, there can be no image of the future. When there is no longer consensus on the meaning of a value it cannot be re-created artificially. A group must create new values and new symbols. The problem is one of invention (Ellul). But in this process there is no way to develop images of the future except by learning how to be instructed by the past (Green). The potential for new images of the future is present when historical facts are pitted against past conceptions of social reality and new images of the past are born (Deloria).

Men and women do not have a choice of not having images of the future (Polak). Nor are we free to decide what our visions of the future will be. Humans rely on mythology and they require stories. Whichever images take root are grounded in a story of the past, and their hidden meanings are revealed through the telling of stories (Green).

CURRENT IMAGES OF THE FUTURE IN THE WEST

Our contributors have identified, often in detail, many prevailing images of the future or at least portions of images that command power and belief today. Some of these images have been considered positive and constructive while others have been labeled negative and pessimistic. The following is not an exhaustive catalogue of the images discussed but rather a representative sample of the more clearly delineated images.

Stanley speaks of the spiritual malaise that has accompanied modernization and how this has altered our sense of the significance of politics. The three futures he describes, which have found acceptance among many contemporary intellectuals, are alike in their eschatological themes and their visions of post-political worlds at the end of secular history. Of the three, he suggests that neo-Platonic functionalism may have the best chance of being fulfilled, given current developmental trends. Stanley argues however that there is an underlying despair evident in all three perspectives because they evidence a lack of faith that people will have sufficient rationality to develop a politics that can discipline human powers for humane purposes. While these three images can be characterized as a form of secular religious experience, *Boulding* is primarily concerned with how the contemporary religious imagination conceptualizes the future and in the eschatological strength of current religious images. Her purpose is to locate some of the resources available to society for imaging the future. Of the four models she examines that command support today, she feels the radical-Christian-secularist model and the sacration model have the most clear-cut images of the future and that they attempt to achieve the ideal balance between utopia and eschatology. In her opinion none of the models are generation-bound, and it is uncertain which ones, if any, will take hold in the future.

Ellul is broader when he distinguishes two different orientations today in the search for an image of the future. The first is a search that can be realized, using the means at our disposal (exemplified by the Great Society). In total opposition is the search that does not consider the means available (namely, the search engaged in by the counterculture). Those who support the first orientation control the means but do not have an acceptable view of the future. Those who espouse the second are capable of generating a view of the future desired by many, but they are ignorant of social organization and dependent on the consumer society. It is impossible, says Ellul, with these radically opposed tendencies to formulate a view of the future acceptable to both.

Like Ellul, *Polak* feels that images which speak only to increasing mastery over nature or a self-centered happiness are destructive. To Polak, the current images of the future generated by the idealists and realists are not split between this and another, better society, but rather are split between those who espouse the here and now (the existential model Boulding discusses) and those who say no to the present and yes to the future they have chosen. He feels the pessimism and negativism of the former are gaining ground, but there are now many signs of a spiritual soul searching for new magnetic images of the future. In geographic terms, he feels there are three main fields to observe. Former images of salvation history and utopian promise (that had their seedbed in Western Europe) are mostly in their death throes. He is uncertain of what he calls the American Dream, but he believes there are powerful mass-appealing images arising outside the West whose values may not be to our liking.

Francoeur agrees that there is a near-total lack of positive and generally accepted images of the future in our culture. Specifically, there is general disillusionment with the utopian promises of medicine, technology, and science. He feels, however, that unless we choose our future we will perish. In his opinion some positive images have already been conceived by small groups of theologians, philosophers, scientists, and other specialists. *Burhoe* shares Francoeur's concerns. A severe breach has occurred in our cultural information. The value controls sacred for human life have been severed from the unchecked growth of science and technology. Human values have remained encoded in ancient literary, mythical, and logical forms, and they are fast losing credibility in motivating people whose world views are shaped by the new subculture of science and technology. If this leads—as Burhoe believes it has to a certain extent—to humans believing that they can create their own destiny independently of the sovereign, evolving, cosmic ecosystem, then humankind may be doomed. Thus Burhoe feels that this particular image of the future is ultimately destructive. Human beings cannot be the final arbiters of their own destiny, nor can they develop viable values independent of nature's constraints and the laws of living systems.

Christiansen also sees this attempt to separate fact and value as having generated simpleminded, irrational, and negative images of the future. These images could lead to a fascistic technologism and homogenization. *Squires* addresses this same theme but carries it deeper. He believes reductionist images, in which the poetic mode becomes subsidiary to the technologic mode, leads to dehumanized notions of human beings because they come to see themselves as observers outside the world. It is the poetic that challenges this dehumanization and shows that human beings are fundamentally immersed in the world.

Mary Bundy and *Elaine Morgan* agree on many points in discussing current images of women and their roles in society. Although they believe the images are changing because of the rising consciousness of women and new technologies, both agree that the current—and dominant—images of women are still based on oppressive male attitudes. Bundy goes deeper in her analysis of oppression, because she integrates the issues of subjugation of women, racism, and class privilege within her exploration of the Male Attitude. To Bundy, most men cannot envision the liberation of women because men have too much at stake in being dominant. Similarly, advantaged white men have too much of an investment in racism and class privilege to envision a different order. *Deloria* argues that images embodying such ideas as complete separatism, cultural integrity, and universal rebellion, as well as images denying the possibility of solving problems within existing institutional structures, have become counterproductive. Moreover, images of social reality that gave all Americans their sense of national identity in the past have been leveled by the efforts of racial minorities in the last two decades. He feels that the be-

ginning outlines—or at least the potential for a new vision—is present, because many minority groups (and whites) are secretly longing to find their way
toward some new conception of what it means to be an American. The problem is that the current conceptual landscape offers no leverage for people to
find their way. In a different but related way, *Green* deplores the thoroughgoing individualism evident in so many contemporary visions of the future.
This individualism runs counter to a basic condition for visions of the future,
namely, the fact that the consciousness of some collective is always involved.

   Weaver sees the patterns of educational growth and the professional
frame of reference in industrial nations as images of the future for developing countries. If this occurs, the attainment potential of most of humankind will be seriously crippled. In short, if the least-advantaged peoples of the
world are to have access to formal education in the immediate future, radical
changes in schooling (and therefore the images of education) will be necessary. *Fairfield* argues forcefully that new images of education are crucial to
the full development of human potential. He sees the current images of education and learning as largely oppressive and nonviable for our survival as a
global people. Allowing for some gradual modifications, he concedes that
these current images will probably prevail in the immediate future but not in
the long run. In a similar vein, *Jungk* feels that a powerful human revolution
is under way and that new educational arrangements and pedagogies have
very often been responsible. Although small in terms of the number of people
holding them, images of creativity, cooperation, simplicity, and participation
being generated by the influential young in this revolution are already having
an important impact and will continue to do so in the future.

   Bell senses that there are certain inspiring images toward which humankind seems to be groping. One long-term historical trend in the West is
the notion of more equality for more people. At the same time, he decries the
excesses and false promises of systematic forecasting and planning even
though such techniques must be used to cope with global problems. In
Brown's assessment of global problems, current images of the distribution of
wealth, the profit motive, national security, the nation-state, poverty, application of research and development, institutional structures, economic growth
rates, social justice, and social development are seen as largely inadequate and
unresponsive to global human needs. He views the demand for equal rights as
the culmination of historical forces that have been at work for centuries.
Kahn, on the other hand, sees many of the issues Brown talks of as failures of
images, as being consequences of stupid planning, the inability to learn from
mistakes, and an improper management of growth. He feels there is an

important split between the images of the "high culture" and the "middle cultures" and that there is a problem of loss of meaning and purpose. In addition, he feels that communism is a defeated ideology although communist morale could be revived.

All of these images, whether considered positive or negative, speak to the full range of human experience: from questions of ultimate purposes and meaning to issues of social structures, economics, and physiological well-being. They overlap at many points and in so doing reveal the enormous complexities of a taxonomy of images. With a few possible exceptions our contributors feel that current dominant images of the future are inadequate, are completely unacceptable, are breeding paralysis of thought, or are creating extreme social divisiveness. This condition is not seen as fatal, however. Given the assumption that there are alternative futures, choice is possible. But exercising this choice has become absolutely essential. At this time the new images needed to inform our choices are felt to be: (1) inevitably and observably taking shape, (2) quietly existing but gaining momentum, (3) drained of their effectiveness by their competitors, or (4) not yet invented. A whole range of new images for the future are suggested, and it is to this issue we now turn.

NEW IMAGES NEEDED FOR THE FUTURE

Ellul and Green do not, as such, describe the images they feel are needed for the future. Their primary concerns are the conditions under which images might emerge. To *Ellul* the traditional values are dead and new ones have to be invented. However, we must avoid the irresponsible attitude of dreaming up any image. Instead we must seek out the one concept that can be implemented that will give us a reason for being and that will allow us to go on creating our future. Only the monumental project of the Third World being able to develop in all of its humanistic dimensions independently of and in cooperation with the West could bring together the two opposed views he describes. Only this project could provide the chance for our society to survive. At the same time, conversion to such a project could give meaning to technological growth, limit the will to transgress, and reassert threatened individualism. *Green* believes three things must be done. We must provide the kind of world that first can nurture hope and, second, does not confuse limited stories of particular pasts with the vision of human limits and possibilities. Finally, there must be a renewed capacity to understand that the story of any particular person can be the story of every person.

Squires feels it is not an image of the future that is needed but rather an image of human beings in their relationships to the world. The rejection of brutal forms of mastery does not mean there must be a return to antiscientific primitivism. *Polak* is another who does not describe a particular image. His concern is that the images needed must speak convincingly to human renewal and the highest perspectives for human society. They must explicitly redefine the new goals for a future life and be more inspiring and stronger than competitive images coming from elsewhere in the world.

Christiansen speaks of an integration of managerial and rational intelligence with symbolic and social intelligence to develop new vigor in our public life. Advancing beyond the current cultural impasse must mean the decline of materialism, pluralism in political organizations, self-control, and conviviality. *Burhoe* calls for images that can unite the two subcultures of human values and science and technology. His solution is a scientifically grounded theology in harmony with divine cosmic purposes. Such a view replaces the traditional belief in a personal god with a fuller understanding of cosmic history and the demands of an evolving ecosystem. This implies the use of religious symbols and rituals for purposes they have always been used for. However, they would be encoded and expressed in the symbol system of the sciences and in forms consistent with a cybernetic view of the world. Burhoe's views are probably closest to the sacration model described by Boulding.

Jungk believes that the emerging values of the influential sector of our youth offer enormous possibilities for normative goal setting. Widespread opportunities for creativity, imaginative thinking, enhancement of the senses, and democratic institutions would result in a tamed and responsive technology and many alternative models for living and working. *Fairfield* would seem to agree with Jungk by the stress he places on images of flowing, openness, networks, and human linkages integrated with and supported by authentic uses of technology. *Francoeur* is also a strong believer in pluralism. Still, he insists we are already supplanting the forces of natural selection and must therefore address the questions of what we want to mean by *human*, as well as what kind of human relations we want to have. Otherwise, we will by default—haphazardly and without being conscious of the implications—create the new person of the future. *Brown* examines these themes too, when he speaks of a new political person combined with a new social ethic. The new society would be less ideological and more humanitarian. It would be based on a new naturalism, with a new child-bearing ethic and the elimination of territorial, religious, racial and sexual discrimination. It would be more cooperative; it would have new global institutions and priorities and greater global loyalties. In effect, it would be a world without borders that accepts the fact that all people have a common destiny.

Like Brown, *Bell* endorses the theme of equality as an inspiring image of the future, as well as the need for taking a dynamic view of the relationships between people and society. He believes we must clarify the new twenty-first century forms that such basic values as equality will take. *Kahn* takes the firm pragmatist's point of view. While not promising happiness with wealth or solutions to fundamental human problems, he believes that rich countries must get richer to make poor countries richer. Proper management of growth can accomplish this with existing resources and technology. The ambiguities of wealth rather than the pressures of poverty will underlie the miseries of the future.

No doubt *Mary Bundy* agrees with many of the goals Brown, Bell, and Kahn propose, but she insists that advantaged, white, male futurists have no intention of giving up their psychological and material investments in race, sex, and class privileges. Moreover, she argues that the global problems and the solutions to these problems that futurists write about are presented as appeals to reason but are in fact dictated by their fears of losing their own vested power. (Interestingly, Kahn himself provides some support for this argument when he points out how the standard of living of upper-class elites goes down as the world gets richer.) Women and other oppressed peoples will have to seize their freedoms because these will not be given willingly. Presumably she might see Kahn's trickle-down theory of development as an attempt to perpetuate an oppressive, male-dominated system—but an attempt that exploited peoples will foil as the tools of power come into their hands. She envisions the end of a civilization that supports advantaged, white, male privilege, and she see it as a victory for exploited peoples everywhere. Her compelling vision of the future is freedom based on liberty and equality.

Morgan is not as adamant as Bundy, though she is just as serious. She feels that the movement toward sexual equality, with many of the same goals Bundy desires, is well under way and will come about inevitably. However, she expects that the goals will probably be achieved more peacefully and within the existing structures of Western civilization and on the basis of trends that are already in motion. Her images of the future include new chemical equalizers for women, the elimination of social, legal, and economic inequities, and changed notions of parenting. *Deloria*'s focus is somewhat different, but his ideas of social reconstruction are directly related to what

Morgan, Bundy, and Ellul, in particular, discuss. The images of the future Deloria feels are now needed should reflect a new center of understanding, a new conception of American history, and a new sense of personal, group, and national identity. They would be images that make possible a coming together and a partaking in each other, unfettered by doctrinal considerations; images that allow the integrity and recognition of past accomplishments of groups but at the same time stress openness to communication across group boundaries; and images that speak to the possibility of a future in which differences between groups can be reconciled at the points where different groups meet each other in the real world.

Weaver's images would presumably focus on more equality in access to formal education, new arrangements for schooling, and alteration of or substitutes for the professional frame of reference. *Boulding* offers no image she personally endorses. Her concerns are to explore the possibility that there might be a "rebirth of God" and to demonstrate that contemporary futurism could learn much from the sociology of religion. *Stanley* would support images that do not trivialize politics, deny sciences as one mode of knowledge or technology as a valid form of human activity, or invalidate centuries of intellectual accomplishment in the West.

Throughout all of this discussion of new images needed for the future we can trace eschatological and utopian impulses or combinations of the two. The diversity of opinion reveals in microcosm the dilemma the larger society faces in the West. Our imaging capacity is not stunted, but we lack any set of common values out of which a new vision could grow. If there is any agreement, it is that we can still exert some measure of control over the future. The greatest fear seems to be that we will not exert this control wisely or that no basis for social cohesiveness will be found. In addition, there appears to be little confidence that systematic forecasting and planning, without new images of the future, will have any important impact on the humanistic resolution of global issues. Most of the contributors' optimism is cautious and guarded. The immediate future is seen as playing a decisive role in creating the social, economic, and political frameworks within which longer-range future possibilities can occur.

AREAS FOR FURTHER STUDY

The foregoing summary has highlighted the main themes, ideas, and conclusions drawn by our contributors. As in any collection of writings such as this where imaginative thinkers are asked to take off on a general theme, we are confronted with problems of levels of meaning, language, and taxonomy. The attempt has been made to untangle some of these problems. In the process, not all of the important issues, questions, and differences of opinion were touched on. Squires, for example, asks whether the European preoccupation with the future is not an aberration, or at least an exception. He also asks to what extent we need common images, that is, what are the limits to a pluralism of images before social divisiveness and serious social instability occur? On another point, Ellul seems to have a different notion of an image of the future than Polak and some of the other contributors. To Ellul, an eschatological conception is the opposite of a real view of the future. Similarly, utopian views lack positive value because they are an attempt to avoid reality and serve mainly to cure the impotence of the intellectual. Moreover, he does not believe an intellectual can have an efficacious image of the future. Bell and Ellul also appear to be in conflict over the future viability of traditional notions such as equality. And Francoeur and Christiansen would probably disagree on the ethics of attempting to define "human" for the future. Other issues could also be mentioned. Taken as a whole, then, the essays are unquestionably a rich source of ideas for further discussion and debate.

Putting this book in a larger perspective, as discussed in the Preface, we find that it continues a tradition of thinking already begun by many diverse thinkers who, directly or indirectly, have contributed to the study of images of the future. Looking at this tradition of thinking in its entirety, including this book, I believe there are ten areas in which additional work is urgently needed. Briefly, they are:

1. the epistemological foundations of thought about the future, including theories of time;

2. how efficacious images of the future come into being and then undergo change;

3. the capacity of a culture to contain disparate images and yet retain a social unity;

4. how to classify, compare, and contrast images of the future;

5. hierarchical structures of images, that is, the nature of those images that form the central core of expectations and within which or from which other subsidiary images are connected;

6. the dynamics by which portions of older images continue to survive and command belief even when the central images have been significantly altered;

7. the social psychology of future time perspective and how images of the future mediate other perceptions of social reality;

8. the commonalities and differences between cultures in terms of images of the future possessed by the cultures;

9. the impact of language in the cultural transmission of images and visions of order;

10. the future development of social and political structures which can foster widespread availability of information and interchanges of ideas on the future by the body politic.

The point of suggesting these areas of inquiry is not to merely assist academic studies and scholarly research. There is a danger that only this will happen and even a further, more ominous danger that the knowledge gained will be used in an exploitive way. However, if our contributors have told us anything, it is that the next couple of decades will be crucial to human survival for centuries to come. If ennobling ideas do not take root, if we cannot find ways to heal the enormous divisions in the West and between the West and the rest of the world, then the picture is bleak indeed for humanity. While a better understanding of images of the future is not a substitute for the actual elaboration of public images, an improved understanding of images may be crucial for opening up and keeping open constructive dialogue on the future—indeed, for keeping open the very future itself.

SOME NOTES ON FINDING A NEW MEANING FOR THE FUTURE

The reader at this point may feel as I do: a deep exhaustion and yet at the same time an intense desire to keep the dialogue going. Our contributors have taken us into the apocalyptic years ahead and shown us the grounds for both despair and hope. From one point of view the questions, ideas, and challenges they pose are too much to bear, too extraordinary for ordinary mortals to feel any active part of or control over. And yet history records great ventures and mass movements in which ordinary people have done the extraordinary when it was demanded. If this is to be true in our age, clearly the time has come for new images of the possible and the opening of new pathways into the future. In closing I will give vent to some of my own feelings on what images are needed and which pathways must be opened.

I believe:

1. The West has lost any reason for being. Simply to further develop scientific and technological tools for their own sake, or to increase our mastery over nature, or to further expand the consumptive society, with its hedonistic license, cannot provide the motive power for a civilization. Some deeper spiritual center and transcendent values are required.

2. This loss of a reason to go on means we have no inspiring image of the future, no dominant vision within whose embrace different expectations can survive and draw strength, no overarching dream capable of infusing all of us with hope and giving us courage to confront and cope with our awesome problems.

3. Images of the future we do have, but they fiercely attack one another and destroy any chances for reconciliation. Our pluralism of images is propelling us inevitably toward extreme social divisiveness and instability.

4. What brings us to this state is that many of our older dogmas and values in the West are dead and cannot be re-created to form a new vision.

5. Nor can a new image of the future capable of healing our divisions be manufactured arbitrarily.

6. In the meantime, our giant institutions and many of our other social and technical tools are out of control. These tools now direct the formulation of human purposes and they have all but taken on a life of their own. As a result the dangers of social, economic, political, and environmental catastrophe on a global scale are imminent; or as an alternative, a worldwide technicist culture inimical to ideals of human dignity and freedom still cherished by many.

7. In response, most current proposals to achieve world peace and development are clothed in humanistic rhetoric but are prompted largely by fears that existing holders of power and wealth are in jeopardy. These proposals merely perpetuate the present and fail to touch the real issues essential to achieve peace.

8. At the same time, certain ideas such as sexual equality and social justice are ideas whose times have come. They cannot be held back, for they are moving into the future landscape with the force of tidal waves.

9. But without an inspiring public image of the future Western civilization cannot absorb these tidal waves and survive; nor can a new beginning be made.

10. We must, then, re-vision the future. And to do this we must first re-vision the past. But here, clearly, our divided society prevents our arriving at a consensus on a new, shared meaning of the past.

If this assessment is correct, we in the West are trapped in a terrible dilemma. We need a vision, but we have none; we have no image of the future capable of uniting us and no consensus on values with which to create a new vision. Nor can we create such a vision artificially. Is there any exit from this dilemma? Must we stumble into the future merely trusting to good luck?

Must we remain subservient to the dictates of our tools and accept their demands as the course of least resistance? Or must we passively wait for some inspiring vision to take root? None of these courses is tenable. I believe the tortuous path to survival, social reconstruction, and a new beginning for the West must take a quite different direction.

We must first accept that we will have to go into the future, at least for a while, without an inspiring image to guide us. Second, as Ellul says, we must engage in some cooperative project with global import to provide the motive power for the bringing of disparate groups together and the joining of their energies. Such a project cannot be prompted by false generosity or a superior attitude of knowing what is good for others. It must go beyond ideologies and doctrines out of the past and be rooted firmly in attitudes of caring, serving, and partaking in others. For this project to occur and these motives to be dominant, I believe with Green and Deloria we will have to re-vision the past. We will have to begin to think of the past as basically the stories of particular groups, some of whom realized their dreams and potential in the sweep of events that made enormous instruments of power come into being. With Squires we will have to see the past as a particular kind of human techno- logical experiment that has reached its limits and from which we must now chart a new course. But even more important, we shall have to see our past as one of journeying and seeking more than one of finding. We shall have to see that people are constantly creating their future as they go forward, that the future is not out there somewhere, like a product, to be discovered. It comes into being as we move toward it. And finally, we will have to have evidence through the projects we undertake that the world contains hope, and because this is so, in time, a new image of the future can be shaped.

I believe the project Ellul suggests of letting the Third World find its own future and develop in all its dimensions is precisely what must be done. Such a project, to me, is analogous (although no analogy is entirely appro- priate) to a person whose earlier life goals are recognized now as inadequate and who is desperately searching for something to give meaning to existence and acquired wealth. Unsure of what future might lie ahead for himself, the person discovers that it is within his power to assist another human being over whose future he has a critical influence but whose future now lacks promise. Prompted by this desire to let the other shape his own vision of the future, the person redirects his whole life and power to this venture. And to- gether both people grow. It is only such a project as Ellul suggests that can impose the limits we so desperately need, give any authentic basis to the altruism the West feels for the Third World, and provide a credibility the world will accept for the leadership we still can offer. Such a project could counter the alienation so many in the West feel today, the suppressed anger at constantly receiving false satisfactions for real needs, the oppressiveness of endless programming toward unrealizable goals, the never-ending conversion of human values into mere technical problems, and the insidious applications of technology that destroy the very basis for community. Such a project, in Ivan Illich's notion of the convivial society, could help restore the belief that people can do much for themselves that they have given up to technological slaves, technical experts, and large institutions.

Ultimately, this project, and the inner conversion it would require, could lead to an uprooting of racism, the liberation of women and exploited peoples everywhere from economic and political oppression, a redistribution of wealth, altered relationships with our social and technical tools, an inversion of our social/economic institutions, different notions of progress and growth, openness to alternative modes of economic production, and a minimum set of worldwide agreements regarding war, pollution, and the use and sharing of the earth's resources. Kahn is right that 1976 provides an enormous opportunity to focus Americans on the next twenty-five years. However, his proposals merely perpetuate the present. What is needed is to help Americans see that a new frontier has opened—not a frontier of land acquisition, accumulation of material wealth, or the fulfillment of some manifest destiny, but a frontier for finding new meanings and reasons for going on living.

In my opinion Western civilization is passing away. So be it. This does not mean that our total inheritance from the past or our leadership potential for the future are lost. It does mean that many of the central dogmas and visions that drove Western civilization forward do not have a prominent place in the future. What does have a place in the future are: (1) the shared conviction that new magnetic images of the future can be born, (2) people who are united by common beliefs necessary for survival and development within a global perspective, and (3) groups that share across their boundaries while, as always, they remain separated by particular visions they are free to follow as long as others may also follow their visions.

For some time we Westerners will have to live in a post-culture. We will have to see that we have played out the myths of our past and that only their shells remain. But at the same time we will have to see that certain of the accomplishments prompted by these myths should endure. And by their endurance we can be helped to understand how to live with a metaphysics of crisis and also that, ultimately, crisis is only intelligible in terms of hope. Perhaps then we can once again develop the mythological structures we need and share the meaning of stories we long to tell.

Contributors

Wendell Bell is professor of sociology at Yale University. He was a coeditor (with James A. Mau) of *The Sociology of the Future* and (with Walter E. Freeman) of *Ethnicity and Nation-Building.*

Elise Boulding, professor of sociology and project director at the University of Colorado's Institute of Behavioral Science, is an active futurist. She translated Fred Polak's *The Image of the Future* and is the author of many articles on futurism and women's roles in society.

A senior fellow with the Overseas Development Council, *Lester R. Brown* was formerly administrator of the International Agricultural Development Service, U.S. Department of Agriculture. He is the author of *World without Borders, Seeds of Change: The Green Revolution and Development in the 1970's,* and *In the Human Interest: A Strategy to Stabilize World Population.*

Mary Lee Bundy is president of Urban Information Interpreters, Inc., a nonprofit corporation founded to lend information support to the struggles of poor and oppressed peoples. Dr. Bundy is a professor in the College of Library and Information Services, University of Maryland. She has been a prolific contributor to professional library journals and has completed work on the *National Prison Directory,* a guide to prison-reform groups in the United States.

Robert Bundy, a planning consultant, has for the past ten years conducted seminars on the future for university, professional, business, and community groups to assist them in imaginative preplanning and rethinking of goals for the future.

Ralph Wendell Burhoe first worked at Harvard University's Blue Hill Meteorological Observatory and later became professor of theology and the sciences at Meadville/ Lombard Theological School in Chicago. Dr. Burhoe is editor of *Zygon: Journal of Religion and Science* and is the author of papers relating the sciences to various religious, social, ethical, and philosophical problems. He is working on a more systematic approach to interpreting religion and theology in the light of the sciences.

Drew Christiansen, S.J., was book editor of *Theological Studies* for three years. He was special editor for their award-winning "Genetic Science and Man" issue and prepared another special issue, "Population and Human Development."

An enrolled member of the Standing Rock Sioux Tribe, *Vine Deloria, Jr.,* has worked extensively in the area of American Indian affairs, including positions with the National Congress of American Indians and American Indian Resource Consultants, Inc. He has also lectured at the American Indian Cultural and Research Center at the University of California, Los Angeles. Deloria is the author of *Custer Died for Your Sins, God Is Red,* and *Behind the Trail of Broken Treaties.*

Jacques Ellul, French lawyer and social critic, underground leader during World War II, and a former politician, is known for his fresh and daring insights into our times. His translated works include *Prayer and Modern Man, Violence, False Presence of the Kingdom,* and *Theological Foundation of Law.*

Coordinator of the Union Graduate School, Yellow Springs, Ohio, *Roy P. Fairfield* has taught social sciences at Antioch, Bates, Hofstra, and Athens College and Ohio University. His writing includes *Sands, Spindles and Steeples,* a history of his hometown, Saco, Maine, and he edited the *Federalist Papers, Humanistic Frontiers in American Education* and *Humanizing the Workplace.* Dr. Fairfield is on the editorial board of *The Humanist* magazine.

Robert T. Francoeur is a professor of human sexuality and allied health sciences at Fairleigh Dickinson University. His recent books include *Hot and Cool Sex: Cultures in Conflict* (with Anna K. Francoeur); an anthology, *The Future of Sexual Relations; Eve's New Rib: Twenty Faces of Sex, Marriage, and Family;* and a text, *Perspectives in Student Sexuality.*

Thomas F. Green, professor of education at Syracuse University, is codirector of the university's Educational Policy Research Center. In 1972 he was a consultant to a firm developing a "new town" with federal funds. Dr. Green is the author of *The*

Activities of Teaching, Educational Planning in Perspective, and *Work, Leisure and the American Schools.*

Robert Jungk is the author of several books on the future, including *Brighter Than a Thousand Suns, Children of the Ashes, The Big Machine,* and *Der Jahrtausend-mensch.* Professor Jungk formerly taught at the Technical University in Berlin, and was an initiator of the first World Future Research Conference held in Oslo in 1967. He now lives in Salzburg, Austria.

A physicist and specialist in public-policy analysis, *Herman Kahn* is director of the Hudson Institute. Among his important books dealing with the future are *On Thermonuclear War, Thinking About the Unthinkable,* and (with B. Bruce Briggs) *Things to Come.*

Elaine Morgan was born in Wales and received an M.A. at Oxford. She is a freelance author and playwright. Her best-known work, *The Descent of Woman,* has been published in ten languages.

Fred L. Polak holds a Chair at the University of Utrecht's Institute for Futurology. Formerly a senator in the Dutch Parliament, he is the author of *The Image of the Future, The New World of Automation,* and *Prognostics.*

Geoffrey Squires was born in Ireland and has lived in England, France, Persia, and the United States, where he worked on educational futures. He has published *Drowned Stones* (Dublin, 1975) and also translates from several languages.

Manfred Stanley is an associate professor of sociology at Syracuse University and has been a fellow of the National Endowment for the Humanities. He is the author of several studies in the sociology of change and development, religion, and education, and he edited *Social Development: Critical Perspectives.*

W. Timothy Weaver, an associate professor of education at Boston University, works in the area of systems development and adaptation. He has designed a training pedagogy for educational development, diffusion, and evaluation specialists for the Educational Policy Research Center at Syracuse University. Dr. Weaver has served as a consultant for a regional medical program and various public-school systems.